Escape Room Tango

by

CC Bridges

Escape Room Tango

Cover Art by *Diana Carlile*

The Wild Rose Press, Inc.
PO Box 708
Adams Basin, NY 14410-0708
Visit us at www.thewildrosepress.com

Publishing History
First Edition, 2022
Trade Paperback ISBN 978-1-5092-4529-1
Digital ISBN 978-1-5092-4530-7

Published in the United States of America

"Friendly competition? Is that why you chose to open directly across the street from me? I filed the permits and the business name with the city. You had to know I was about to open." She watched confusion grow on his face. It made him look younger, almost vulnerable. She quashed any sympathy she had. "Don't tell me. You didn't do the market research?"

He shrugged. "I chose the strip mall because Tony's dad owns it, and he gave me a good deal on rent."

"Well, that sounds like a smart marketing plan." She heard the edge in her voice. She had no patience for incompetence. Before she started this venture, she had done her homework, including taking business classes at the local library. Like her dancing, she poured all her time and attention into her business. To meet someone who didn't do basic market research, who chose a location due to the cheap rent, well, that got her back up.

"My master's degree is in chemistry, not marketing," he snapped. "I don't know everything."

"Shocking to hear you admit it."

He stared at her for a moment, his hands clenched into fists at his sides. "Are you seriously not going to let me into your room?"

She almost laughed. In any other situation the words would be incredibly suggestive. Instead she shook her head. "I'm sorry. I have to protect my work."

"This isn't over." He stomped out of her office.

Dedication

This book wouldn't have been written without the support from my husband and son, and the 150 or so escape rooms we completed together. I also wanted to thank all those who've accompanied us on our escape room journey, even if we had to really convince some of you to join us. I'm looking forward to the next 150 rooms, and who knows, maybe another book?

Chapter 1

The timer continued to tick down, the seconds disappearing into ether. Elena couldn't look away from it. Two minutes left to disarm the bomb. She bit her lip and forced herself to turn away from the countdown. She couldn't make it stop.

She and Phoebe had done their parts. Now they could only stand and watch Quinn as she worked two wires through the tiny holes in the clear plastic maze on the wall. Sweat dripped down Elena's back, and her fingers twitched.

Quinn's finger slipped, and for a moment the key teetered on the edge, about to fall down a long path that would take her a while to pull it back up again. They didn't have that kind of time. But she managed to get the second wire in and catch the key before it fell.

Elena let out a relieved breath. "You got it."

"Almost," Quinn whispered, her face contorted in concentration. Beads of sweat gathered at her temples, bright against her blue hair.

Elena checked the timer again—a flat-screen TV mounted in the corner of the room—only a minute left. Damn it, that's why she hated these kinds of tedious puzzles in escape rooms. The point was to have fun. Giant plastic mazes on the wall that only one person could work on while the others waited were not what she called a good time.

None of her own rooms would be designed so poorly.

"Got it." Quinn fished out the key and tossed it to Phoebe, who used it on the last lockbox in the entire room. Inside she found a stereo wire, which she handed to Elena, who ran back to the main "bank" area.

She plugged it in—the final wire left in a twisted mess, connecting letters and numbers in a sequence that had taken her twenty minutes to decipher. As soon as she did that, the keypad lit up, and she entered the code she'd figured out fifteen minutes ago. If it hadn't been for that stupid wall maze, they could have been out of here ages ago.

As soon as she hit enter, the incessant beeping stopped, lights started to flash, and a voice said over the loudspeaker, "Congratulations, you disarmed the bomb and escaped the room!"

"Oh yeah!" Phoebe pumped her fist and held out both hands for a high five.

Feeling only slightly ridiculous, Elena hit one hand while Quinn slammed the other. Both women had big grins on their faces. Elena's heart pounded in her chest, and she felt warm and flushed as if she'd just spent an hour on stage and had come back for the curtain call. They'd done it.

The door popped open, and their game master—a kid who looked barely old enough to drive, wearing a faded Star Wars T-shirt—greeted them. "Great work, guys! Did you have any questions about the room?"

Elena had more suggestions than questions, but she didn't want to be here all day giving out pointers to her potential competitors. They quickly made their escape, gathering their coats from the rack along the door, armor against the blustery March cold, before venturing out to the parking lot.

"Okay, so what the hell was that?" Phoebe grumbled as she pulled out her keys. "How much of that room was busy work? The puzzles weren't even any fun."

"Tell me about it." Quinn flexed her fingers. "I think that last puzzle gave me carpal tunnel."

Of the two of her employees, Phoebe seemed to enjoy doing escape rooms more. Quinn viewed it from a more practical lens, which made sense since her role at Elena's business involved working behind the scenes, making sure the technology functioned. Phoebe would staff the front, and her enthusiasm would help drum up business.

Once Elena managed to actually open. After six months of fighting with the city about her construction permits, she finally had a date. She did have a little time for some last-minute tweaks, and every room she tried out for herself helped her plan better rooms.

She waited until she slid into the back seat of Phoebe's sedan before asking, "Okay, ladies, what have we learned?" She clicked her seat belt on and made sure not to watch while Phoebe pulled into traffic. Elena couldn't even think about driving without getting nauseous and hadn't been behind the wheel of a car in two years.

"That lots of technology doesn't make up for a shitty room," Phoebe said. "Yeah, I mean that final bomb was cool looking. And how you opened the door between the two rooms? That double mirror? I kinda loved that."

Quinn pulled out her tablet from the glove compartment. Her fingers tapped the screen as she took notes. "I think we all left feeling more frustrated than

3

anything else. Okay, so what else was annoying besides the wall maze?"

Elena thought about it for a moment, reviewing the puzzles they'd completed to solve the room. "Finding solutions to locks that we had to wait to use."

"Yeah, that was super frustrating."

Which meant Elena really needed to double-check the puzzle chain in Uncle Enzo's Study. She had been designing that room in her head for months, and while she was sure of her story, the last thing she wanted was to duplicate the frustration she felt in other rooms. That meant no puzzles that led nowhere or were annoying to her customers. She had one particular chain that might prove tricky if the players found the key before finding the lockbox hidden in the bookcase. "Quinn, make a note to change the location of the lockbox in the bookshelf in Uncle Enzo's room."

"Got it."

Quinn had a natural attention to detail, in addition to being a great tech person. She kept careful spreadsheets of everything, and Elena found herself relying more and more on the blue-haired woman she'd met in the laundromat across the street.

"Opening day is in one week. I want everything to be perfect." Elena caught herself wringing her hands and forced them to stillness. It was an old habit she hadn't fallen into since she'd been a young dancer, fretting before getting up on stage.

Her mother had always held Elena's hands, when she was a baby ballerina, and helped her to breathe in and out before stepping out onto the stage. *In and out. Calm.*

That calm had deserted her with the screeching

sound of car brakes failing. The sound that had ended her career.

In and out. Breathe.

"It's going to be awesome." Phoebe glanced back for a split second.

"Eyes on the road." Elena grabbed the bar on the car door. So much for her calm.

"I have everything on order," Quinn continued, thankfully not mentioning Elena's freak-out. "Have you thought about getting some beta testers in? It would be great if we had some online reviews before we opened."

Elena frowned. None of her friends were local, and all were in the midst of the dance season. But she really needed someone outside of her employees to test the room. "Do, uh, either of you know anyone who might volunteer?"

Phoebe flexed her arm in an "I can do it" gesture. "I'll ask some guys at my dorm. I'm sure they'd be willing to do it for some pizza. Speaking of pizza…"

"Lunch at Spano's?" Quinn suggested. It had become their go-to place for food, considering it was in the strip mall directly across the street from the building Elena had bought and renovated for her escape room business. She enjoyed their mostly home-cooked Italian food in addition to their scrumptious pizza.

"Of course!" They'd eat and pick apart the room some more.

Phoebe turned her car into the strip-mall parking lot, taking the right turn with a little too much force. Elena swallowed the lump in her throat and held tighter to the handle on the door. At some point she should be able to ride in a car without panicking. Maybe she could blame Phoebe's driving. That would only work if she didn't freak out when she got into any car.

"Holy shit, do you see that?" Phoebe had stopped the car in the middle of the lot and not in a space either. Elena leaned forward to see what she was talking about, and the bottom fell out of her belly.

In the formerly vacant store next to the pizzeria, someone was finally taking the tarp off the sign that had been installed a few days ago. The storefront had been vacant for months, undergoing lots of construction work, but not a hint of what might be inside. Today the sign proudly exclaimed *The Greatest Escape* in polished metallic letters. Red and gold balloons had been tied to the pillars outside, and a grand-opening banner stretched across the glass windows.

Someone had opened an escape room business directly across the street from Elena's, and she hadn't noticed a damn thing.

A horn blared, and Phoebe swung the wheel around and maneuvered the car into one of the lined spots. She threw the gearshift into park, and they sat there in silence for a moment.

"Maybe it's not what we think it is?"

"What, maybe it's a 1960s movie shop?" Elena took in a deep breath and let it out again. *In and out.*

"No, it's definitely an escape room." Quinn had her head down, immersed in her tablet. "I'm on their Facebook page now."

"How did they do this so fast?" Elena couldn't believe it. Getting the permits, hiring the contractors, and renovating her building had taken months. Of course, she'd bought one of the classic homes in the mixed residential/business zone across the street. Doing construction on an already empty storefront might not have needed as much work or time.

She dug her fingers into the back of Phoebe's seat and pressed her nose close to the window as if she could see inside the storefront. Who was this jerk? She'd sunk everything she had into her business, spending time trying to get it right, to build something she could be proud of, and this mystery person just swung into town and did this?

At least it wasn't yet another Escape-o-Rama franchise. She couldn't have dealt with that. How could she have competed with someone that had built-in customers and web presence? At that point she'd have to pack it all in and start over somewhere else.

"Not fast. The website was registered six months ago," Quinn said. "It's to The Greatest Escape, LLC, so I don't know anything about the owner."

"Yet," Phoebe cut in. "I'm going to go inside and give that asshole a piece of my mind. Would it have killed him to notice the sign across the street?"

They'd been advertising The Escape Space with a coming-soon banner for the past month. Elena had set up a website and Facebook page to go with it. Her business hadn't been a complete surprise. Except The Greatest Escape had managed to open up sooner than she had. A pounding started in her ears, and heat swarmed all over her. She clenched her hands into fists, leaning into the anger that burned inside her.

"Their bookings page just went online." Quinn finally looked up from her tablet. "They have openings today."

"What are you saying?" Phoebe turned to face her. "We book and go in there like it's just another room we're scoping out?"

Elena sat back and narrowed her eyes. "Yes. That's exactly what we'll do."

Quinn took only moments to book the next available opening, which was in fifteen minutes. Phoebe found better parking, and then, after Elena did her deep breathing, it was showtime.

Elena didn't think much of the place from the outside. It matched all the other storefronts in the strip mall—utilitarian, with concrete columns holding up the roof that extended over the walkway. Only the painted sign that proclaimed the name *The Greatest Escape* in blocky gold letters gave any indication about what was inside. Otherwise, it looked no different from the laundromat.

The lobby, however, was another world completely. Long and rectangular, it had a row of chairs along one wall and another in front of a large flat-screen TV. The wall opposite the entrance had a gorgeous mural painted on it, showing a number of locks and gears in silver and gold, perfectly positioned around an artful lettered version of *The Greatest Escape*.

A front-desk area, similar to that of a doctor's office, sat off to the right. It separated the waiting area from the rest of the lobby. A man stood up from behind it and walked over to greet them.

His smile struck her first. It lit up his face and caused crinkles to appear in the corners of his dark eyes. And those eyes—he had sleepy bedroom eyes, the kind that reminded her of spending all night and into the next day with a lover. A jolt went through her, and for a moment, Elena couldn't speak.

Then he introduced himself as the owner.

Chapter 2

"My name is David Brant. I'm the owner." He didn't know why his words made the dark-haired woman glare at him, but David didn't really care.

He only had eyes for the redhead. She had stolen his attention from the moment she walked into the lobby. He'd been excited about welcoming his first customers, his intro speech on his lips. Every word left his mind the moment he saw her.

She held herself differently than the other two women, with her shoulders back and neck extended. Her cinnamon-colored hair hung over her shoulder in a long braid. He wanted to pick up that braid and tickle her nose with it to make her laugh, anything to see what her smile might look like. Her green eyes speared him with their gaze, rendering him temporarily mute.

He held out his hand. "Pleased to meet you…" He trailed off, hoping she'd take him up on the offer.

She took it, her grip firm and decisive. "Elena."

"That's a lovely name." He grinned, realized he was acting like an idiot, and stepped forward to greet the other two women in the same way. They were all his customers and deserved the same courtesy. "Can I take your coats? There are hooks back here."

He'd designed the lobby to be comfortable but clearly a place of transition. With any luck, his customers wouldn't spend much time here at all before being escorted into one of the three escape rooms in the back. If he wanted to be successful, he needed to have a constant flow of customers.

That didn't mean his lobby couldn't be fun. He'd placed Rubik's cubes and other mind-teasing puzzles on the coffee table near the chairs along one wall. He included a water cooler for those who arrived thirsty. If they were hungry, he'd happily direct them to Spano's Pizza next door, owned by the family of his best friend, Tony.

Without Tony, he didn't think he'd have ever pulled the trigger and made this fresh start by opening his own business.

"Of course, thank you." Elena handed over her coat.

David collected it and those belonging to the other two before hanging them.

"Have you ever done an escape room before?" he asked, trying to keep the conversation going.

"A few. But this place is new to us." Elena seemed to be the only one willing to speak.

Not that he minded, he liked the sound of her voice. Man, Tony was right. Before the ladies had walked in, he'd been telling David he had to get back in the dating scene, go on the rebound, get it out of his system. Clearly, his words held some truth if David had immediately started checking out his customers. Well, one notable customer in particular.

"Opened up today." He couldn't help the pride in his voice. He walked over to the front desk and picked up one of the customer tablets. "In fact, you're my first customers. Can each of you sign this waiver, please?"

"What are we waiving?" the dark-haired one asked. Her name was Phoebe or Chloe or something that ended with E. "Our rights to sue if we die in there?"

Oh boy. He kept his voice light. "It's a document stating you understand you'll be locked in a room for an hour."

"That's the whole point, isn't it?" The blue-haired one took the tablet and stabbed at it. "What software are you using for these?"

Wow. Not questions he'd expected on his first day. He should have prepared better.

"Don't mind Quinn." Elena smiled. "She loves computers, coding, all the geeky stuff."

"I have a friend like that, too. He'd take my computer apart if I didn't stop him." He collected the tablet once they'd all signed.

"Since we're your first customers, can we get a tour?"

"Of course. Follow me." He wanted to show off his place. Once things got busy, he wouldn't likely have the chance again. He led them down the main hallway, gesturing to the giant murals decorating the walls. They matched the themes of the rooms on the other side and had been done by one of the local college students.

He was especially fond of the one outside the Underwater City Room. The deep blues really popped against the white wall. "You'll be doing the Prison Break Room today, but I will have two more rooms up and running this week."

No need to stress himself out so soon. Plus, he had always been a tester. Try something, evaluate what worked and what didn't, and then try it again. His attention to detail had made him a good scientist. Hopefully, it would make him a good businessman as well.

"Did you design the room yourself?" Elena reached out to touch the mural and then pulled her hand back at the last second. He didn't blame her. It did look too pretty to touch, but he'd had it covered in epoxy to protect it from fingerprints and dirt.

Her words sparked a tiny bit of guilt in him. He had gone the easy route and purchased some ready-made rooms. "No. But I assure you, these are some pretty amazing rooms. I tested them all myself."

"What company did the design?" The blue-haired one again.

"Lofty Designs. Why do you ask?" Because really, he hadn't expected anyone to be this curious.

Elena stepped in front of her friend. "We've done a lot of escape rooms, so we don't want to do a room we've done before someplace else, you know?"

That shouldn't happen. This company had promised they wouldn't sell the same design to anyone within a hundred miles of him. David needed to move this tour along. "This is the room you'll be doing. Normally, I'd show you the safety video in the lobby—"

"Safety video? Is it dangerous?"

"Of course not," he said. "Unless you do something like stick your fingers in an electric socket or try to climb into the ceiling." All things he told people not to do in the safety video.

"We're not stupid."

"I didn't… That's not what I…" He found himself floundering. He finally cleared his throat and found the right thing to say. "Don't blame me. Blame my lawyer. I'm going to assume you know basic safety, then?"

Elena's lips twitched as if she were trying not to laugh. He was rapidly losing control of the situation.

Time to launch into the speech he'd prepared if his addled wits could remember.

"You'll be locked inside for an hour. There will be a monitor where you can interact with the game master and receive clues if you need them. We give unlimited clues here. Please don't take any pictures, but you can use your phones. I assure you, the internet won't help with any of the puzzles inside."

He continued, his words speeding up. Why had he made this speech so long? "You won't need to climb on anything. Nothing is hidden in the ceiling. If something is plugged in, please leave it plugged in. If it doesn't move, it's not supposed to. Any questions?"

The dark-haired one raised her hand, but the other slapped it down. "I think we're good," Elena said.

David wasn't so sure of that. "Here's the scenario. You're in prison for a crime you didn't commit. Due to an incident in the yard, you know the guards will be busy for the next hour. Time to execute your escape plan! But remember, if you don't escape in an hour, the guards will return and put you back in lockup."

He opened up the door and led them to the "prison cell" inside. Three sets of handcuffs had been laid out on the bare bed pushed up against one wall. "Who would like to go first?" He held out the cuffs.

"You've got to be kidding me."

Of course the dark-haired one protested, again. Thankfully, Elena stepped in once he pointed out they were only plastic props. He'd had the option to include real handcuffs with his purchase, but he thought these were safer. They could be broken with a strong snap if need be.

Elena was the last one to get cuffed. She gasped as

he slipped the plastic over her slim wrists.

"Too tight?" he murmured.

She shook her head.

"Don't worry, you'll do fine." He met her eyes and smiled.

She smiled back, finally, and for a moment only the two of them were in the room.

He swallowed and let go of her wrists. "Your game master is Sean. He will help with any clues when you need them. The timer on the monitor over there will start once I leave. You have one hour."

Then he closed the door behind them and turned the lock. He hurried back to the control room where he'd left Tony and his employee, Sean, one of the college students he'd hired to game master. The two had probably been watching the entire time on the cameras that covered every inch of the place.

"If you're going to turn into a giant dork every time a hot girl comes in, you might want to reconsider working the front." Tony smirked and spun around in a task chair as David entered the control room.

A flush of warmth hit David, and he hoped he wasn't blushing. Tony had always teased him about his romantic interests, from even before he first met his most recent ex, Laura. At least Tony hadn't been standing next to him when David had made the introductions. No telling what inappropriate thing would have come out of his mouth. One time during freshman year at college, when David was awkwardly trying to ask out one of the girls in their gaming group, Tony had burst in and said absolutely the wrong thing, and she'd never spoken to him again. David had learned his lesson after that—he hadn't introduced Tony to Laura until after they'd been dating for a few months.

"I'm just nervous because they're my first customers," David said to explain away the blush.

Tony sat next to Sean, who seemed very pointedly not looking at Tony as he stared at the computer screen in front of him that showed the split-camera view for the Prison Break Room. Three other desks took up the rest of the space in the room, all with similar computer setups for when David had the business fully staffed. It looked a bit like a security command office when all the screens were on and displaying their respective locations.

Right now the desk next to Sean held an empty pizza box. Sean had a dribble of tomato sauce on his chin, and David itched for a paper towel. Tony was such a bad influence.

No customers would ever be back here. Tony and Sean could be as disgusting as they wanted, no matter how much it annoyed him.

Tony tilted his head to one side and narrowed his eyes. "I don't know, are you dead or blind? All three of them are smoking hot."

David crossed his arms over his chest. "I don't know if you can tell through the cameras, but two of them are Sean's age. That makes them practically babies."

Why did he let himself get drawn in to Tony's bullshit? After knowing the guy for almost twenty years, he should know better.

A red flush started on Sean's cheeks, and he glanced over in David's direction and then back at his screen. The headphones he wore that let him listen in to the room were not noise-canceling—by design. He might need to run to the front if something came up and David wasn't around.

"You're embarrassing Sean." Tony slapped Sean on the back.

Sean, to his credit, didn't react.

"You're thirty-five, not fifty. Plus you're on the rebound. Dating coeds should be your next step."

"Don't be gross," David said. "They are customers. And I came back here to see how they do with my first room."

Tony gave Sean a knowing look and jabbed his elbow into Sean's arm. "At least you can appreciate the view. Huh?"

Sean ducked his head. "The one with the long dark hair is kinda pretty."

"And she's got a nice rack, too." Tony whooped as if he were the college student.

David loved him like a brother, but could the guy grow up at some point? "Out." He pointed. "You don't even work here, and I won't have you ruining my staff."

Tony laughed his way out the door. He lifted his hand and gave a final two-finger salute before exiting.

David settled into the vacated seat next to Sean, feeling like ten times the hypocrite. Tony might have said it crudely, but David really had come here to watch Elena, especially while she still wore the handcuffs. Something about her had drawn him in, and he needed to know more. Watching her solve his escape room would go a long way to telling him a lot about her—how she thought, how she worked with her friends. Here in the control room, David was free to indulge in his curiosity.

He didn't have to feel guilty about that. He was a single man. He could enjoy watching a pretty woman, as long as he wasn't being creepy about it. Oh God, he was being creepy about it. He had been spending way too

16

much time with Tony. David needed to get over Laura and move on, the proper way, not by going on the rebound or eyeing up the women in his escape room.

"They're doing really well," Sean offered. He seemed a bit stiff, his shoulders tight. Of course, this was a big deal for Sean, too. No matter how many times they'd run it as a simulation, nothing substituted for the real thing. Now Sean had to pay close attention, to be ready with the right hint if their clients asked for one. If he lost track of where they were in the room, he wouldn't be able to figure out the proper clue to give them. Also, someone might try to break something—either on purpose or accidentally—and Sean would be responsible for stopping them.

"You're doing great," David encouraged. Despite whatever he had going on in his brain, he couldn't forget his employees. Sean was a good kid, and he put up with Tony without complaining. David couldn't afford to lose him, especially after all the training they'd done. "I'll be here to help if you need it, okay?"

"Got it." Sean nodded. He gripped the mouse a little tighter, but some of the stiffness in his body loosened a bit. David figured that was as good as he was going to get.

He leaned forward to get a better view of the screen. He gave in to the impulse to watch Elena—yeah, he had a good excuse, to help out Sean here, but he didn't deny his own interest in the woman. He wouldn't ever see her again, and he had too much professionalism to do something like slip her his number. He wasn't Tony, for God's sake.

But he'd watch for as long as he could.

Chapter 3

Elena realized the door had no knob the moment after David left and she heard the lock click. The door had even been painted the same gray color as the rest of the wall, with only the grooves to indicate an opening there at all. They wouldn't be escaping through that way. Still, the lack of doorknob disconcerted her.

"Elena." Phoebe held up her cuffed wrists and gave her a pointed look before glancing at the camera in the corner and frowning.

"We'll talk about it later," Elena whispered, not knowing how sensitive the microphones were in this room. "Right now let's focus on getting out of here."

Quinn ignored both of them to search under the single bed on a metal frame. She came back with a long wooden rod. "First step, let's get out of these cuffs."

She walked over to the bars separating them from the rest of the room. On the wall perpendicular to them, a set of keys had been hung on a hook. The rod was just long enough to reach the keys. Elena held her breath as Quinn worked the keys off the hook and carefully brought them into their cell—not easy with her hands cuffed.

"Thank God," Phoebe muttered, holding out her hands and letting Quinn unlock her. She returned the favor, and then Elena got out of her cuffs.

Despite being props, they felt surprisingly real.

Elena rubbed her wrists and scanned the room. The set design was incredible—the cinder-block design on the walls, the metal bars, the toilet against one wall, and the guards' station she could see just outside their cell. "All right, let's start looking."

She attacked the small wooden dresser next to the bed, opening up each drawer. Inside she found a baseball bobblehead figure. The base had been altered into a much more solid wood than it should be. *Aha.* Clearly a puzzle piece. It might unlock a magnet lock or be a part of a larger puzzle.

"Got a box with a four-digit lock." Phoebe pulled it out from behind the toilet. "That's totally gross, by the way."

Quinn was sorting through the stack of books on the tiny bookshelf. "What are the odds these are just a red herring?"

"Unless something points us to the books, pretty good, I'd say." Sometimes designers would throw props into the room that didn't mean anything but kept players from focusing on the real game elements.

Elena squinted at the posters on the wall. Something about them looked fishy. She lifted the curling edge and found writing underneath. "Gotcha."

Black ink had been scrawled on the gray walls, laying out an escape plan. They'd probably use this information later as well. But she fixated on step one—*use map of the cell to escape.* "Anyone find anything that looks like a map?"

Quinn lifted the second poster. "Not yet. But here they mention their favorite quote is on page thirty-two…"

"Of what book?"

"Check them all." Elena looked back at the dresser. Something about the surface—it looked almost indented, like something belonged there. She tried running the bobblehead along the top, but that wasn't the trigger at all.

"Got it. Phoebe, that lock is three, three, four, five."

Phoebe went to work on the box and emptied its contents on the bed—blocky wooden puzzle pieces. A very distinct pattern was embossed on one side of each block.

"Is that a map?" Elena picked up a piece and turned it over. It had to go on the dresser. She started to assemble it and got most of the way before she realized they were missing a piece. "Crap. Look for more of these."

In the background, soft music played. She looked up at the monitor where a timer ticked down. Was David watching them? He'd said they had a game master, but this was the first room, so he might be monitoring to make sure everything went okay. She'd be watching every single room when her business opened, but Elena would be operating on a much smaller scale.

This place was huge. She hadn't expected the empty store to have so much space. Four escape rooms? How was she going to compete with that when she had only two ready to go next weekend?

If David had been a jerk, Elena could go on hating him. But he'd been so kind to them, not like the arrogant owners she'd met before. He'd smiled at her, revealing honest-to-God dimples in his cheeks. His brown eyes had a glint in them, and something in the way he looked at her...

"Got it." Phoebe held up the missing piece, a

triumphant grin on her face. She placed it on the dresser top, and the metal bars slid open.

"Oh, nice tech." Quinn paused to take a look at the magnetic lock on the bars while Elena and Phoebe squeezed past her.

The second half of the room had been set up like a guard's station—with a computer, file cabinet, and a row of bookshelves. Elena noted the indented space on a bookshelf. On a hunch, she grabbed the bobblehead from the cell, and it fit the notch perfectly. Unfortunately, four more notches stood empty—and she wasn't sure what order they needed to go in.

"If either of you finds any more bobbleheads, I need them here." She turned around to find Quinn frowning at the computer screen, which was blank.

"Do you need a way to turn it on?"

"It is on, but I think it's one of those screens where you need special glasses to see." Quinn gestured at it.

"If you look at it from an angle, sometimes you can make it out." Phoebe bent her head sideways and kept twisting around.

Elena ignored them and attacked the file cabinet where she found another bobblehead. "Keep searching. We'll worry about the computer later." Sometimes they couldn't complete a puzzle until they found all the missing information. They shouldn't waste time playing with the computer until they found what they needed— in this case most likely special glasses.

They did have to go back to the cell a few times to get data from the plan written behind the poster. Mainly the baseball teams that the guard liked ranked in order from best to worst, which was how they ordered the bobbleheads. One was missing.

Eventually, they figured out the code for the lock holding one of the file cabinet drawers shut. Inside Quinn pulled out a few pairs of glasses, which were what enabled them to finally view the computer screen.

" 'Prisoner transfer,' " Quinn read. " 'Input the location of transfer.' Great, did we see that anywhere?"

"That must be a reason for the map of the US on the wall." Phoebe stood in front of it and frowned. They hadn't used the map to solve anything yet, and Elena should have known it would come up.

She ran her fingers along it, looking for any clue about the destination the computer was requesting. But it felt smooth. Nothing was bold or highlighted, and she frowned at it. "Do we need to ask for a clue?"

"Oh, hell, no." Phoebe popped back into the cell. "Did you notice there are coordinates listed on the little map we used to get out?"

"Give them to me."

Phoebe called out the number, and Elena matched the longitude and latitude.

"Got it. It's San Quentin."

Quinn's fingers raced across the keyboard. Elena looked up at the timer, not happy with having only ten minutes left. They didn't know how much they still had to do, and she didn't see an exit point.

A drawer on the desk popped open, revealing the final bobblehead. Quinn picked it up and placed it on the shelf where it belonged. In response, yet another drawer on the desk opened. Damn it, that wasn't the last puzzle? She'd hoped the wall would open once they put the last figure in place.

Elena pulled open the drawer and pulled out a screwdriver. "What?" What were they supposed to do with this?

They stared at each other for a moment, then scattered, looking for what they needed the tool for. Elena noted the screws holding the map to the wall, but disregarded them. She wandered back into the cell and noted the very large vent. It didn't quite connect completely with the wall, and the screwdriver fit the oversized screws perfectly. "I hope this is right."

She bent and unscrewed the vent, then popped it out from the wall. A piece of black fabric greeted her, which she pushed out of the way to see a crawl space. "This way, ladies!" Elena ducked, careful not to hit her head—she'd done that a few too many times.

Phoebe and Quinn scrambled behind her. But just when they thought they were done, they came to a door with a keypad and flashing lights.

"Damn."

"Did we see a code for this? I didn't see a code for this!" Phoebe turned around and went back into the cell.

Quinn stared at the lock, and a light appeared in her eyes. "We don't need a code. The code is the flashing green lights. And the red lights are the time we have to input it. It changes every cycle, see?"

Elena did, after a moment. "Can you figure it out?"

"Sure. Only problem is that I don't know if the zero is the first light or the last light." Quinn scrambled to the keypad and started entering numbers.

In here Elena didn't have a screen to look at. She had no idea how much time was left. Her heart pounded too loudly, and adrenaline coursed through her. She could smell her own sweat mixed with sawdust and paint. Were they going to make it? She was not going to lose to her competition!

"Damn it. Zero is at the end." Quinn watched the lights cycle through again, and once again Elena couldn't do anything but kneel there. God, she hated this kind of thing.

Phoebe came stumbling back into the crawlspace falling on one knee. "Do you have it?"

"Now I do." Quinn punched in the final code, and the door popped open. Colored lights flashed just outside the room, and a recorded voice said, "Congratulations on escaping the room!"

They emerged into the same hallway but out of another door.

David came down the hallway, a big smile on his face. "Congrats! You did great. You had two minutes left!"

They could have done better.

Chapter 4

David vibrated with excitement. Putting together and beta testing the rooms didn't compare to watching real live customers working out his puzzles. Granted, he had purchased these first few rooms, but he had every intention of designing the next on his own. That didn't mean he couldn't take pride in a business he had put together from the ground up. He might not have created the puzzle chain, but he'd helped install it and learned every nuance of the room so he could jump in and help if a customer needed it.

These ladies hadn't needed his help at all. They'd rocked the room, not even asking for a clue. Poor Sean hadn't even had to type anything, although he'd been at the ready, hands on the keyboard, with sweat dripping down the sides of his face. It hadn't been a test for him at all, but he got the first room out of the way. He'd be less nervous next time.

David should thank them for that, and the words were on his lips when he saw the angry expression on Elena's face. She straight up glared at him, and her eyes blazed with fire. He nearly took a step back in the face of it. Was she pissed about the last puzzle? He had to admit it was a bit of a dirty trick, having something so complicated at the end of the puzzle chain. Still, when he'd approved the design, he couldn't resist leaving it in. It made the room so authentic.

He couldn't meet those angry eyes and found himself looking down as if he were a kid in school being told he had detention. He ended up looking at Elena's feet, noticing for the first time the odd shoes she wore. They reminded him of the orthopedic shoes some of his mother's friends trotted around in. Maybe she was a nurse or some other profession that spent a lot of time on her feet.

He'd come up with a dozen scenarios if he stood here speculating all day. The shoes bugged him because they didn't fit, and he needed things to fit. Of course, what he really wanted was to ask her out. She was gorgeous, and she'd solved his puzzles. God, what more could he ask for?

David cleared his throat and forced himself back into his customer-service personality. Because they were customers, not his personal dating service. "Please follow me to the lobby." He gestured down the hall, resisting the urge to bow as well. "We have bottles of water and bracelets for you."

Tony had been the one to hook him up with a business that could print anything, and he'd gotten David a good deal on little rubber bracelets with *The Greatest Escape* printed on one side and the name of the room completed on the other. Customers loved swag, and swag that showed off his business name made a great conversation piece. Plus, it made for an incentive to come back and complete their collection, since each bracelet came in a different color to match the theme of the room. At least Tony was good for something. He had a better sense for business than, well, romantic entanglements. David nearly laughed at the thought.

"That final puzzle, was it an Arduino or a Raspberry

Pi?" The one with blue hair pointed with her thumb toward the final door.

He started walking down the hall while he thought about the question. He'd never considered what to tell technophiles about his room designs. He hadn't thought anyone would care. "You should meet my friend Tony. You both speak the same language."

"I take it that means you don't know?" Her question had an arrogant tone to it. Wow, yeah, she and Tony would really get along. Either that or kill each other on sight.

Why did she care so much? Could they be secret reviewers? David had heard about that online, people going into escape rooms and then writing up reviews on blogs. He'd chatted with some of the other owners on the private Facebook group about what to do if he ever encountered them. Of course, if they were secret reviewers, how was he going to know? Maybe this was the clue, why they asked all these questions about his technology.

He kept the smile on his face as he replied, not wanting to offend her if his hunch turned out to be true and they were secret shoppers. "It means I like to keep a sense of mystery. Why worry about the man behind the curtain?"

Escape rooms were meant to be fun and, in his opinion, more fun if they didn't show the workings behind the room. It's why exposed wiring in rooms made him absolutely nuts. Customers couldn't get lost in the illusion of a pharaoh's tomb if the wires beneath the sarcophagus gave it away. David prided himself on providing an immersive experience, and that meant not giving away his secrets.

He picked up his pace, wanting to get to the lobby to avoid answering any more questions. If they were reviewers, they'd have to come clean before they got any more information from him. Once they made it to the lobby, he picked up the silver tray with bottles of water and the bracelets.

"You weren't kidding about the bracelets." The dark-haired woman Sean had liked grabbed one and slid it on her wrist. The Prison Break bracelets were made of black rubber, but the other rooms had been color coordinated with their respective murals. "Where did you get these?"

He ignored the question for the moment and set down the now-empty tray. He walked over to where he'd set up the camera and tripod while they were in the vent. At that point he'd known they were almost finished; all they had left was the final puzzle. Two baskets sat propped next to the wall, both filled with large cardboard signs. The ones in the winner basket said things like *we did it* and *Escape Room Master* while the loser one had phrases like *so close* and *almost made it!* This group would be using the winner versions. "Would you like to take a picture for our Facebook page?"

Elena froze in the middle of examining her bracelet as if he'd said something shocking. "No, thank you."

"Come on. You're my first customers." He had a legitimate reason for wanting a picture of them. Pictures of actual customers on his Facebook page would do wonders for his engagement and entice others to try the room. However, he could hear Tony's voice in his head, laughing at him for being a coward.

Damn it. He should just ask for her phone number. No need to be creepy. He was out of practice with this.

28

Being stuck in a relationship for two years that suddenly ended would do that. He almost wished Tony were still here to say something inappropriate. Then David would look much better in comparison.

"No, dude, seriously, we can't. I have a restraining order out on my stalker ex-boyfriend, and I can't have my face on a public Facebook page." The dark-haired one leveled wide eyes at him, and her explanation caught him off guard. He didn't know how to respond to that.

She went to grab their coats, and the three draped themselves in winter apparel quickly, far too quickly for David to think of anything to say other than, "Well, I hope you enjoyed yourselves. Please come back and check out one of my other rooms."

He waved as they shuffled out the door, the bell above jangling loudly. He watched them leave and murmured to himself, "Please?"

****

Elena couldn't shake the feeling of David's eyes on her as they left. She didn't look back to see if he still stood there, staring at them. Maybe he'd gotten suspicious. They'd asked one too many questions. And they refused to take a photo for his page. Normally, she didn't mind because most of the rooms she did as research were not her direct competitors.

But for her picture to be the first one on David's Facebook page? No. Fucking. Way.

Phoebe turned around and opened her mouth, murder in her eyes. Honestly, Elena had been impressed Phoebe managed to hold it in the entire time they were in the escape room. Elena grabbed her arm and steered her in the right direction. "Wait until we get in the car." Who knew how well sound carried in this strip mall?

They piled back into Phoebe's sedan. Elena looked back once, positive she saw David still standing in the doorway. "Phoebe, drive around the block. We don't want him to see us pull in across the street."

Maybe David stood in the doorway to keep watch for other customers. She had no reason to think he was still watching them. She might be taking this cloak and dagger thing a bit too far, what with the corporate espionage and low-speed car chase.

"First of all." Phoebe pulled them out of the lot onto the street, accelerating to match the flow of traffic. "Putting us in handcuffs? That's against fire code."

Elena had spent weeks poring over rules and regulations before the fire inspector came to review her rooms. She'd needed her typical attention to detail to make sure everything was up to code, or else the city would stop her from opening. She knew exactly where else David's room failed. "Plus the lack of emergency exit. Remember? That door didn't have a knob on the other side. He'd better hope no one has a bathroom emergency."

"Is that what the toilet in the cell was for?" Quinn pulled out her tablet again and started jotting down notes.

"Oh, that is so gross," Phoebe said. "And totally illegal."

Elena frowned. In some ways, David's room impressed her. "It might have been gross, but it felt like a prison cell. I'd have to give him points for the immersion factor."

"Having never been in prison, I'm not so sure about that," Quinn said. "But other than ambiance, was it a good room?"

"It depended a lot on hiding things," Phoebe mused,

30

driving them leisurely through the streets. She could have turned back a few times but kept going. "There were some cool tech puzzles, but overall I'd rate it as average."

Elena played with her seat belt, giving in to fidgeting. She couldn't disagree with Phoebe. All the puzzles were variations on ones they've seen before, except for the very last one. "I loved how he decorated. Those murals are gorgeous." The thought of doing something like that hadn't even occurred to her. She'd kept the original woodwork and paint of her historical building. "Everything there is so shiny and new."

Phoebe seemed to pick up on her distress. "Hey. It's totally different from your rooms."

"Exactly. I don't have the same level of technology." Her business was doomed before she had even opened.

"Stop that. Quinn, smack her. I'm driving." Phoebe finally took a right, driving back toward The Escape Space. "What you created is awesome. Don't let some asshole get you down. We are totally going to rock that opening next week. Tell her, Quinn."

"Totally," Quinn agreed, looking up from her tablet. "Phoebe does have a point. Your work is different enough to stand out, I think. We can emphasize that in the advertising."

"About the opening…should we move it up?" Elena could see dollars drifting away the longer David stayed open before she did. He'd grab the market share and was likely to get customers who were shopping in the strip mall. She really needed that college-student clientele to come through.

"We can't. All the flyers are already printed with the

date," Phoebe reminded her.

What she needed was a truly grand opening. Something so big it would make everyone forget about David's rooms. She closed her eyes. How could she do that? All of her capital was sunk in the business. "Then we need to ramp up the advertising. We need to book every single one of those slots."

Even David hadn't done that. His afternoon schedule had been completely empty.

Phoebe pulled into the gravel lot on the side of The Escape Space, what used to be the backyard of the converted house Elena had bought. They rolled to a stop, and then she turned and leaned over the seat to look at Elena. "I'll talk to some guys on my floor. This would make a great frat initiation."

Yes. This was what Elena had over David, an in with the college crowd. "Do that. Get as many people as you can to come give it a try. We're going to want our Facebook page flooded with photos. And, uh, Quinn, do you think you can find us a tripod?" Seeing David's made her think it would be useful to have—no shaky camera, blurry pictures for their webpage.

"I'll find one."

Elena took a deep breath. They were going to rock that opening, and she'd show David who had the greatest escape room.

Chapter 5

David's phone buzzed as he finished typing in a clue to help the currently very stuck group of customers in the Prison Break Room. They were his last group of the night, reserving the ten-thirty slot. It was now very close to eleven thirty, and they didn't look like they were going to make it. For the past ten minutes, they'd circled the desk, not knowing what to do with the bobbleheads they kept finding. Someone eventually figured it out, and now they stood around staring at the screwdriver, discussing what they should do with it. David needed to intervene before they started using it on the computer.

He shifted his headphones to around his neck, so he could still kind of hear what was going on in the room, and answered the phone. "Hi, Momma. I didn't forget to call. I'm still working."

"It sounds like it's been a productive day." She chuckled. "I'm about to go to bed, and I wanted to check in and see how it all went."

Use the screwdriver on the vent cover in the cell, David typed out, since his original hint hadn't done anything to spur the team along. They stared up at the monitor with the hint until finally someone ran to the vent. Even if they got it open in time, he doubted they would be able to figure out the end puzzle with so little time remaining.

"I think it was a good first day. I only had one room

33

open to see what the traffic was like." He had very little downtime during the day, which might have been due to the novelty of a new escape room opening. He needed to keep the traffic coming if he wanted to be successful, but he'd worry about that tomorrow. Right now all he wanted was to head home and sleep after the long day.

He'd sent Sean home an hour ago, confident he could run the last room himself. Only after he was gone had David realized he was also going to have to restage everything for tomorrow's early bookings. Why hadn't he thought of that earlier? Now he'd have to stay even later. *Mental note—next time keep the college kid around to do the cleanup.*

Who was he kidding? He'd go home to a dark and empty house, without even a pet excited to see him when he walked through the door. Before, when Laura still lived there, he'd come home from work so late he'd slip into bed, and she'd barely stir at his presence. Leaving work at a normal time would have been the unusual.

Maybe he should consider putting a cot in the corner of the control room. Why bother driving twenty minutes when he could sleep right there? At that point he should consider selling his house and ditching the mortgage. God, how had this become his life? No one waiting for him at home, a fridge full of expiring takeout, and a pile of laundry sitting around waiting for him to decide if it was clean or dirty. No wonder he didn't want to go home.

"And how was it?" His mother's voice drew him out of his sudden bout of self-pity.

"Busy in the evening. I had one booking this afternoon." Oh, but what a booking it had been. David couldn't stop thinking about his first customers, the three women who'd come in and conquered his first escape room without a hint. No, he should be honest with himself. Elena had captured his attention. He regretted not asking for her phone number. He should have taken the chance when he had it, instead of sitting here wondering what she would have said if he asked. He couldn't have been the only one to feel that spark when their hands touched, could he? Now he'd probably never see her again and kicked himself.

Of course, he couldn't tell his mother any of that.

"I'm meeting new people," he said instead, which was true although skirting the issue on his mind currently. So many people had walked through his doors, yet none had been as memorable as Elena. That was probably a good thing since he couldn't afford to be that distracted as he ran his business.

"That's nice, dear. Any pretty girls?"

"Mom." How did she always know? David never could hide anything from her, and this time he didn't even have anything to hide.

"Well, you know I'm not getting any younger." Her voice rose at the end.

He knew she was hinting about grandchildren. She'd always joked about that, but the reminder bothered him. No, she wasn't getting any younger, and she still lived all by herself. It made David worry, especially now that he couldn't easily pop up there to make sure she was okay, not when he had a business to run. "You should get to sleep, Mom. It's late."

"Oh, please, I won't turn into a pumpkin. Maybe I can make it down next weekend, and you can show me what all the fuss is about."

Finally, she'd be able to see the results of his hard work. Before all the props had been installed, his place had looked like a bunch of bare walls with paint slapped on. His mother had never seen everything completed, and she was in for a treat. He immediately started to plan what he would show her first. Maybe the Underwater City Room. As a math teacher, she'd really appreciate the puzzles in there.

"Sounds like a plan. Love you, Mom."

He ended the call and checked in on his customers still trapped in the tunnel outside the prison cell. The timer counted down to zero, and the failure buzzer sounded. He needed to go let his customers out of their prison cell.

The group came out disappointed but told David they wanted to know when his other rooms were open. He handed out a flyer with the room descriptions, the water, and bracelets before having the customers all pose in front of the logo for a picture. No one else had given him a hard time about the Facebook photo. No one but Elena.

Damn it, could he ever stop thinking about her? Her striking hair, her sharp eyes, the way she carried herself with grace, and most of all, the way she'd smiled at him. He'd most likely never see her again, not unless she came back to do another one of his rooms. He could only dream of that happening.

****

Elena spent the rest of the day working with Phoebe and Quinn, putting the finishing touches on the rooms and the technology. They made notes about what still needed to be done, and she made phone calls to some of Phoebe's friends to come beta test the rooms that week. Tomorrow she'd need to go buy some extra locks and batteries. She never could have enough of those. She had been in too many rooms where the flashlight batteries had failed and ruined the entire experience. Not on her watch.

Finally, she sent Phoebe and Quinn home for the night. "I don't have enough money to pay you overtime."

"Yet!" Phoebe called from the front porch. "Just you wait. We'll be raking in the cash next week."

"I hope you're right." Elena shook her head and laughed. She nodded to Quinn who stuck her earbuds in her ears and headed down the street. Quinn lived only a few blocks away, which would be helpful once they had late-night bookings.

Elena closed the door behind her and locked it. The silence echoed throughout the empty building. They'd shut down all the computers, so for the first time she didn't hear the hum of the electronics. The lack of sound made everything echo. She pulled her phone out of her pocket and queued up a playlist of some of her favorite songs. She nodded her head to the beat as she headed upstairs.

She did one more walkthrough of the two escape rooms, her hands touching every polished wood surface and lock. These rooms held her creativity and hard work. She had put so much of herself into them. All she could do was hope that her customers liked them. She had to accept much of her success or failure was out of her hands.

Especially with the newcomer across the street. Elena had factored in saturation of the market—it's why she chose this town over any other since New Brunswick lacked an escape room business. But now it would be blessed with two opening at the same time. At least Phoebe was right—Elena's rooms were nothing like

David's. They couldn't even compare. Hers were far more traditional while his had flashy technology.

How much money had he sunk into those rooms? She knew from experience that those third-party companies charged ridiculous prices for complete creations. Elena had discarded even the idea of purchasing from them on cost alone, but more than that, she wanted to be the architect of her own designs. She had a story she wanted to tell, and she used her escape rooms to do that.

She couldn't blame David for buying his rooms although she could blame him for not noticing she was about to open up across the street. Damn him and his sleepy bedroom eyes and his hardworking hands and the way he smiled at her...

Elena went back to the main floor and opened the door built into the bottom half of the staircase to access her basement apartment. She'd loved this about the house. It felt like she was entering her home through a secret passage. Customers wouldn't be able to see it, and no one would know she lived right downstairs. The steps creaked, showing their age, as she made her way down the narrow staircase.

The lights flickered on, and her wireless speakers picked up the music from the phone, filling the apartment with sound. She'd thought she'd love living by herself after years of sharing apartments with multiple roommates in New York City. But Elena found she couldn't take the quiet.

She missed Jesse lounging on the bed, flipping through the TV while icing his feet as she sewed elastic into her pointe shoes. Hell, she even missed Sharon, who had a tendency to talk through her nose in the most annoying way. When Phoebe and Quinn were here, she didn't have time to be lonely, to listen to the sounds of silence.

Soon, if things went well, this entire building would be filled with people, at all hours of the day. Maybe then she would long for the quiet.

She had spent so much time on her escape rooms she hadn't gotten around to completely unpacking. She had moving boxes stacked in the corner, and part of her knew she was avoiding the contents. Some things from her past should stay boxed up. Costumes, shoes, and other mementos would only remind her of what she'd lost.

Elena sat on her bed and carefully untied her orthopedic shoes, wincing at the swelling in her feet. She'd spent too much time standing today. They'd told her it would get better, and every day she did feel a little stronger. She had never been patient. She'd always pushed through pain, always focused on the dance. But pushing too hard now could hurt her permanently.

She worked through her physical-therapy exercises with the same care and dedication she used to apply to her dancing. Her feet had been her instrument. They'd held up her body as she twisted and twirled into impossible poses. They'd been broken and put back together, but she'd never fly through the air again.

Elena reached for her phone and changed the music, this time to something a little more upbeat. No use getting depressed about what she couldn't change.

Her email dinged as she scrolled through her playlist, and curious, she opened the app. She expected the email from The Greatest Escape asking her to rate their room, but another, more-intriguing email caught her attention with the subject line *An Opportunity*.

She read it quickly, then once again slowly. It made her scalp prickle. If she went through with it, this could give her the advantage over David and his too-perfect rooms and his big bright smile. She tapped a response before tossing the phone on the bed and flopping backward, immediately second-guessing herself.

The music flowed through her, and she felt the notes all the way to her bones, just like up on stage. It had been something that never left her even after she stopped dancing. She decided to use this song in the Uncle Enzo room for background noise. The rising tension would be the perfect companion as players worked their way through the puzzles, slowly discovering the truth about their long-lost uncle.

She had that over David's rooms. Elena understood story and drama. With nothing more than a smile, she could make a stage come alive.

She'd show him exactly what he was up against.

Chapter 6

"I found a guy on Craig's List who's selling a coffin for pretty cheap," Phoebe said, not looking up from her computer at the receptionist's station in the lobby. The click of the mouse sounded unnaturally loud in the sudden silence.

Elena lifted her head from checking train schedules on her phone. She looked over at Quinn, who sat on the floor wrestling with wires and circuit boards. Quinn didn't seem inclined to say anything, so she bit the bullet and asked, "What would we do with a coffin?"

"We could put it in Uncle Enzo's room. Isn't it supposed to be his wake?" Phoebe suggested.

Elena gave it some thought. While she had to admit the idea of having a coffin in the room would be incredibly dramatic, it wasn't exactly the feel she was going for. "The objective is to find his will. The assumption is that he's been dead for a while. And the last thing I need is for someone to climb into the coffin and get stuck in there."

Quinn snickered. "I can imagine what the fire marshal would have to say about that."

Well, that put the kibosh on any plans to use the coffin for a Halloween event. "Sorry, Phoebe, you can't buy the coffin."

"Someday." Phoebe shook her fist at the computer screen. "You wouldn't believe the things people sell on the internet…"

"Don't buy anything while I'm gone." Elena grabbed her handbag, which was large enough to hold her nice shoes. She had to wear her orthopedics to walk to the train station but planned on changing right before her appointment. She wore sensible slacks and a blazer over a white shell. Her winter coat would cover it all up until she was safely inside. This March weather could warm up any time now.

"Where are you going?" Phoebe stopped her perusing of the web market and finally looked up. She tilted her head to one side. "And why so snazzy?"

Elena let out a sigh. The other night she'd been so sure about going to this meeting, but this morning she felt conflicted about it. "I'm going to meet with Sven Svenson."

Phoebe and Quinn exchanged looks. "Who?"

"He's the owner of the Escape-o-Rama franchise. Don't look at me like that." Both of them had rolled their eyes and tossed their heads in response.

"Why exactly are you going to meet with that guy?" Phoebe asked.

Elena knew they wouldn't like what she had to say next. She sat back down, figuring this conversation might take a while. "He contacted me about a franchising opportunity."

"One second." Phoebe held out her hand as if she were warding Elena away. "Whatever happened to Miss Do-It-On-Her-Own, None-Of-This-Franchise-Crap?"

"I know," Elena said. "And normally, I'd never even consider it."

"Don't tell me you're worried about that asshole across the street?"

"Of course I am." Her voice rose as she spoke. "And a franchise comes with name recognition and a built-in customer base. I'd have an edge over him, and at this point I think I might need it."

David had more rooms than she did. He had the ability to grow. And apparently, he had enough capital to purchase slick-looking designs and gorgeous murals. She was proud of her work, but she didn't want to be compared to David. She needed something to give her an advantage.

"But your original reasons for not doing it are still valid." Quinn gestured with what looked like a tiny wrench.

"I still think I should see what he has to say. He went to the trouble of contacting me."

"That's shady as hell," Phoebe insisted.

"We can argue about it later. I need to get to the train station before I miss my train." Elena checked the schedule on her phone one more time.

"I can drive you," Phoebe offered.

She shook her head. "I can't keep relying on you to take me places. Besides, there's nothing wrong with taking public transportation."

"Spoken like an ex-New Yorker," Phoebe teased. "Where's the meeting?"

"At his office in Edison." Not far. Only a few stops over. Shouldn't be too bad.

"Seriously? What are you going to do once you get to Metropark? Take a cab? What if your train's late, then what?"

Elena opened her mouth to respond, but Phoebe wasn't done.

"You can't just leave an important meeting like this

in the hands of public transportation."

"I thought you said this meeting was shady." Elena threw up her arms.

"Boss, I'm gonna have to bring you into the twenty-first century. Let me introduce you to Uber."

"I prefer Lyft myself," Quinn interjected.

"I know what Uber is," Elena snapped.

How could she explain it to them when she didn't quite understand herself? Since the accident, she hadn't felt comfortable around cars. Sometimes she could be a passenger and be fine, and other times her heart would squeeze itself in her chest until she could barely breathe. She'd come to rely on Phoebe's driving and eventually trusted Phoebe enough to not worry about freaking out in the back seat. Most of the time.

But could she let a total stranger drive her? Elena swallowed. She knew it was illogical—trains and buses were driven by people, after all. She'd come this far relying on public transportation, but she'd never be free if she couldn't let go of this one illogical fear.

Maybe someday she could get back behind the driver's seat of a car, but today wasn't it. Perhaps this was a tiny step on the way there.

"Fine, get me an Uber." She tossed her phone to Phoebe.

Phoebe looked down at it, tapped at the screen for a second, and then tossed it over to Quinn who sighed. "Don't ever let Phoebe install anything on your phone."

"Got it."

****

The Uber driver got Elena to her destination early. She had to brace herself against the wall of the building and wait for her breathing to settle down. Tiny crescents marked her palms from her nails digging into her skin for the entire ride. She took out her phone and made sure to give the driver five stars. Quinn had emphasized how important that was. And, hey, he'd gotten her here despite her rocking back and forth in her seat.

She let out a little laugh and knocked her head back against the wall. She'd done it. She'd actually done it—gotten into a car with a stranger and managed not to throw up or otherwise embarrass herself too much. Score one point for her.

She was going to have to do it again to get home.

Okay, one step at a time. She entered the office building and took off her coat, draping it over her arm. She couldn't wait for spring to finally show up so she could stop lugging this heavy thing around. A directory printed in gold on the wall told her where to go. This building rented out suites to multiple corporations, but she found the bright Escape-o-Rama logo listed on the eighth floor. She walked to the elevator, the sound of her dress flats echoing on the polished marble. She'd left the orthopedics at home once she'd committed to the Uber idea.

The elevator opened to yet another hallway, and Elena took a minute before heading to the appropriate suite number. *I am a fellow business owner. I am here for an opportunity. It doesn't matter that he's a multimillionaire and I'm not.*

She threw her shoulders back, her spine ramrod straight as if she were going out on stage with perfect posture. She pulled open the door and glided inside, nodding at the receptionist sitting at the desk. "Good morning. I have an eleven o'clock appointment with Mr. Svenson."

The young woman pushed up her thick black plastic glasses and got to her feet. "I'll just let him know you're here." She left her desk and walked to one of the doors down the corridor to the left. The receptionist wore heels so high just looking at them made Elena's ankles ache.

Along the wall were framed posters, all advertising different escape room themes done by Escape-o-Rama. They were done in the style of old circus posters and looked to be hand-illustrated. Elena stopped in front of the one for The Speakeasy. The artist had done a damn good job portraying a young woman dressed as a flapper, with a tommy-gun car-chase scene behind her. Too bad the actual escape room wouldn't be so exciting. She made a mental note to check that one out at some point, to see if they'd done anything different. Speakeasies were a common escape room theme.

The art reminded her of the murals in David's business. They all had vibrant colors that drew the eye and invited the viewer to want to know more. Elena would have to look into something similar. It was too good a marketing opportunity to miss out on. Maybe Phoebe knew some artists at her college who might be interested. She'd have to remember to ask when she got back.

Of course, seeing the art made her think about David again. Why couldn't she get him out of her head? She needed to focus on finishing her rooms and taking the market by storm. If she kept comparing herself to him, she wouldn't accomplish anything. They had completely different rooms and different styles of doing things.

The receptionist returned, somehow able to walk soundlessly on those stilts. "You can go right in."

"Thank you."

The first thing Elena noted as she stepped through the door was the smell of popcorn. A glance to her right showed the source—Svenson had a giant popcorn cart, the kind found at a carnival. It chugged right along, spouting out pops of warm, buttery popcorn, filling the air with its rich scent.

Her mouth watered.

The popcorn maker wasn't the only thing that looked to be rescued from a circus. A crane machine sat in the opposite corner. The walls had been painted with red-and-white stripes, making it feel like the inside of a circus tent. Elena fully expected Sven Svenson to be wearing a top hat and carrying a whip.

Instead he wore a pair of acid-washed jeans, an Escape-o-Rama T-shirt, and a cashmere blazer over the entire ensemble. He crossed the room and held out his hand with a smile, his pin-straight blond hair brushing the tips of his shoulders. "Ms. Evans. So good to meet you in person."

She shook his hand, making sure to tighten her grip as she gave her most dazzling smile. "Mr. Svenson. Pleasure."

"Please, it's Sven." He gestured to the popcorn maker. "Would you care for something to eat or drink? The popcorn is fresh."

"No, thank you." She might have been tempted, but the least professional thing she could think of was sitting there munching kernels while they talked business. "Are you planning a carnival room?"

"I can see why you might think that." He walked over to the cart and used a silver scoop to fill a red-and-white box with popcorn, which he took back to his desk. "Have a seat."

Elena kept her coat in her lap as she took the seat closest to the door, a dark-green and chrome monstrosity that was surprisingly comfortable as she sank into it. She crossed her legs and attempted to look comfortable.

"I'm in the entertainment business. Escape rooms are only one aspect of that. I own several arcades down the shore. They've treated me well. But people are looking for the next big thing. In a world of digital crap"—he made a gesture with one finger—"people are looking for the physical connection. The analog. That's why escape rooms have become so popular."

"That's one way of looking at it," she conceded. She'd always been a tactile person herself, so she could sort of see his point.

He nodded. "I'm sure you encountered that in your previous occupation."

"Excuse me?" She stiffened. He couldn't mean...

"You were a dancer, weren't you?" He smiled, setting the popcorn down. "I googled you. I assume you googled me as well."

A flare of rage raced through her. How dare he? She knew about the horrible pictures on the internet, newspaper articles of the accident with nasty headlines like "Famous Ballet Dancer Will Never Dance Again," and that had even been before she'd known that for certain. A few pins in her ankles had ended her career.

She shouldn't be this upset. Of course he'd research any potential business partner. But he'd stumbled onto something she didn't want to discuss. Her past career influenced her work, yes, of course, but she preferred to focus on her potential now. The past was just that, in the past. Svenson should be doing the same—focusing on the future—unless he was thinking he could get some bonus points for knowing things about her.

It left a sour taste in her mouth, the scent of the popcorn too cloying now. Elena put a mental check in the "no" column in her mind. Still, she smiled as she said, "I'd hoped we could talk about the future instead. Like the opportunity you mentioned in your email."

"Ah, yes. My franchise. You understand that usually people approach me. I have the most well-known franchise of escape rooms in this state."

She bit her lip to refrain from mentioning Escape Tactics, the international escape room franchise company. That one was still getting a foothold in New Jersey—it had only one location so far. But Svenson didn't seem at all threatened by them.

"New Brunswick was a market I could never quite crack. And then, out of nowhere, there are not one, but two escape rooms opening." He leaned forward, spearing her with accusing pale-blue eyes.

Forgive me for not informing you first. She kept the sarcasm to herself. "Imagine my surprise when I found out another room was opening so close to my location." Right across the street. She still couldn't quite believe it.

"You see the wisdom in considering a franchise opportunity. I've taken the liberty of drawing up the paperwork. You can have your lawyer review it if you wish. You'll see it's all on the up-and-up." He opened a drawer in his desk and withdrew a manila folder, then slid it across.

She had to lean forward to grab it. She opened it and couldn't hold back a gasp. "That's the upfront cost? For the name alone?" It was far higher than she'd imagined. "I'm not going to waste your time, Mr. Svenson. I can't afford the price of admission."

"If you'll look at page three, you'll see that is easily addressed."

Elena flipped through the pages. She skimmed the words twice to be sure she understood. "In exchange for the upfront cost, you'd be entitled to a percentage of all of my profits?"

Phoebe had been right. This was super shady.

"Exactly. You don't have to worry about not having the startup capital. I make things very easy for my franchises."

She closed the folder and pressed her hand on top, the coldness of the cardstock seeping through her fingers. She licked her lips, unable to keep up the smile she'd managed for most of the meeting. "Thank you for your generous offer—"

He clearly didn't catch the light sarcasm there based on the grin he still wore.

"—but it's not right for me."

His smile never changed, but his eyes narrowed. "Excuse me?"

Had no one ever turned him down before? She put the folder back on the desk, between the popcorn and a pencil cup shaped like a clown's head. "Financially, it doesn't work for me. Thank you." She started to stand.

"I suggest you reconsider. This opportunity will turn your little no-name escape room into a well-known respected chain."

"Another cog in the machine," she said, her mask slipping. The last thing she wanted.

He leaned back in his chair and folded his hands in front of him like a B-movie villain. "Machines work for a reason. Take the folder. Think about it some more. Call me when you're ready to deal."

She knew her answer would stick, but Elena picked up the folder anyway. Tucking it beneath her coat, she turned to leave.

"And Ms. Evans?"

She stopped at the door and looked back.

"Remember you're not the only escape room in New Brunswick. Perhaps your competitor won't be so quick to say no."

She opened the door and left without a word in return.

Damn him and David and every man who thought they knew better than she did. Elena had poured her heart into her business, and that's what would set her apart from both of them. She'd show them all.

Chapter 7

"I told you I'd make it."

David smiled at his mother as she burst through the glass doors of The Greatest Escape. The sharp March wind followed her in and temporarily chilled everyone inside. She wore her tan winter coat, which only emphasized her bright burgundy curls.

He hugged her and smelled the rich vanilla of her Shalimar perfume. She'd worn the same perfume ever since she left his father. David always thought of it as her badge of freedom. Smelling it now brought a sense of comfort, the kind that usually came with a bowl of chicken soup. He was glad she'd been able to come.

"My turn." Tony slipped in for his own hug. "How you doing, Ms. C?"

"I told you, Tony, it's Marilyn." She stepped back to pat him on the cheek. "When are you going to go back to school, huh?"

He grinned at her. "Once you accept my marriage proposal."

She laughed and swatted at him. "You're horrible."

David shook his head. If he brought up going back to college, Tony would probably punch him. Instead, Tony flirted with Mom. Typical.

"Make sure you come by for lunch. My dad would be mad if you missed his eggplant parm."

"Of course."

Tony waved at them before heading out of the lobby. Despite the fact that he didn't work there, he had made David's place his home away from home. He probably needed to get away from his dad for a little bit. David was happy to provide the service.

"Let me give you the grand tour." He took his mother's coat and hung it up on the hooks in the lobby.

"Oh, that reminds me, I brought you a gift." She reached into her purse—a giant thing that he knew from experience held everything from her wallet to first aid supplies—and pulled out a book. "The entire thing is a puzzle."

He took *The Encyclopedia of Mystery* from her and flipped through it carefully. It in no way resembled a normal book. The first page held instructions for clipping out some of the pages within, based on solving a cipher. He grinned. This was exactly the kind of thing he loved. "Thank you! I can't wait to get started."

"And I can't wait to see your place." She held out her arm, and he linked their arms together as he led her into the back, pointing out the murals along the way.

He decided to show her the Underwater City Room first, since no one was currently playing it. Sean guided a group through the Prison Break Room, and David could hear their squealing and exclamations as they walked past. The Underwater City he'd rated the most difficult of all his rooms, and he was darn proud of it.

The designers had done a magnificent job, creating something out of a steampunk fantasy land. The finishes were all dark wood and brass, from the benches along the wall to the faux instruments in the engine room. And this was just the submarine. The players would eventually open up the doors into the mysterious lost city of

Atlantis.

"The story is that you're on a sub that's been disabled by a giant octopus." David opened the door for his mother.

"Shades of Jules Verne?" She laughed, ever the teacher.

"I hadn't actually thought of that." He waved her over to one of his favorite puzzles—a group of three dials with various symbols painted in gold. "And once they do this, then pop…"

The set of doors against the back wall popped open, revealing the small hallway "airlock." He stepped through and placed his palm on the panel opposite the opening. He reached out to his mother. "Take my hand and touch that metal panel behind me."

Mom obeyed, causing the second set of doors to open and revealing the undersea city.

The designers had outdone themselves here, creating faux-marble columns and statues to make the city look ancient. The sand-colored floor glittered in the soft lighting, and the sound of roaring water filled the room.

Mom went to the center, spun around, and sighed. "All right. Maybe now I understand why people want to do this."

He grinned, but when he looked back at his mom, the smile faded from her face. "Ma?"

"You're here late every night, aren't you?"

"I started my own business, Mom. You know that kind of thing takes a lot of work." He could already see where this was going, and he tried his hardest to steer her away from that frame of mind.

It didn't work.

"If you're here all the time, how will you meet anyone special? I mean, I thought Laura..." She must have realized that was not the road to go down and changed tracks. "I would like to see you settled."

"I don't have to be with someone to be settled." He truly believed that. However, he couldn't help but admit he liked the idea of coming home to someone. But Laura had never supported him, not really. He'd finally accepted that they weren't meant to be.

He opened his mouth to tell his mother he'd met plenty of women here at the escape room. Although none of them had caught his attention like his first customer—Elena. David still couldn't stop thinking about her. He'd even sent a follow-up email to the account she'd signed the waiver with, a simple *how did you like the room*, but he hadn't heard anything in response.

Instead what came out was "I don't want to be like Dad."

She pressed her lips together tightly. He knew she didn't like talking about him, and normally, he would not even have brought the man up. He didn't know what the hell had come over him now. Maybe being in this weird fake underwater city gave him the courage to bring it up. Or maybe he couldn't shake the fear that his anger issues had been what really caused the breakup with Laura. Anger that was too much like his father's.

To his surprise, his mother smacked him upside the head. "Did I not do a good job of raising you? Are you saying I was not a good mother? Are you?"

"What? Ow! Mom, no."

"Then stop saying things like that. The best thing your father ever gave me was you. You may have his genes, but everything else came from me. Any woman would be lucky to have you."

"Geez, Mom, only you could guilt me into feeling better about myself."

"Then my work here is done." She did look satisfied with herself, a little grin on her face. "I met someone."

He blinked and did a double take. "As in…someone you're dating?"

Who was this guy? How had she met him? Did he treat her right? David needed more details.

Details he wasn't going to get because at the moment Tony called from the other room, "David, where are you?"

"In here." He came out of the airlock. What was Tony doing here? He had gone back to the pizzeria to work.

"Come on, you have to see this."

That didn't sound ominous at all.

In the lobby, Vanessa and Sean, both his employees, were staring out the front picture window. Sean…who was supposed to be game mastering a room right now.

"Sean, aren't you in the middle of a room?" David barked as he joined them at the glass. He wasn't sure what the heck they were looking at. Outside sat the parking lot, like it always did. But across the street one of the converted houses on the block had balloons and a large banner proclaiming *Grand Opening*.

"Sorry, David. But Tony came in screaming about this…"

"What is this?" He still couldn't see what they were going on about. He looked back at his mom who shook her head and shrugged.

"It's the grand opening of The Escape Space," Tony said with jabs of his finger at the window, punctuating every word. "It's another escape room business. Across the fucking street! Oh, pardon my language, Ms. C."

"What does that mean for you?" His mother came forward. "That there's another escape room over there?"

"We were totally here first," Tony exclaimed. "They shouldn't be allowed to do that."

David rubbed his forehead, feeling a headache coming on. "It's a free country, Tony. You know there are two dollar stores on this block. Oh yeah, and another pizzeria around the corner."

"It's not the same, and you know it."

To be fair, escape rooms were still a rather specialized market.

David lifted his hands in an attempt to calm the room. Right now everyone looked ready to charge across the street and battle for him. While that felt nice, it was probably not smart. "I'll go across the street and say hi. It's the friendly thing to do, and that's what this is, friendly competition."

Tony scowled at him. "I've got a better idea. Why don't you book one of their rooms and check them out without telling them who you are?"

"That's sneaky and underhanded," David protested.

"Right, just like opening an escape room across the street from yours." Tony pointed emphatically outside.

"There is an opening at twelve thirty," Vanessa piped up from the booking computer at the front desk. She had snuck back there while David and Tony argued. "You could totally join in with that group, and no one will notice!"

David winced at her enthusiasm. Every time she spoke was a few decibels louder than it needed to be. He'd hired her for that energy but preferred it in small doses himself. "Mom is visiting. I don't have time to go do an escape room."

"I'll be fine here, dear." She sat in one of the comfy chairs in the lobby, sinking into the cushion. "Tony will entertain me and bring me food."

Tony bowed in her direction. He took her hand and kissed it. "Of course."

"Oh my God, if the two of you are going to be like that, then I'm going over there just to get away from you." David turned to Sean. "Go back to your room. They probably need a clue by now."

Sean gave a half-hearted salute and ran back down the hall.

David turned to Vanessa and sighed. "Book me for the twelve thirty. I'm still going to go over and have a nice friendly chat first."

Tony snorted. "Yeah, like that's going to go well. Take my advice, be sneaky."

David shook his head. He pushed the glass door open and looked back once. All of them stared at him, and he waved nervously.

He didn't know why his gut twisted as he ran, shivering, across the parking lot, dodging a car backing out without looking first. He had visited plenty of other escape rooms and chatted with their owners, talking about the rooms he was planning on building. Of course, it was right across the street, but he didn't think it would be a big deal at all.

That was, until he opened the front door of The Escape Space.

"You!"

Chapter 8

Elena stood back and soaked in the spectacle of her grand opening. Phoebe had suggested balloons, and they'd partnered with a local florist to get a substantial discount for some mutual advertising. The spring wind buffeted the silver and scarlet balloons and encouraged customers to come inside.

They'd spent the entire week beta testing and then fixing the problems found by the frat brothers Phoebe had conscripted. The guys had had such a great time they promised they'd tell their friends. One had even joked about making it a hazing activity. Elena didn't care as long as it brought the bodies in the door.

Phoebe's grassroots marketing seemed to have worked. They had filled most of the bookings for today, and tomorrow was starting to look good, too.

Take that, David and your so-called greatest escape. She glared across the street.

She had no way of telling how his business was doing. Other than, of course, obsessively refreshing his booking page to see how many openings he had and calculating how much money he was making. Elena also had to worry about him suddenly franchising with Svenson, which would give him an advantage.

She didn't think David would franchise. He'd seemed too proud of his business for that.

Then again, what the hell did she know? She'd only

met the man for a few minutes. She had absolutely no reason to keep thinking about him. She needed to keep her focus on the competition—figuring out how she could beat him at his own game.

"Check us out! Today we're offering free bagels. You can book online or over the phone." Phoebe handed out flyers to people who walked past. That was the nice thing about being on the residential part of the street; they had quite a bit of foot traffic.

And because Phoebe was Phoebe, she'd managed to get strangers to come in and partake of the free food. They left full of bagels and coffee and carrying flyers and postcards with an image of Elena's building—so very different from David's—and their website URL.

Elena would get into her costume later. She had plenty of time before the first booking this afternoon. Right now she stood with Phoebe, handing out flyers and smiling at strangers.

Her phone buzzed just as a car pulled up along the street. She didn't even have to look at it to know Jesse had texted his arrival. She recognized him through the window.

She grinned. She hadn't seen that familiar noggin in a long time.

He got out of the car and waved to the driver who sped away as soon as Jesse stepped onto the curb. Elena ran in for the hug and nearly knocked him over. He smelled like he always did, of mint and baby powder. They'd been partnered so many times on stage, to the point where his body felt more familiar than her own. She'd been afraid that he wouldn't be able to make it. He couldn't always get time off during the season, and he still had an entire month of shows ahead.

"Good to see you, too, Elena," he said into her hair.

They separated, but she still held on to his hand. "Phil didn't come?"

"It's tax season. He's working overtime like crazy."

"How did you manage to marry an accountant again?" She draped her arm loosely around his waist, so she felt it when he stiffened.

She'd been on her way to Jesse and Phil's wedding when she had the accident. Accident was a strange word for it. She'd been driving along when the brakes on someone else's car failed, and they plowed through a stop sign and right into her tiny rental. There had to be a better word to describe such a life-changing event.

"Just lucky, I guess." He forced himself into a smile. The crinkles didn't reach the corners of his eyes the way they did when he really meant it.

That hurt, that he still felt guilty. She never blamed him, but she had been too chicken to bring it up. Instead it lay between them like this tense fog that neither of them could ever quite get past.

"Let me show you the place. Oh, let me introduce you to Phoebe." Elena waved her over.

Phoebe's eyes lit up as Elena said, "Phoebe, this is Jesse…"

"Hello, tall, blond, and handsome." Phoebe looked him up and down.

Elena tried to see what she saw—Jesse's strong defined legs, the way his broad shoulders filled out his dark-gray cardigan.

"It's Jesse actually."

"Stop it. He's married," she told Phoebe and then, with a wicked look in Jesse's direction, said, "and he's too old for you."

"Ouch." He touched his chest and pretended to stagger back. "That one got me right here."

Elena shook her head. "I'm going to take Jesse in for a tour. You can stay out here for a little longer but then go inside and man the registration desk. We'll have customers soon."

"You got it, boss."

She felt a wave of nervousness as she led Jesse up the front porch and through the open doorway. The lobby wasn't much to look at right now, since most of the comfy seating had been removed so they could set up the table with bagels and coffee. The plan had been to draw in customers with free food, and so far it had been working.

"Lobby." She gestured. "Behind that door are my office and the control room. You know, where the magic happens."

Jesse laughed as he followed her up the stairs. Elena grabbed the railing and hid a wince as she took the first step up. She'd been on her feet too much in the past week, trying to get this together. Tonight she needed to make sure she got in a good long soak and put her feet up.

"Both rooms are upstairs." She didn't look back at him. As a fellow dancer, he might be able to tell when she was hiding pain. That was a conversation she didn't want to have right now.

"This stairway is stunning." He ran his hand up the polished wood of the railing. "This entire place has such character."

"I know. It's why I bought it and didn't bother renting something industrial." She had fallen in love with the house, with its fancy woodwork and streamlined wainscoting. The last person to renovate it had taken care with the space, leaving all the classic details behind. She knew it had been a good investment—walking through it had given her so many ideas for escape rooms, and if the business didn't go well, she could always rent it out as a law firm again.

No. Her business would succeed. It had to.

"You had to spend a lot of time restoring this." He gestured to the cherrywood floors, the smooth white color on the walls. It still smelled slightly of paint, no matter how many times she tried airing the place out.

"It was in surprisingly good condition. A lawyer had rented it out before and kept it in decent shape. The real work went into the rooms themselves." She stood in front of the Uncle Enzo's Study Room, and her face went hot. This was it—her baby. And if her best friend in the world hated it…

Elena took a deep breath and threw the door open, gesturing inside. She tried to see the room as he saw it for the first time.

Tall bookcases lined the wall opposite. A heavy mahogany desk stood in the center of the room, with a tall black leather chair behind it. Guarding the opposite wall sat a green leather loveseat over a rug such a shade of dark red it looked like blood. Her best find had been the grandfather clock she'd scavenged at the flea market. It didn't work, of course, which made it easy to modify.

In essence, it should look exactly like the study of a stuffy old man. But after looking closer, her clients would notice the locks on boxes, drawers, even the clock itself. The paintings on the wall started to look a little suspicious. Why was there a painting of the life cycle of a flower anyway?

He shook his head and applauded. "Who'd have thought this would be the result when I took you to your first escape room?"

"Go ahead," she teased, throwing her arm around his waist again. "Take all the credit."

Jesse had taken not only her, but some of the other dancers in their company. She had been skeptical—locked in a room for an hour with work acquaintances and they had to work together to solve their way out? But she'd needed the break from rehearsals and darning her pointe shoes, so she'd acquiesced. She hadn't expected the rush of excitement—the sheer joy when completing a puzzle correctly—or the panic when the timer slowly started to tick down to zero. It'd felt like the moment before heading out on stage, when her heart raced and her blood pooled in her ears, reminding her she was alive.

She was still alive. Not dancing, maybe never again, but still right here.

"It's beautiful. You did a fabulous job." He ran his fingers along the desk, picking up and turning over the very obvious paperweight shaped like a dragon. Jesse barely looked at it, paying no attention to the clue stenciled underneath.

"Thank you." She showed him the puzzle chain, including the mechanism inside the grandfather clock that Quinn had helped her with. It was the part of the room that made her nervous since so many things could go wrong.

The scent of pizza greeted them when she led them back out of the room to the landing. She had wanted to show him the other room, but her belly growled, and she figured eating sounded like a good idea.

"Want to grab some pizza? I'll show you my office. Unless you have to go?" She had forgotten to ask if he had a show tonight. He'd have to take the train back into the city soon if that were the case.

"It's my night off." He trotted down the stairs behind her. He inclined his head at Phoebe who was handing out paper plates of pizza. The boxes had replaced the bagels and would do for the afternoon shift.

Phoebe winked at Jesse. "I chose that slice especially for you," she said.

"Old enough to be your father," Elena said in a singsong voice as she got her own slice and propelled him down the hall.

"Yeah, if I had a kid at fifteen," he protested.

She missed this—teasing Jesse, laughing with him. They had been partners for so long she got used to having him around, almost like an extra limb. Their bodies had often been entwined, and he felt like an extension of herself. Of course, that had been their on-stage personas. Jesse had belonged to Phil from the moment they met.

Elena showed him into her office. It shared a door with the control room so she could quickly go to Quinn's aid if necessary. But she had the equipment for running a room set up here as well, across her folding table that served as a desk—three computer screens: one linked to the cameras, one showing the output of the monitor in the room, and the last a map of the puzzles to be solved, as well as speakers and a keyboard.

Quinn had set it all up. Elena had lucked into a gold mine when she met her at the laundromat.

Jesse, of course, gravitated to the poster hung on one wall. She'd regretted it the moment she did it, but that production of Swan Lake had been her favorite—her first time as principal, with Jesse as her partner. Some things about the past she wanted to remember.

"Elena," he said quietly, the pizza still uneaten in his hands. "Are you happy?"

She dropped into her seat, pushing aside the keyboard to set down her plate of pizza. "What kind of question is that?"

"It's exactly what it sounds like." He turned to face her. "After the accident—"

"It wasn't your fault," she interrupted firmly. No matter how strongly she said it, guilt lingered in his eyes. Maybe she should accept she couldn't say anything to make him feel better.

"All right." He nodded. "But you have to admit, this isn't what most dancers do after retirement."

After a forced retirement. She clenched her teeth. Just because she didn't blame him didn't mean she wasn't still angry about the turn her life had taken. "I can't see myself teaching. I don't have the patience."

She gestured to the computer screens, showing the empty escape rooms. "And I need...I need passion in my life. I need to love what I do. To have a reason to wake up every morning."

"And this is that?"

"It's going to have to be." She held his gaze.

Jesse stared at her, and she didn't know what he saw, but he stepped away from the poster and half sat on her desk. "Then I will support you no matter what."

"Thanks."

"And Phil did offer to do your books. I'd accept his offer. He's a really good accountant."

She opened her mouth to tease him about Phil some more—what else was he good at?—when a commotion outside her office got their attentions.

After a fast heavy knock against her door, Phoebe poked her head in. "Uh, boss. Can you come out here a sec?"

Elena got to her feet, wincing slightly at the twinge in her left ankle. She limped out to the lobby and stopped dead at the sight of David standing there.

"What's going on here?" Elena looked between David and Phoebe, who had a guilty expression on her face. The clock behind her read *12:00*, and something itched at the back of Elena's head—she needed to get into costume in order to greet the twelve-thirty booking. They'd start showing up any minute now. She didn't have time for this.

She was aware of Jesse at her side. His presence gave her enough support for her to stride forward and cross her arms, facing David head-on. She might have to look up to meet his eyes, but he wasn't anywhere near as tall as Jesse.

David glanced between her and Jesse, and something caused him to narrow his eyes and square his shoulders. "I am here for the twelve-thirty booking."

"And I told him he's not welcome here." Phoebe glared daggers at the back of David's head.

Elena resisted the urge to rub her forehead. She got why Phoebe had said it—the girl was too protective of this place, though that's pretty much what Elena had wanted when she hired her. Normally, she would have let David in if he'd paid like a normal customer. But she had to back her employee's play.

"Phoebe will make sure your money is refunded," Elena said, hoping to not escalate this further. "Is there anything else?"

Phoebe took a deep breath, and Elena was glad she'd stood up for her.

David stepped closer and lowered his voice. "May I have a word in private?"

She hesitated. She had no reason to fear this man, yet... She glanced around the lobby at the potential customers still eating pizza. This scene shouldn't go any further. "Of course. My office?"

"Elena," Jesse said in an undertone. He narrowed his eyes at David and looked about ready to pounce.

She squeezed his arm. "I'll be right out. This shouldn't take long at all."

She turned and went back into her office, quickly switching off her computer monitors before David entered the room. She turned to face him and gestured to one of the extra chairs.

"I'd prefer to stand, thank you."

She leaned against her desk. She didn't want to sit down and make herself even shorter than this guy.

"At least now I know why you never responded to my email asking what you thought of my room."

She needed a second to understand what he was talking about. "Did you use the email from the waiver? I gave you my spam account. I rarely check it."

"Do you make a habit of jerking men around?"

"Look." She forced herself to breathe through her nose, to not let this jerk get to her. "You're the one who opened out of nowhere after I spent six months getting this place up and running. You've got a lot of nerve showing up here and acting like this is my fault."

"That's not what I'm doing. I just wanted to see your rooms. What's wrong with some friendly competition?"

"Friendly competition? Is that why you chose to

open directly across the street from me? I filed the permits and the business name with the city. You had to know I was about to open." She watched confusion grow on his face. It made him look younger, almost vulnerable. She quashed any sympathy she had. "Don't tell me. You didn't do the market research?"

He shrugged. "I chose the strip mall because Tony's dad owns it, and he gave me a good deal on rent."

"Well that sounds like a smart marketing plan." She heard the edge in her voice. She had no patience for incompetence. Before she started this venture, she had done her homework, including taking business classes at the local library. Like her dancing, she poured all her time and attention into her business. To meet someone who didn't do basic market research, who chose a location due to the cheap rent, well, that got her back up.

"My master's degree is in chemistry, not marketing," he snapped. "I don't know everything."

"Shocking to hear you admit it."

He stared at her for a moment, his hands clenched into fists at his sides. "Are you seriously not going to let me into your room?"

She almost laughed. In any other situation the words would be incredibly suggestive. Instead she shook her head. "I'm sorry. I have to protect my work."

"This isn't over." He stomped out of her office.

Elena followed and watched him storm out of the building. She looked over at Jesse who said, "Are you all right? Am I going to have to beat someone up?"

"I'll let you know if that becomes necessary." She had a feeling she wasn't seeing the last of David. She found herself looking forward to the challenge.

Chapter 9

David made it two weeks before he cracked.

He'd left The Escape Space shaking with anger but managed to hold it together when he got back to The Greatest Escape. After the conversation he'd just had with his mother, he did not want to prove her wrong. Especially when all he wanted to do was punch walls and throw things, neither of which were conducive to running a business.

Mom had only shrugged when he explained his annoyance at being forbidden entry into Elena's room. "You've got better things to do with your time."

Which happened to be true. He barely had a moment to have lunch with her before having to run back and fix a broken prop and then game master for a surprise booking of his third room. All the while he had to keep an ear out for any incoming customers since, with the three of them in the control room, nobody could work the reception desk.

All in all, he was far too busy to worry about his competition.

Except. He couldn't stop thinking about her eyes—the way they'd flashed when she told him to leave. Her hair as it shone beneath the lights. Her voice—sultry and slightly breathless.

Damn her—for being someone he couldn't have.

Every time he drove to work, he passed The Escape

Space, the gray brick house taunting him from the middle of the block as he turned into the strip mall. He would crane his head, looking at her gravel lot, and try to gauge how many customers she had.

Doing that bordered on obsessive. He fully admitted he crossed that line today when he sat in front of his computer and pulled up her website. David clicked on the description for the first room.

Your great-uncle Enzo has passed away suddenly, and you have been informed that he left you something substantial in his will. As you didn't know you had a great-uncle Enzo, this is rather disconcerting, but you're not going to miss the chance for some free money. There's only one catch. We're not exactly sure where he hid his will. You have one hour to find it before the lawyers start dividing up his estate. But are you sure you really want his money?

"What the heck does that mean?" He leaned forward as if getting closer to the screen would make it any clearer. The second room he found even more intriguing.

You've been given a backstage pass to a premier ballet performance. Excited to meet your favorite dancers, you arrive at the allotted time. However, no one is waiting for you backstage. The doors have been locked shut behind you. Something terrible has happened, and you have an hour to find your way out or risk becoming part of the show...forever.

He loved the creative themes she'd come up with. He'd done a fair share of escape rooms. The first one had been a team-building exercise at work before the company had been bought out. He'd found he couldn't stop with just that one and quickly sought out every escape room within an hour's drive. He'd seen numerous bank heists, plenty of zombie apocalypses, some ancient tombs, and the ever-popular serial killer's lair.

But Elena's themes intrigued him. He wanted to see what she had designed. And he was pretty sure she'd been the one to design them. He hadn't seen any rooms with those themes advertised on the common escape room designer websites he frequented. Also, she'd been so possessive of them when she kicked him out. He itched to see what he'd missed.

The bell on top of the door rang as Tony entered carrying a to-go bag from the pizzeria.

"No more pizza, please." David sat back and rubbed his belly. "I never thought I'd get sick of it."

"One of the perks of spending all day next to a pizzeria. Soon you'll hate even the smell of garlic." Tony placed the bag on the desk in front of David. "It's eggplant parm. Thank me later."

"Why can't I thank you now?" David unwrapped the bag and pulled out a Styrofoam container and some plasticware. His stomach rumbled, and he realized he hadn't eaten anything since lunch. When had it gotten so late?

"Seems quiet in here." Tony gestured to the empty lobby.

Just then they heard a scream from the back. He sighed. Why did someone always feel compelled to scream? The room wasn't that scary. "I have two rooms in progress. Sean and Vanessa are running them. I'm watching the lobby in case we get any walk-ins."

"Not bad, not bad." Tony paced until he got to the window. He never could sit still. "You realize her parking lot is full?"

"It's a tiny lot," David bit out, the taste of the

eggplant turning bitter on his tongue.

"And she has a discount on a Wednesday. Did you know that?"

Of course he did. "I'm not stalking her."

"I'm just saying you should look into that discount thing." Tony turned around and shrugged.

"Didn't we have that discussion about how you don't work here?" He waved his fork, wishing Tony would change the subject. After David was denied access to The Escape Space, Tony had been equally affronted and kept bringing it up, like a dog with a dirty old bone.

"I could," Tony said softly. "You really could use another hand with the tech. What happens if the Arduino blows again?"

That had happened last week. Something—possibly a power surge—had shorted out the circuit board on the last puzzle in the prison room. David had called the company he'd purchased the puzzle from, but they could only offer a replacement, and that wouldn't be here for weeks. Tony had been able to find a new board and fix it all himself. He'd refused to charge David for his services.

He sat back. "What would your dad think about that?"

"I can do both. It's not like I get paid to work at the pizzeria. I'm not a fifteen-year-old kid anymore."

David didn't want to touch any of that. Tony and his dad had a lot of issues, and while Tony had a point most of the time, he still lived off his parents' money. "Maybe…"

He was interrupted—thankfully—by the door opening and the bell jangling loudly as the customer pushed a little too hard. Three more people followed into the lobby.

"Hello, welcome to The Greatest Escape." David quickly shoved his food back into the bag and got to his feet. "How can I help you?"

"We have a seven o'clock booking," one of them said after a moment.

David didn't think he had anything running at seven exactly. He pulled up the schedule on the computer to check. "Which room did you book?"

"Um, I'm not sure…Kate?"

The youngest looking of the group pulled out her phone and scrolled. "Yeah, got it. The Ballet."

David stopped looking at the schedule. "I'm sorry. You're looking for the place across the street. The Escape Space. This is The Greatest Escape." He could feel the daggers Tony was glaring at him from across the room.

Tony stepped forward. "But, hey, why don't you try one of our rooms? I highly recommend the Prison Break. It's a scream."

As if on cue, someone screamed from the back again.

"Sorry, man. Maybe another time."

"Yeah, we already paid for our room."

They shuffled out, the bell ringing again and again as they held the door open too long. David got up after they left and pulled the damn bell down. He tossed it into the trash with way more force than was necessary.

"I don't think it's the bell you're mad at." Tony hopped up on the desk and swung his feet.

"No." He clenched his hand into a fist. Tossing the annoying bell had felt good, but the last thing he wanted was to destroy his own property. He paced the length of the lobby, then paused to stare out the window across the parking lot. "If only I could get a look at one of her rooms."

"What if you could?"

David whirled on Tony. "You're not suggesting breaking in?" For a brief, tantalizing moment, he considered it.

Tony shook his head. "Do I look like a burglar? No. I ordered a wireless button camera from the 'interwebs,' and I've been dying to try it out. We send someone in to do the room, and we'll have full access to anything he sees. Of course, it can't be you, or me, since I'm pretty sure they've seen me at the pizza shop…"

Just then cheering echoed from the back. Sean emerged from the control room to lead his group to get their photos taken. Sean, with his perfect square chin and his baby-blue eyes and his "aw shucks, ma'am" personality. Sean, who could charm a wooden door. Sean, who none of the women across the street had ever seen before. David and Tony locked eyes.

"Sean," Tony said.

"Sean," David agreed.

Chapter 10

"Stop wiggling so much. You're making the feed jumpy."

They implemented Tony's plan a few days later, on a quiet afternoon when the room Sean usually game mastered didn't have any bookings. Tony had replaced one of the buttons on Sean's shirt with a tiny camera that looked identical to the other buttons. Sean filled the shirt, his massive shoulders stretching out the white fabric, but it was the only button-down he owned.

He apologized for that several times. Sean was like a giant puppy that way. David patted him on the back and told him it was okay.

"Remember what we talked about." Tony punched something into his phone and handed it to Sean, who put it in his pocket. "We'll only have sound once you put your earpiece in, but don't be conspicuous about it."

"And try not to look like you're talking to yourself." David debated the logistics of this yet again. Between Sean's inability to lie and Tony's tendency toward experimenting with tech before it was ready, this could go horribly wrong. "Go in, do the room. Have fun."

"And be sure to walk around slowly and get a good look at everything." Tony had sent him on his way—out the back of the building so no one saw him coming out of The Greatest Escape.

They watched the feed in David's private office in

the back, transmitted from the camera to David's computer. At first the picture jumped around. Sean couldn't hear Tony's annoyed command to stop wiggling, not yet. As soon as he was in the room, the plan was for him to slip in the earbud with the mic attached.

"I should have made popcorn." Tony tapped his fingers against the desk.

David stared at the video, watching as Sean crossed the street—carefully, at the crosswalk. The view was slightly distorted—the camera was in the middle of Sean's chest, and since Sean was so tall, the view seemed a bit shorter than David's normal eye level. The image did jump around a bit, but as soon as Sean stood still, it stabilized.

Sean climbed the steps to The Escape Space, opened the door, and entered the lobby. Phoebe greeted him with a smile, and she was so expressive David could read her lips, although he missed a few words here and there.

"Welcome to The Escape Space. Can I help you?"

Sean apparently responded, because Phoebe gestured to the other people waiting in the lobby. They were careful to put him in with other people who'd already booked the room. If he went alone, they might get suspicious. Then she handed him a waiver—a paper waiver, on a clipboard with a pen.

"Well, you're up on them when it comes to tech," Tony said as Sean scrawled his name and email on the form.

"That doesn't mean anything. I've seen plenty of places with paper forms and fantastic tech in the rooms. There's a time and a place for technology."

Tony made a humming noise and continued to shake the mouse.

They watched a few minutes of nothing while Sean chatted with Phoebe. She kept smiling the whole time, so perhaps Sean wasn't totally crap at this. David had worried about his inability to lie since Sean had a tendency to blush and stammer when confronted. They'd told him to stick with a single story—he wanted to try out an escape room, and none of his friends would go with him—and keep smiling.

It seemed to be working.

Phoebe gathered the group and motioned toward the stairs. Because of the angle of the camera, David could only see the bottom of the staircase. Which was why he didn't see Elena until she had descended onto the last step.

He swallowed at the sight. She wore a deep-blue dress in the style of a 1920s flapper. Her hair had been pulled back tightly, leaving her neckline gloriously exposed.

He leaned forward, transfixed by her collarbones. "Can you zoom in on this?"

Tony, thankfully, didn't pick up on why. "Yeah, but let's save that for individual puzzles in the room. I'd like to get an overview of the big picture."

"Right, right." David sat back, embarrassed. He wished he could hear what she was saying. Something in him wanted that soft smile on her lips to be for him.

But no, she was playing a part, setting the stage for her guests. He'd heard of escape rooms with actors before, but he didn't know if Elena herself participated in every room. How would that work?

She led the group up the steps, and Sean's camera had a fabulous view of her feet—wearing simple flats, not the orthopedic monsters this time. They came to a landing with a wooden door. Elena said something, then threw open the door and let the group inside.

Sean walked past her, and yes, this was what David had been waiting for—to see the room design. However, he couldn't help but be disappointed when Sean turned around and Elena closed the door with her on the opposite side.

"Now, Sean," Tony muttered.

Sean stepped to the side, and they had a view of the other customers in the room, scattering to different corners. Muffled static came through the computer speakers, and suddenly they had sound.

"So, uh, what did you guys find?" Sean asked, his voice echoing.

Tony winced and adjusted the sound quality.

"Four-digit lock," someone said.

"Look, there's a ledger on the bookshelf. Didn't she say something about this?" Another person started paging through the tome.

"Try to get a good look at everything," David said into the microphone.

For a second, his hands blocked the camera, and then the view cleared as Sean circled the room. He started with the grand desk, kneeling to get a good look at the drawers, two of them locked. One of the drawers opened, and he pulled out a piece of paper. "Hey, is this useful?"

He put it on the top of the desk, knocking over the paperweight. The rest of the group came over like chickens to feed.

"Here's your chance to look at the other stuff," David ordered.

Sean continued to the bookshelf, past the painting

on the wall until he finally reached the grandfather clock. The thing was massive and looked beautiful, all intricately carved wood with inlaid enamel. Sean's fingers brushed the lock on the front mechanism.

"It all looks first-gen to me," Tony said. "Locks and puzzles."

David scribbled down notes as Sean and his new friends continued to work out codes. Someone figured out that the painting on the wall swung open, revealing a wall safe. Inside they found more "evidence"—of what David wasn't sure. Now he really wished he'd heard the room's intro.

On the back of the evidence was a cipher—the symbols had been all around the room. After a few minutes of scrambling, they finally had the code to the grandfather clock.

Inside was a lever.

"Should we push the button?"

"But we don't know what it does!"

Sean ignored the giggling group and reached out to pull the lever.

David found himself holding his breath. What would happen? Sean whirled around, and the picture went blurry. When the video feed cleared, they could clearly see the bookshelf had swung open, revealing a second room behind it. David leaned forward, wondering what exactly would be in the second room.

Sean bent down to enter the opening, the camera still shaky. Inside was dark and decorated in red, and David needed a moment to figure out why. "Is that a wine cellar?"

"In the 1920s? Don't you mean a speakeasy?" Tony chuckled.

"Not quite." David tried to tune Tony out. He wanted to absorb as much of the room as possible.

However, in the back of his mind, he couldn't stop thinking about Elena in that blue dress—the way she smiled, how the color lit up her eyes, the curve of her neck. He grabbed his knee and squeezed, forcing himself to concentrate. This might be his only chance to look at one of Elena's rooms.

Sean's compatriots were just as enthusiastic here, finding locks and more of the evidence they were looking for. They needed one hint—delivered through the monitor over the door. Sean had to do a sort of shimmy to get it visible on camera, and David didn't want to know what that looked like from the other side.

They needed to uncap the wine bottles on the table. The letters for the final puzzle were written beneath the caps. Odd choice. David didn't think anyone would go about untwisting wine caps without having a hint first.

They opened the final door—a huge wooden thing with a curved top—and the group drew back and screamed, revealing a skeleton on the other side. A skeleton with a piece of paper on his chest with the word "will" written on it in letters so large David could read it on the grainy computer screen.

"Congratulations." Elena's voice came from somewhere, and David ordered Sean to turn around so he could see her again. She stood in the doorway that the bookshelf had hidden, still in the blue dress that made his mouth go dry and something darker twitch in his midsection.

"You've found your uncle's will. Now, considering what you've learned, will you still accept the money?"

What they had learned was their uncle had been

heavily involved in bootlegging, and one of the victims of his illegal activities had been locked away in his wine cellar. Half of the group argued for taking the money anyway, but ultimately they decided not to.

That mattered for when they took their photos—they held signs saying *we didn't take the money!*

David smiled. That was a cute touch. It made their choices in the room seem important afterward. He actually liked that.

"Hey, Sean, can I talk to you for a minute?" Phoebe pulled Sean aside after the photo, after the others started to leave.

"Oh shit," Tony muttered. "Sean, abort, abort! Get out of there!"

David didn't think Sean had anything to worry about. Phoebe continued to smile sweetly, the camera perfectly lined up to her face. Then she looked directly at the camera and plucked it off Sean's shirt.

The feed went dark.

Chapter 11

After performing for the group in Uncle Enzo's room, Elena went to the control room as she did after every session. She didn't game master this room despite putting on the show beforehand. No, Quinn handled that. Elena managed the other room, The Ballet. Phoebe had trained on both experiences and could help out in a pinch. Unfortunately, they still needed her up at the front to manage bookings. Otherwise, Elena would be putting on a different costume and performing for that room, too.

Maybe she should reconsider doing that. Getting into dance gear again, even for a role, would be too painful.

She took a seat next to Quinn, watching on the monitors as the group worked together, searching the room. Elena got a little thrill from watching her customers do this, try to figure out the puzzle chain that she had created.

"Not a bad group," she said. They found most of the items right away and seemed to work well together.

Quinn pulled out one of her earpieces so she could still hear the room as well as Elena. "Yeah, but you see that big blond guy in the corner?"

"Hard to miss him."

"He put an earbud in his ear and fiddled with his phone about two minutes into the room. That's weird, right?"

"He didn't take any pictures or anything like that?" Elena wheeled her chair closer, trying to see what was bugging Quinn.

"No. But…" She shook her head. "Watch."

Elena did. While the guy did participate with the group, every so often he'd wander around the room, getting rather close to things…with his chest?

"I need to get his name." She stood and went to the front to get the packet of waivers.

When she got to the lobby, she explained to Phoebe what was going on.

Phoebe followed her back to the control room. "Which guy?"

"Him." Quinn pointed at the screen.

Phoebe leaned forward. "Ah, the hottie with hips like Michelangelo's David?"

Elena stopped ruffling through the papers and stared at Phoebe. "I take it you didn't spend a lot of time looking at his face, then?"

"And abs like…and shoulders…mmm." Phoebe licked her lips. "Sean. His name is Sean."

"Surprised you can still form words," Quinn said. "Look. There he is fiddling with his belly again. That's weird. Isn't it weird?"

"Totally weird," Phoebe agreed. Her gaze was glued to the screen.

Elena didn't see anything odd in the waiver. Sean Wilson. Had a college email address. Something about the name, however. "Where did I last hear someone named Sean?"

"It's not like it's an uncommon name," Quinn pointed out.

Phoebe snapped her fingers. "Sean. Wasn't he our

game master at The Greatest Escape? We never got to meet him, but..."

"Son of a bitch." Elena dropped the clipboard on the desk. "You don't think that asshole would do that? What am I saying? Of course he would. He'd totally send in one of his employees to check out my rooms."

"And what? Secretly film it? That shirt is so tight it's not like he's got a camera in there..." Quinn trailed off. "Let me google a thing."

"Hold on a second," Phoebe said. "We don't have any proof. Let me interrogate him afterward."

Quinn opened a browser window on her computer and typed furiously. "What? Are you going to use your feminine wiles on him?"

"They're called boobs." Phoebe jiggled her chest.

"Well, they are certainly distracting." Quinn stopped typing and wiggled her eyebrows.

"What would your girlfriend say if she heard you?"

"She'd be just as distracted..."

Elena rolled her eyes at both of them. Still, Phoebe had a point. "All right. Talk to him. It's not an interrogation. It could be nothing."

"Or it could be a whole lot of something."

****

Elena didn't always go back to the room at the end of the hour. Sometimes she was busy running the other room, so Quinn was the one to ask them if they'd accept the ill-gotten money. This time she made sure to be the one to tell Sean's group they'd won.

She tried not to look directly at him. But she couldn't help wondering if he'd somehow managed to smuggle something in here. The more she thought about it, the angrier she got, a cold anger that burned in her belly. David was starting something here, something she didn't like.

Phoebe pulled Sean aside, and Elena saw the other customers out, inviting them to check out the second room when they had time. As soon as the door shut, she whirled around, in time to see her pluck something from Sean's shirt.

"That doesn't look like a button." Phoebe's voice was as sweet as molasses.

"Um. Shit." He stared down at his feet and scratched the back of his head, looking like a big kid.

"You realize filming our escape rooms breaks the terms of the waiver, right?" She continued to smile.

"What?" He looked shocked. "Nobody told me that!"

"What exactly did they tell you?"

God, Phoebe was good. Elena hung back and let her play Sean like a fiddle. This whole mess was almost worth the trouble to see him blushing and trying to stumble his way out of it.

"Look, my boss asked me to check out the room. I didn't mean any harm."

"Your boss. The guy across the street?" Phoebe leaned in, brushing her hand across his chest. That, Elena was pretty sure, was not part of the interrogation. Shame he worked for the competition, because the two of them would look cute together.

He nodded miserably.

"I'm afraid I'm going to have to ban you from here for life." Elena stepped forward.

His head snapped up, and she guessed he'd had no idea she was listening.

"Oh God. I am so sorry…"

"Save it. Get the hell out of here." Elena gave him her best death glare, and he hightailed it out of the place so fast he ran into the doorjamb with a loud thump. Elena and Phoebe both winced at that.

"Can you believe that guy?" Phoebe swept her arms out in a huge gesture. "Shame he's hot."

Elena laughed. She had to. Otherwise, she'd be annoyed, and she was tired of feeling annoyed and angry. She dropped onto the couch in the lobby and then kicked her feet up onto the coffee table. The flats didn't really have much ankle support, and if she didn't baby her feet, she'd be feeling it later.

"What are we going to do about it?" Phoebe asked.

"What do you mean, do about it?" Elena rubbed her forehead. She needed to check the time on their next bookings, and she'd left her phone in her office. "I banned him from coming back."

"You know what I mean. The Greatest Escape. He can't get away with this." Phoebe continued punctuating her words with her hands. "We told him he couldn't see our rooms, and he...cheated. That's what he did. He cheated."

"You shouldn't have told him that," Elena said softly. She hadn't wanted to address this at all, but now that Phoebe brought it up, she had to.

She went still. "But you backed me up."

"Because you're my employee, and I'd never let either you or Quinn take a hit. But look what happened—he found a way in anyway, with a recording device. That's so much worse."

"Don't blame me for him being an asshole." Phoebe pointed, presumably at the location across the street. "You saw his room. He didn't even have a safety switch for an emergency exit."

"Phoebe…"

"That's dangerous, and you know it. Did you ever call the fire inspector about it? You should."

"You're changing the subject."

She huffed. "Yeah, I am. I hate assholes."

Elena smiled at that. "I know. I do, too."

Phoebe sat next to her on the couch, looking utterly miserable. "Are we good, boss?"

"Yeah. Check with me before doing something, okay?"

"Something like calling the fire marshal?" She looked hopeful.

"Phoebe."

"Come on. That's not safe, and you know it. Out of everything he's done, that's the one thing that keeps me up at night." She bit her lip.

Elena thought about the plastic cuffs against her wrists, how it felt to turn around and find no doorknob after being locked into an actual prison cell. That was part of the experience, but the city had certain standards for a reason. What if someone had a panic attack in the room? Or if something caught on fire? David needed to be responsible, and from their brief conversation in her office, he clearly hadn't thought about the safety implications before starting his business.

"All right. Call them."

Phoebe bounced to her feet and reached for the phone at the receptionist's station. Elena's belly twisted, and she hoped she wasn't making a horrible mistake.

****

Sean came back to The Greatest Escape with his head down and his tail tucked between his legs. David wanted to pat his head and give him cocoa, because that's how pathetic he looked. But Sean was his employee, not his pet, so David didn't let any of his sympathy show on his face. He held open the door and gestured to one of the seats in the lobby.

With his head ducked down, Sean sat in the chair. "Am I fired?" He asked, clasping his hands together between his knees, his blue eyes wide.

"Of course you're not fired." David rubbed his forehead. Why had he let himself be swayed by Tony's version of logic? That never turned out well. "We shouldn't have asked you to go over there in the first place."

"Are you kidding? It was an awesome idea." Tony bounced on the balls of his feet. If Sean looked like a dejected dog, then Tony was a Chihuahua on steroids.

"You got your button cam confiscated, and Sean is banned for life. How is that awesome?" David demanded. How could Tony be so clueless? Even more than that, how could he not see how much this hurt Sean?

"We got an absolutely perfect bird's-eye view of her room. We know your rooms are so much better. And…" Tony whirled on Sean. "He doesn't want to go back there anyway, does he? I mean, do you?"

His cheeks turned bright red. "Well…" he started, then seemed to shrink in on himself when both David and Tony glared at him. "One of the girls there is kinda cute."

"Elena?" David said right as Tony said, "The blue-haired chick?"

Sean shook his head. "Phoebe. The one who took the camera."

"Buck up, kid. There are plenty of fish in the sea."

"Yeah, Tony is not the one to listen to when it comes to women," David couldn't resist pointing out. The last thing he needed was Sean taking advice like this from Tony.

"Says the guy whose longest relationship with a woman is with his mother." Tony scampered out of reach to avoid the fist David threw in his direction. Tony rarely crossed the line, but this time his words made him see red. That was the problem with being friends with someone for so long—Tony knew exactly how to hurt him.

David pointed to the front door. He was done with Tony's bullshit for today. "Out. You don't work here, remember?"

Tony laughed. "I need to go order a new button cam anyway." He darted out the door before David could respond to that. They were absolutely never ever trying something like this again. They'd gotten caught the first time. What made Tony think they could try again?

He sighed and dropped into a seat. "He's an asshole. He may be my best friend, but he's still an asshole."

Sean didn't seem to know what to do with that information. He looked about ready to jump out of the chair and hide somewhere. David probably shouldn't be unloading his problems on a college kid who was only here for the nine bucks an hour. They'd already put him through a lot today.

David took pity on the kid. "Your room has a booking in fifteen minutes. Go reset it and get ready."

"Yes, sir." Sean sprang to his feet and hightailed it out of the lobby like his ass was on fire.

Damn it, Tony. David never should have gone along with the stupid plan. Although…he'd enjoyed the chance to look at Elena's room and, if he was being honest with himself, the chance to see her all dolled up in costume. It had really added to the atmosphere of the room, especially since it seemed to fit into the historical house where she'd built her escape rooms. He loved the ones where he could lose his sense of reality and really immerse himself in the story.

Plus, she'd looked amazing in that dress. He groaned and threw his arm over his eyes. He could not be crushing on her. He was a grown-ass man, not a teenager. Plus, she'd made it very clear she wanted nothing to do with him.

David got to his feet and walked to the window, staring across the street. She wouldn't let today slide. Not the Elena who stood toe to toe with him in her office, defending her space. They'd cheated their way inside, and she would not forgive them for that. What would the consequences be?

He found out two days later when the fire marshal showed up.

Chapter 12

David taped the cardboard sign to the front of the glass door. It said *Closed for renovations. Check our Facebook for reopening date!* Underneath the handwritten text, he's pasted a QR code with the link. He took a step back to make sure it was symmetrical. Sean had originally hung it up so lopsided David worried about the kid's vision. Maybe he needed glasses.

"What's going on? What renovations?" Tony appeared suddenly behind him, causing David to startle and drop the duct tape.

He bent over to scoop up the roll. "Can you clear your throat or something? You move like a ninja, I swear to God."

"That's the real reason you needed a bell above your door." Tony gave him a shit-eating grin and then tilted his chin at the door. "So? Why are you shutting down? I thought you hadn't decided on that fourth room yet."

Tony meant the space in the back. David still hadn't decided on a theme for it. He wanted something special, not the same escape room he'd seen done a million times before.

"Remember the fire-inspector guy who showed up yesterday? He shut me down until I make some changes."

His jaw dropped. "You're shitting me."

David pushed the door open and stepped back

inside, Tony at his heels. "Wish I was. Turns out a couple of the rooms break fire code."

In retrospect, it should have been obvious. He needed to have emergency exits or at least a way for customers to exit his rooms quickly in case of something going horribly wrong. And some rooms, like the Prison Break Room in particular, were like a case study in what not to do. The fire inspector had shaken his head multiple times when David led him through there. However, David couldn't simply add an emergency open switch. He would have to rethink the layout of the entire room, not an easy feat when he'd purchased the design.

"That's bullshit."

"No, Tony, that's facts. Honestly, he's right. Some of these violations were a lawsuit waiting to happen. What if someone had a panic attack in the Prison Break Room?"

They walked down the empty hallway to the room in question. David had sent Sean and Vanessa home and hoped he'd have a business for them to return to.

"Didn't you get everything inspected already?"

David shook his head. "This wasn't that kind of inspection. Although to be fair, your dad's friend helped with the original permits."

That's how you did it in Jersey. Greased the right palm and since Tony's dad did in fact seem to know everyone, David had followed his lead. It had not turned out in his favor.

"Why the heck did he show up, then? How random is that?" Tony skidded to a stop. "Shit."

He shrugged. "I have no idea…"

"Dude. This happens right after Sean's cam mission? They totally narked on you."

93

"First of all, who says 'narked' anymore? Second, 'cam mission'?"

"Shut up."

Tony might have a point. The arrival of the fire inspector certainly had suspicious timing. "Even if they did call him…we did kind of illegally film their room."

"Which was a damn good idea. Now we know what you're up against, which, I might add, is not much. Locks and keys? Your rooms are so far ahead of hers."

"Right now I don't have any rooms until I get this fire code thing straightened out." David turned his back on Tony and strode down the hall toward his office. He had a lot of phone calls to make if he were going to get things fixed sooner rather than later.

"And until you do that, you're out of business." Tony fell right into step behind him. "Are you going to let this go?"

"What do you want me to do? Honestly? Run over there and tell them off? What the hell is that going to accomplish?" David burst into his office and slid in front of his computer. He needed to find the phone number of the contractor he'd worked with initially. Maybe the guy could make some quick changes.

Tony stood in the doorway, and for a second he had a look on his face, the kind of look that meant trouble. It was the same expression he'd worn when he almost got them both kicked out of college by climbing the roof of the observatory. David had had to do some fast talking to get them out of that one.

"Fine. What puzzles need redesigning? I can help you with that at least. Better than waiting for someone else to come in and do the tech."

That would be a big help. Tony had bailed him out

once before, and this way David wouldn't have to deal with waiting for the company he'd purchased his rooms from. Said company was apparently too busy to come do basic maintenance on their props.

"Thank you. That would be great." David hesitated. "I know we had a conversation about you working here…"

Tony waved him off. "Consider me hired."

"I haven't paid you."

"I work cheap. Pop next door and pick up a pizza?"

David laughed. "A pizza that your dad will probably comp for me? I guess I am really making out on this deal." He got up. His stomach growled, reminding him that he hadn't eaten yet. The entire day had been taken up by this whole mess.

"Of course you are. You have my not-inconsiderable talents at your disposal." Tony slid into the chair David had just vacated. "By the time you get back, I'll have your problems solved."

If only it were that easy. David paused for a moment in the doorway. Tony still had that gleam in his eyes. Now, granted, that might be because he was excited about doing some redesigning of the room. But David couldn't shake the feeling Tony was planning something underhanded.

****

Elena heard Phoebe's squeal even with her office door shut. She'd taken the opportunity to close herself up with her books and run the numbers. After a few hours of this, she'd picked up the phone, seriously considering calling Jesse and having Phil take over. She had many talents. Accounting wasn't one of them.

At least Phoebe's exclamation got her out of her

chair. She'd take any excuse for a break at this point.

"Phoebe? Are you all right?" She ventured down the hall to find her at the receptionist's desk, the phone pressed tightly to her ear.

"Are you kidding me?" Phoebe shrieked, clearly not done with her conversation.

Elena blinked. She couldn't be on the phone with a customer, or they were going to have a very frank discussion about customer service. She looked up at Elena, held up her hand in a gesture to wait, and then went back to her conversation.

"You can't do that. It's un-American. Well, yes, I know you're not American… Fine. We'll just order pizza from someplace else."

Phoebe slammed the phone down and sank backward in her seat. She threw her head back and groaned.

"What the hell was that?" Elena gestured.

"I tried to order pizza from Spano's across the street."

They practically had Spano's on speed dial. Especially on busy Friday nights, Phoebe would order food and demand Elena and Quinn eat between game mastering. Elena appreciated the leftovers, since she often stayed up past two a.m., resetting the rooms or running games for surprise, and sometimes very drunk, customers.

"And?"

"We're banned. They refuse to sell us any food. Apparently, the owner is friends with David." Phoebe's cheeks flushed red.

Elena couldn't help the giggle that escaped. Of all the absurd things she'd heard today, that went to the top of the list. "We've been blacklisted from the pizza place?"

"It's not funny. They make the best garlic knots in town." Phoebe leaned on her elbows, but then she too started to giggle. "Oh God, is this in revenge for the fire marshal?" She did a quick imitation of David. "You'll never have pizza again! Not in this town!"

Quinn emerged from the control room, her wireless headset hung around her neck. Phoebe's outrage must have reached her even back there. "What's so funny?"

"No pizza from Spano's anymore. They've banned us." Even saying that out loud was ridiculous. "The owner is friends with David."

"Oh, interesting." Quinn pulled out her phone as she sat on the edge of the desk. "I saw a closed-for-renovations sign up when I went over there for bagels this morning."

"Wait, you mean we shut him down?" Phoebe clapped her hands together. "Sweet."

Elena swatted at her. "No, not sweet. I want to beat him fair and square, not because the fire marshal made him close."

"Then he should have done it right from the beginning." Quinn scrolled through her phone. "I'm ordering Chinese. What do you guys want?"

"Better hurry before we're banned from the Chinese place, too," Phoebe grumbled.

"I don't think he has that much power." Although didn't David say he picked that location because he was friendly with the owner of the entire strip mall? Crap, Elena would have to find a new dry cleaner and bagel place. "I'm going to go out and grab menus from some other pizza places."

Having a backup plan was always a good idea.

She gave Quinn her order before leaving the building. Elena took a deep breath of the spring air, glad the weather had finally decided to warm up. April always was one of her favorite months. Getting out would be good for her anyway, help her clear her mind from all the numbers.

The parking lot across the street looked jammed, as always. But now she knew none of those cars were going to The Greatest Escape. This was her chance. Elena could finally get the jump on David, show him and everyone exactly how good her rooms were.

After all, at the moment, she had no competition.

Chapter 13

Elena showed the last group of the day out the door, glad they were leaving with smiles on their faces. Once she made sure they had gone—and didn't pause on the porch to discuss every intricate element of her room— she turned back to the lobby and plopped down on the couch. She yawned so long her jaw popped. She winced and rubbed beneath her ear.

She'd managed to take advantage of The Greatest Escape being closed. Quinn had stepped up advertising at local businesses—except for Spano's, which still refused to sell them pizza—and through other online avenues that were mysterious to Elena. Their bookings had increased to the point where she had to turn people away—well, encourage them to come back another day.

It made her wish she had enough time to work on that third room.

Right now the increased business made that impossible. She worked until two a.m. almost every night, accommodating late-night bookings and then spending the extra time to close down and prep the rooms. Her extra lock box was running low, and she needed to make a run to the hardware store soon. She still didn't understand how quickly her customers ruined locks.

Quinn emerged from the control room with her silver backpack slung over one shoulder. Phoebe had started packing up her own stuff, filling the massive purse she carried everywhere. As soon as they left, she would go back up and clean the rooms, making sure everything still worked and no one had left her any surprises.

Like the time she'd gone back up and found a used condom in the fake trash bin. Elena still didn't know how they'd managed it. They'd been on camera the entire hour. She'd have to check for blind spots in the room or, at the very least, add a rule about no hanky-panky in the room.

"Have a good night," she said, her voice breaking on yet another yawn.

Quinn looked over at Phoebe, who nodded. Then both of them pulled up chairs around the couch.

"Listen, boss," Phoebe said. "We think you need to take a break."

Elena looked between the two of them. Both young women wore extremely serious expressions on their faces and had all but cornered her on the couch with their choice of seating.

"Is this an intervention?"

"You're here all the time. Fuck, you even live here." Quinn pointed downstairs. "That's not healthy. You take the shifts when Phoebe or I have off. But when do you get downtime?"

Elena rubbed her eyes and leaned forward. Her head felt fuzzy, and her body ached to her very bones. She did not want to have this conversation right now. Maybe in the morning when a twenty-ounce cup of coffee had her fresh and wide-eyed.

Lately, even the extra-large coffee hadn't been enough.

"I can't afford to hire more staff just yet," she said. "But I appreciate your concern."

Phoebe leaned forward and shoved a brochure in her lap. "Maybe you need to get out of here for a little bit."

What was this? A spa or something? Elena opened the brochure, shocked to see information about an escape room conference down in Atlantic City. Despite herself, she flipped through, curious. "Your solution is for me to do more work?"

"We know you. You're not happy unless you're working. But this gets you out of the house, a view of the beach, and some ideas to get you excited about this place again." Quinn shrugged. "You keep talking about that third room, but you don't have any time to work on it."

"And, um, maybe consider closing one day during the week?" Phoebe suggested. "Mondays are pretty slow. Give yourself a day off."

"And who's going to run the place while I'm gone? This is on a weekend when we're the busiest."

Quinn and Phoebe wore matching grins. Phoebe leaned forward. "We got this. You know Quinn and I can handle both rooms. It's just one weekend, boss. Let yourself have a little fun."

She looked at them, narrowing her eyes in sudden suspicion. Did they want her gone for some reason? "You're not planning on taking revenge on Spano's Pizza while I'm gone, are you?"

Quinn rolled her eyes. "You got me. You're the only thing stopping me from donning night-vision goggles, breaking in, and stealing their pizza recipe."

"I'm serious."

"Seriously, the only thing that might get stolen is Sean, based on the way Phoebe keeps making cow eyes when he comes in for work."

"Hey!" Phoebe's cheeks flushed a bright red. She clamped her lips together and glared at Quinn.

"Come on. Why do you think he parks in front of here when he's got the entire lot across the street?"

Elena hadn't even noticed that, and she should have. Something like the same car being parked on the street right outside seemed so obvious. Maybe they were right and she needed a break from this place.

"Maybe I could turn him." Phoebe rubbed her hands together. "We can have a double agent on the inside."

"No trying to seduce David's employees," Elena said forcefully. She got to her feet, letting the brochure fall onto the couch. "I'll think about it, okay? Now get out of here before I make you both help with the vacuuming."

That got them to scatter. Elena locked up after they left, watching Phoebe's car speed along the street and Quinn walk down the block to her own apartment. Much as she loved them both, she really could use some quiet.

Elena continued her close-up routine, finding comfort in doing the exact same thing she did every night, ending with mopping the floor in the public bathroom. She made notes on which locks needed replacing—one in Uncle Enzo's room was already starting to stick, and she swore she'd just swapped that one out.

She did a final circuit, shutting down the lights and checking the locks before descending the back stairs to her apartment below. Her body ached, but her mind raced, far too wired for sleep. Plus, she still needed to do her daily physical-therapy exercises. She kept up with them religiously.

Elena turned on the TV and sat on her bed. She unlaced her shoes and rubbed her ankles, fingers catching on the scars. Sometimes she imagined she could feel the metal inside although she knew it for the foolishness it was. She'd work through her movements while watching TV and then ice her feet afterward, like she used to do after rehearsals.

After a long day, her mind was so fuzzy she didn't notice at first what played on the screen. She had basic cable, so PBS turned on by default when she switched on the TV. Tonight they were showing a ballet performance, and she realized she'd been in this production. She leaned over for the remote and hit *info*.

Swan Lake, Five Boroughs Ballet Company.

It felt like a lifetime ago. She gripped the plastic so hard it cracked beneath her fingertips.

But she could not stop watching.

For a moment, it felt like any other time she'd watched herself on video, dissecting her performance, figuring out how she could do better, be better, each movement precise and absolutely perfect. And then hours upon hours training at the studio until her thighs burned from practicing the jumps, her calves ached, and her feet reminded her that she was alive.

Tears streamed down her face. Elena turned off the TV, unable to watch anymore. It was the first time she'd seen an old production, and it reminded her vividly of what she could no longer do. She picked up her phone, considering texting Jesse. But he'd probably be sleeping right now, and after performing earlier tonight, he'd need his rest to start it all over again the next morning.

She didn't want him to know she was upset. He'd only take it to heart, and she did not want to hear that crushing sense of guilt in his voice, not again, not when it seemed they both finally had moved on. She wanted him to keep dancing for as long as he could, even though she could not be at his side.

Oh, but she missed it.

Elena stared at the blank screen. She had a new life now, a new purpose, something that made her happy. It was time to stop living in the past and move fully into the future.

Instead of texting Jesse, she pulled up messenger and shot Phoebe a note.

—Fine, you win. I'll go to the conference. But no retaliation while I'm gone. That includes stealing Sean.—

Without waiting for a response, Elena put her phone on charge. She limped upstairs to get the brochure. PT could wait a little longer tonight. Phoebe had helpfully clipped the train schedule on the back, and though it would suck, the journey was doable. God, she had such good employees. They were efficient, and they actually cared about her.

Elena logged into her laptop and registered for the conference before she could change her mind.

This would be the last night she'd cry over her lost dance career.

Chapter 14

Elena put the lanyard around her neck, taking a moment to run her fingers over the plastic encasing the card with her name printed on it. Underneath *Elena Evans* it read *Owner: The Escape Space*. That made it official. Here she was, at a trade show for escape rooms. As an owner.

Elena thanked the woman at registration, picked up her program, and walked over to the side to get her bearings.

The conference—Escape-a-Con—had booked part of the Atlantic City Convention Center and thankfully had included shuttles to the casino hotels on the boardwalk. She found it cheaper to get a room there than at the conference hotel right across the street. She appreciated how much the city had changed since the last time she'd been here performing. A short walk from the main hall led to a downtown filled with shops and restaurants. She remembered much of the entertainment had been confined to the boardwalk area, and that had all changed.

Like she had. She took a deep breath and reminded herself this was exactly why she was here—to forget about the past and embrace her future.

She took a moment to flip through the program before deciding to walk around and see what was available. Huge banners hung from every surface, advertising sessions, seminars, and companies. Most of the action seemed to be moving toward the trade floor, so Elena followed the crowds of people, their voices raising and lowering like the ebb and flow of the ocean.

The trade room stretched out as far as the eye could see, consisting of booths with bright colorful signs. She walked between the rows, eyes wide at the variety of things being sold, from props to entire escape room experiences. She stopped in front of a stand with what looked like a suitcase with table legs attached. Inside it held all sorts of escape room components: locks, boxes, puzzles, and code wheels.

"Interested in a pop-up event?" The salesman came over. "We make all kinds of products you can take with you. Advertise your business at local baseball games, street fairs, even set up next to the Girl Scouts."

Elena never liked using puzzles someone else had designed. However, the idea of a little traveling escape experience intrigued her. "Do you have a card?"

"Certainly." He smiled and handed her one with brightly colored letters spelling out *Bob's Pop-Up Designs*. "If you purchase something at the conference, it's twenty percent off."

"Thank you." She had no way of bringing anything like this home on the train with her. "I'll check back later."

She stopped at another booth that sold variations of images on canvas encased in heavy frames. Some had compartments behind them that slid open at various triggers. The vendor demonstrated how covering the eyes of the painting of a young girl caused the slot beneath to slide out from the bottom of the frame.

Elena could plan an entire room around that. She

would have to incorporate some kind of story around the girl—why was there a portrait of her, or why did covering her eyes cause something to be revealed? Did the girl see something she never wanted to remember? This might be something she could use for her third room. She took one of his cards as well.

Quinn and Phoebe had been right. Coming here had sparked her creativity. She found herself coming up with lots of ideas, and while she couldn't actually use them all, it was fun to think about. Maybe a spaceship room wouldn't be so farfetched after all.

She looked at her watch. It was nearly time for the workshop on marketing to begin. She flipped to the program and checked the map. The seminar locations were on the second floor. She found an escalator—thankful she didn't have to climb another set of stairs—and walked along the hallway until she found room 2B.

The room was smaller than she'd expected, with a projector set up in front of a white screen. Several rows of chairs had been set up in front, and most had already been taken. She slid into one of the available seats in the last row, tucking her feet beneath her and wishing she'd thought to bring a pen and paper to take notes. Perhaps she could sneak some pictures of the slides with her phone.

As the speaker stepped up to the podium, the door to the room banged open. Elena turned to glare at the newcomer, and her mouth dropped open at the sight of David heading straight for her.

****

David had left the contractors in Tony's capable hands. One thing Tony excelled at was telling other people what to do. Most of the redesign ideas had come from Tony in the first place. David figured he'd better stay out of the way and decided to take advantage of being closed to attend Escape-a-Con. He could always write it off on his taxes.

Because honestly, how much could someone really talk about escape rooms? A lot, it turned out. David had paged through the program, fascinated at the variety of workshops—everything from story design to prop making.

He honed in on the one titled "Marketing plan—how to turn your room into a corporate hangout." If he could get in on the corporate gig, he would rake in a hell of a lot of money. Corporations loved that team-building stuff.

He managed to make it into the room before the presentation began, though he cringed at the sound the slamming doors made behind him. He hated being late. David scanned the chairs quickly, looking for an empty seat. A shock of red hair caught his attention. *Seriously? What were the odds?*

He slid into the empty chair next to Elena and said, "Hello."

"What are you doing here?" she hissed.

"Why wouldn't I be at an escape room convention?"

"No, I mean, here, here. This room."

"Just lucky, I guess." And he meant it. He would finally get a chance to talk to her outside of all the shenanigans.

The presenter cleared his throat menacingly, so David turned his attention to the on-screen presentation. He could feel Elena's glare, like a physical presence, stabbing him in the side of the head. He hadn't come here to ruin her day. He was honestly interested in the topic.

He tried to focus on the presentation. He wished he'd brought a pen and notebook to take notes. Even in grad school, he'd been the guy with the old-school note-taking obsession. Everybody else printed the professor's notes file. David needed to write things down to really understand them. He couldn't pay attention to half of what the guy said.

Especially with Elena sitting right next to him. She even smelled like cinnamon. He'd think of her every time a hint of that spice crossed his nostrils. Damn it, from the moment she walked into his business, she had fascinated him. Getting that glimpse of her room—the one she'd designed all on her own apparently—had only made him more curious. Who was she? He needed to know more.

Maybe today was his chance. They were on neutral ground. Escape rooms, yes, but not his or hers.

She shifted her legs, and their calves touched briefly, warmth along his jeans. Her cheeks went pink as she pulled away. "Sorry," she murmured.

"No problem. These are the most uncomfortable chairs I've ever sat in. Do they want us to walk out in the middle of the poor guy's talk? Do you think if I sat on the floor, it would help?"

"Don't you dare." She covered her mouth, but not before he saw her lips turn up in a smile.

That smile was worth sitting on uncomfortable metal through the next forty-five minutes of the not-very-interesting talk—that went over the posted ending time by five minutes. The next presenter had to come in and commandeer the room. David shuffled out with the rest of the group, sticking close to Elena.

"What did you think of the presentation?" He

couldn't think of anything more intelligent to ask and winced at his own words.

She regarded him for a second. She shrugged. "I'm not sure my place is cut out for corporate events. For one thing, I like my customers to have fun."

He laughed. "My first escape room was one of those team-building things. You're right. There's a bit too much pressure for it to be classified as fun."

"But you kept at it despite that?"

He shrugged. "I caught the bug. I imagine you know how that is." He had to say something to keep the conversation going. He didn't want to stop. "Where are you heading to next?"

She crossed her arms over her chest. "Why?"

"I think it would be more *fun*"—he emphasized the word—"to check out a few things together."

"Oh, really? I find that surprising."

"Why? Because we're competitors? You know Steve Jobs and Bill Gates were best friends?"

To his delight she burst out laughing. "They were not. That's bullshit."

"Thomas Edison and Tesla?"

"Mortal enemies," she replied.

"Reagan and Gorbachev."

"Now you're just making shit up."

"I haven't stopped," he admitted. "Let's try a seminar that's not quite so dry. Look. Top-ten things people do in escape rooms when they think no one is watching."

"I bet number one is make out." She looked at his program and started off down the hall.

He had to scramble to keep up. "I had a marriage proposal in one of my rooms," he told her. "Before I had to shut down."

She winced at that. "Look, that's another thing. Aren't you mad about…the fire inspector?"

"So you did call them." He jabbed the air in triumph.

"You were handcuffing people in a room with no emergency release," she pointed out.

"You're absolutely right." And she was. Which was why, unlike Tony, David hadn't protested the changes. He didn't want an unsafe business. He wanted people to have fun, not panic attacks, in his rooms. "I am, so you know, taking the opportunity to add some puzzles, so you'll have to try the prison room again sometime."

She stopped walking and shook her head. "See, you say stuff like that, but then you get Spano's Pizza to stop delivering to us in retaliation."

Oh, damn it, Tony. "What? I didn't… I had nothing to do with that. I'll fix it when I get back."

"Right." Elena turned, pivoting on one foot in an artistic twirl. "Aren't you coming? I'm dying to know what number ten is."

He laughed and followed her into the next seminar room.

****

Elena shouldn't do this. She should have let David go to this seminar without her while she did things that would actually help her business. She could not forget that he was a threat.

But he made her laugh. And he didn't seem too upset about Phoebe calling the fire inspector on him. Elena would have bet he'd be livid about that. Instead, he'd smiled and said she was right. And he looked really good in those dark-wash jeans. In the workshop, she had caught herself gazing at the way the fabric tightened on his thighs, like even the denim couldn't stop itself from embracing his muscular legs.

This time she made sure to scoot her chair a little bit farther from his. She didn't want to risk them touching again. He didn't seem to notice.

Unlike the first workshop, this one had a very loose format. The presenters were game masters from a variety of different escape room companies and had the experience to back it up. Number one was, indeed, public displays of affection. Although, apparently, it did go beyond making out.

Elena recalled the used condom she'd found in one of her own rooms and shuddered. "Why would someone do that? They know they're on camera."

"Maybe that's part of the thrill," David said in a low voice next to her ear. "Being watched? And locked into a room for an hour? Can't you see how that's a little bit erotic?"

Although his words and voice might have been flirting, her mind instead flashed to one of the last rooms she'd been exploring in the trade room downstairs. She slapped her hand over her mouth to keep the guffaw from escaping.

He frowned at her.

"Clown rooms," she said, trying not to break up completely.

He snorted, drawing several annoyed looks from their neighbors. "Well, you might not know this, but some people find clowns very erotic."

And then she lost it, dissolving completely into giggles and missing the next few minutes of the presentation while she got her breath back. She tried to pull it together, at least long enough to hear the last bit of the presentation and the Q and A.

The biggest problem, apparently, from the questions received, was property damage. Customers who took apart things they weren't supposed to, who got into walls, dropped ceilings, who tore apart furniture or broke props that were expensive and irreplaceable. Why would other owners even have glass diamonds as a prop anyway? Elena had made sure to use plastic wine bottles in her room. The last thing she needed was shards of glass everywhere.

"I did have someone break the cuffs," David said. "Before the fire inspector came. Tore right through the plastic chain. I think they took the escaping part a bit too literally."

"You're lucky they didn't break through the actual wall." She hadn't had anything get broken, but she was starting to think she was lucky, based on all of these horror stories. Or maybe she hadn't been in business long enough.

The lively panel ended, and they followed the crowd back out into the hallway. Everyone was sharing stories, and for a moment Elena listened in, trying to hear even more outrageous tales.

"I'm surprised no one has made a sitcom based on escape rooms by now," David said.

"You have to admit, it's still pretty niche."

He gestured to the crowds of people as they navigated the hallway. "Plenty of people here to disagree."

"It's hardly a good sample size. These are all owners and prop creators. How many average people know what an escape room even is?"

"It's our job to let them know."

They came to a junction in the hallway, with signs pointing to more workshops and the keynote speaker in the main hall. Elena stopped, and David did as well.

She didn't know if she wanted to keep walking with him or find a way to extricate herself discreetly. She had enjoyed laughing with him, but she couldn't forget this man directly threatened her business.

"Are you staying for the second day?" he asked.

"Yes. But I'll have to leave early to make my train…" That was true, but it was also to keep him from demanding any more of her time.

"Maybe we can have coffee tomorrow? I'm staying at Caesars on the boardwalk."

Not the same hotel, at least. That would have been too much of a coincidence, with all the hotels and casinos that dotted the ocean.

When was the last time someone had asked her out for coffee?

Since the accident, she'd been moving ahead full throttle, constantly working toward something. First she'd been focused on healing and learning to walk again. Then she'd had to manage the lawsuit and trying to figure out what to do with her life. And then she'd been consumed by building her escape rooms, growing her business, and working, working, working…

Her belly twisted, and she didn't know why the bottom suddenly dropped for her. She'd been too busy seeing David as a rival, despite her attraction to him. Maybe it was time to stop. Just stop.

He held out his hand and pulled a ringing phone from the back pocket of his jeans. "I need to take this. It's my mom."

He moved off to the side and put the phone up to his

ear. "Hi, Momma. What's up? Of course I got here okay…"

Elena took the opportunity to melt into the crowd and walk away from David. She couldn't deal with him, not now. Maybe not ever.

Chapter 15

David shook his head as he stuck his phone back into his pocket. He'd resigned himself to his mother still worrying about him although he felt slightly insulted that she'd called to check up on him. He could handle the two-hour drive to Atlantic City perfectly well. Of course, she'd always say she didn't trust the other drivers on the road.

Elena had taken the opportunity to escape. He chuckled at his own joke. He shouldn't have expected her to wait around while he talked to his mother. Most people didn't understand David being so close with Mom, but only because he rarely shared his past. At one point he needed to protect her as much as she protected him. Laura had never understood that.

Stop thinking about Laura. Those days were gone. He had a new life now, a new purpose.

Too bad he couldn't ask Elena out. They'd had a great time together in those workshops. He loved making her laugh. He had enjoyed the way she couldn't contain her giggles, and how she slapped her hand over her mouth to try, but it only made her eyes sparkle. He wanted to have the chance to get to know her, outside of this ridiculous rivalry.

Obviously, she didn't think the same, considering she'd run off. It hurt his ego a bit, that she couldn't look past him owning her competition, that she didn't feel the same spark between them. He was so out of practice with this stuff, because he had been sure she was attracted to him, too.

Or maybe he couldn't tempt her away from all the escape room joy that currently surrounded them. That had to be far more interesting than sitting around with him. His jokes weren't that funny. They'd both come here to learn more about the business and improve their own. He probably should start working on that and stop mulling over what he couldn't have.

David sighed and took out his program. He still had plenty to do, and he could always run into her again. The convention hall was huge, but the con itself took up only a portion of it. In a few hours he could go to the escape room owners' mixer. It promised free food, and that was better than getting dinner by himself. He'd hit the trade floor for a bit and then go grab some grub.

****

"If you're not spending a million dollars on advertising, what is the point? I keep very careful track of my Google ad metrics. I highly recommend having a dedicated employee doing that. Getting yourself out there is your bread and butter."

David kept his expression blank. He'd made the mistake of taking the empty space at this high-top table to hold his drink and plate of food. He should have realized this guy had been alone for a reason. He'd introduced himself as Eddie the Escape Room Master, although David hadn't caught the name of his business and couldn't read the badge that had gotten twisted around on the brightly colored lanyard. Eddie hadn't stopped talking about advertising since David had set his plate down.

"That's a little beyond where I'm at right now." David made the mistake of trying to take part in the conversation. Of course, he couldn't think about advertising while his place was still shut down. Once open, though? He couldn't imagine spending millions of dollars when he'd be better off hanging some flyers around the local college campus.

Eddie pointed with one finger as he spoke. "It's never too early to look at Google ads. You want to be the first thing that comes up when someone searches escape rooms."

David took a step backward in order to avoid getting poked. "I'll look into it." Maybe if he started agreeing with the guy, he wouldn't get the finger again. Why had he decided to come to this mixer? Had he thought all fellow owners would be as beautiful and interesting as Elena?

"Of course, the business is shifting. I'm offering experiences, not just escape rooms."

It sounded like he was about to start on a whole new tangent. David tried to smile between bites of his fried chicken. At least he could enjoy the food, despite the company. And chewing kept him from having to respond.

"I think my next project will be to purchase a broken-down carnival and turn the entire thing into an escape room." Eddie stared out into space. "Picture it. From the moment you walk in, the entire thing is puzzles."

It didn't matter what Eddie said next. David didn't hear him. He could only focus on the person who'd walked into the room—Elena.

****

Elena never could turn down free food, and when someone handed her a flyer for this mixer, she'd jumped on the opportunity. Inside, the room bustled with people clustered in groups at the high-top tables arranged strategically around the room. The buffet had been set up along one wall, and the line didn't seem long at all. She'd timed her arrival perfectly—late enough to not have to wait for food.

She hopped in line and filled her plate with a variety of items, including some fried chicken. It looked amazing—crispy, with thick breading and spices. Finally, she grabbed a bottle of water and looked around, trying to find a place to set down her plate and eat.

A woman smiled at her and waved Elena over to the table she shared with a man sporting an impressive goatee that reached the middle of his chest.

"Hello, I'm Elena." She set her plate down.

The woman held out her hand, and Elena shook it.

"I'm Diana. This is my husband, Sam. We own Escape in Time."

"You work together?" That boggled Elena—how could Diana stand working with the person she was married to? They'd spend all day running the escape room and then go home to each other. Wouldn't that get claustrophobic?

"She does it all. I'm just the eye-candy." Sam put his arm around his wife and tugged her close.

Diana laughed and curled into the embrace before pulling away. "I handle room build and design. Sam works the business end."

"You each have your own strengths." Elena took a bite of her food. She chewed and swallowed before continuing. "I have two employees, but I do all the

119

puzzle design myself."

They chatted about their rooms—Diana had created a Shakespeare-themed room herself. She described how she used her background in theater to design the puzzles. Years spent building sets and props came in handy because escape rooms were essentially that—small theaters.

Elena really liked her.

They exchanged cards, and she promised to check out their rooms sometime. She went to dump her empty plate in the trash, and when she turned around to grab her water bottle, a very familiar smile greeted her.

David. Of course he'd come to this event.

"You found me," she said. He was close enough the heat of his body reached her, and she could even smell his scent, something like spearmint and musk. She stepped back, uncomfortable with that knowledge.

"Were you hiding?"

That caught her off guard. She didn't want him to think he scared her, because she was not a coward. "It seemed like you had an important phone call to attend to."

"My mother." He shrugged and ducked his head. "She worries about me."

Elena swallowed down the ball of grief that lodged in her throat. It had been so long since she'd last heard her mother's voice. "That's... Appreciate her while you have her."

The expression on his face turned worried. He held out a hand, and for a moment she feared he'd try to do something like hug her.

"Are you okay?"

She waved him away, blinking back the tears that

had threatened. "I'm fine. My mom died when I was in high school." Cancer. It hadn't been quick or painless, not like her father's death. "And my dad passed about ten years ago. For some reason, it hit me when you mentioned your mom."

Breathe. In and out. Those lessons her mother taught her would always be with her. What would her parents think of the life she'd made for herself? Would her mother be disappointed she hadn't stayed in the dance field? That she had run as far away from it as she could after the accident?

"I'm sorry." He looked at her, eyes soft.

"You shouldn't be." She lowered her hand and looked around for her bottle of water, although at this point she might want to grab a new one.

"Well, if it isn't my two favorite New Brunswick escape room owners." The voice slid down her spine like ice on a chalkboard.

Elena turned so she stood next to David, their fingers brushing as they both faced off against Sven Svenson. She shouldn't be surprised to see him, yet she hadn't expected him to mingle with the peons beneath him. "Mr. Svenson. What are you doing here?"

He chuckled, but his laugh sounded forced, like a villain who'd escaped from a comic book. Svenson wore a purple suit, a brightly colored pin in the shape of a wizard's hat affixed to his lapel. The brightness of the colors made his skin look paler than usual, and his light-blue eyes stabbed her like lasers. "I am an escape room owner, am I not? It's always lovely to scope out new clients. I mean, fellow owners."

She could feel David stiffen beside her.

"I told you," David said, the words sounding forced

as he spoke, "I have no interest in franchising with you."

Svenson never dropped the smile. "I heard you're having a bit of a tough time out there. It can't be easy, two no-name escape rooms in the same town, right across from one another. You're competing for the same market. Imagine what my name could do for you."

Elena had heard this spiel before, and apparently so had David. He'd had the good sense to turn Svenson down just as she had. Maybe he wasn't so bad. "Neither of us is interested. You should probably go look for someone who is."

He tucked his hand into his jacket and pulled out a purple business card. "You say that now, but I look forward to that day you do call me. Make no mistake, that day will come."

She took the card to be polite, only to crush it between her fingers as he stepped away. "I don't like that guy."

David snorted. "Understatement. He gave me the hard sell on franchising with him. Like I'd pay him a hundred grand for the name. That didn't even cover any of the prefab rooms."

"And those rooms suck."

"Exactly."

She smiled at him. He wasn't so bad, really. Shame he'd had to set up shop across the street from her.

****

David found himself lost in Elena's smile. It seemed like something special, meant only for him. Not only did it light up her eyes and brighten her face, but that slow curve of her lips raked over him, soft and intimate. What had he done to deserve this gift? He needed to know so he could do it again. Warmth filled his chest, and he lifted one hand, about to reach out and caress her cheek.

Hell, he'd tell off Sven Svenson a million times if that had been the reason she smiled like that.

Maybe he'd been wrong about her escaping earlier. Maybe she did feel the spark between them. He picked a bad time to pursue it—they were surrounded by way too many distracting things—but maybe this was his chance.

He didn't want this connection between them to end. David opened his mouth to ask her to hang out with him for the rest of the convention. Maybe get that coffee together. But before he could say a word, someone squealed and ran over to them, enveloping Elena in a hug.

A mixer filled with people was probably not the best place for private conversation.

"Lorraine! I'm so glad to see you." Elena hugged back.

She stepped away from David but turned and gestured toward him, which surprised him. This wouldn't be a case of her using this person as an excuse to run away again.

"This is David. David, this is Lorraine. She owns an escape room up in Montclair. She's one of the first people I talked to about opening my own business."

This Lorraine looked a bit older than the two of them and wore her hair up in an orange scarf that contrasted nicely against the brown tones of her skin. She had a warm smile and eyes that crinkled in the corners. David found himself liking her instantly. He grinned as he took her hand and gave it a hearty shake.

"This girl just walked in, with her red hair and crazy eyes, and asked me for tips right after finishing one of my rooms, with a record-breaking time, mind you."

Her words painted a vivid picture. He could see Elena doing it, picturing how she must have looked when she loved an escape room, eager to learn more. If only she had been that enthusiastic about his rooms.

Lorraine shook her head. "How do you know Elena?"

"I own the escape rooms across the street from her," he said drily.

She gave Elena a look and patted her on the shoulder. "Later on, you and I are gonna have to talk."

"I'd be happy to. How long are you here? What are you doing next?"

"I have a booth," Lorraine said proudly. "I partnered with Night Eye Designs. They built a self-resetting room for me, and we're demoing it down in area C."

"A self-resetting room?" David blinked. How the heck was that possible?

Lorraine pulled out her phone and started tapping. "Are you both here tomorrow? I have an open slot at ten. I can book you right now."

He hesitated and glanced over at Elena for guidance. She looked thoughtful and chewed on her bottom lip, like she didn't know what to say.

"I'll be here," he said.

Elena nodded. "Yeah, me, too."

"Great. I'll see you both then. Look for my business name on the banner. Exit Escape." Lorraine tapped on her phone and whirled away, bouncing out of their sphere as quickly as she had bounced in.

"So," David said. "Want to check out the rest of the convention with me?"

As long as nobody else interrupted them in the next five minutes. He would body check anyone else who got close.

Elena gave him a look. "All right. But first, dessert."
He followed her back to the buffet.

Chapter 16

Elena cranked open the window of her hotel room and sighed at the sea breeze that wafted in. She breathed deeply of the salt air. With the pounding of the waves on the surf a few feet away, she'd sleep soundly tonight, soothed to dreamland by the most delicious white noise.

Her phone buzzed from the bed. She leaned over to grab it and accept the video call from Quinn. After a moment, both Quinn and Phoebe looked back at her from the tiny screen.

"Hey, boss," Phoebe said. "Having fun?"

"Actually, I am." Elena sat on the bed and started working off her shoes with her free hand. "There's so much to see. I've barely scratched the surface of day one."

"Did you buy us anything?" Phoebe asked.

Quinn elbowed her.

"What?"

Elena laughed. "Not yet. How is everything going there?"

"Fine. I've got one room running and another coming in about twenty minutes." Quinn gestured to the barely visible computers behind her. "There was just one incident with drunk frat boys."

"Oh no."

"It's fine. We handled it. Phoebe handled it."

Elena decided she didn't want to know. If it had

been serious, they would have told her. Maybe.

"All right. I should be back before the rooms booked for tomorrow evening." At least if the trains actually kept to their schedule. That could go either way, especially on a weekend.

"Take your time. Have some fun, boss. Go throw a twenty on the roulette wheel or something."

"I'd be better off throwing it in the ocean." Elena shook her head. She had managed to get both shoes off and started massaging her sore ankles. Tomorrow she'd regret all the walking. "It's funny. I ran into David down here."

"David? David who... No fucking way, you don't mean the jerkface from across the street?" That was Phoebe. Never tactful.

Elena bit her lip. She still had good reason to hate David, but... "He actually was kind of nice."

Phoebe narrowed her eyes and got close to the camera. "Boss?"

"He could have been a jerk about the fire inspector, but he wasn't. He said we were right to call. That's weird, right?"

Quinn shrugged. "Maybe he's not such a douche-nozzle after all."

"Do me a favor and never say that word again." Elena couldn't help giggling, though. "Oh, the good news is that he said when he gets back, he'll make Spano's lift the ban. You'll be free to order pizza again."

"I don't know. I've lost two pounds since the ban."

Quinn elbowed Phoebe. "Now that everyone is playing nicely, can we focus on escape rooms? Do you know what you want to do for your third room yet?"

"I have a lot of ideas. I have to pick one."

"And close on Mondays so you have time to work on it."

Elena rolled her eyes. "Yes, mom." The word caught in her throat, meant as a joke, but after the emotional conversation she'd had with David earlier, she couldn't help but think of her lost family and how Phoebe and Quinn had slotted into her life more like family than employees. Warmth flooded her. "You're right. Now, both of you get back to work."

"Good night, boss."

"Night." Elena ended the call. For a moment she remained flopped on the bed, too tired to move. If she didn't get up and get a bath started, she'd fall asleep right here.

The nice thing about this casino hotel was the ridiculously sinful bathtub. She didn't have one in her little basement apartment, so she intended on taking full advantage of it. She pushed herself out of the bed and then limped over to the bathroom and played with the taps until the temperature was absolutely perfect.

She'd stayed in many hotels over the course of her career as she'd traveled throughout Europe. Some were little more than dormitories with shared bathrooms. She had come to truly appreciate the better experiences. If she only had a single night someplace, she'd made sure to use every amenity. Like tonight.

She hadn't always gone back to those hotel rooms alone. She liked to think she'd left a string of broken-hearted men across France and Italy. They'd had a good time. Knowing she'd be gone soon meant she'd never had to risk her heart.

David was a very good-looking man. As she watched the water swirl in the white porcelain, Elena remembered how he'd filled out his jeans, the denim tight against his ass, the kind of posterior she could sink her hands in as she pulled him closer, inside deeper. She crossed her legs as she sat on the toilet, shocked as the flush of arousal flooded her.

She'd known she was attracted to him, but her anger had always gotten in the way. They'd had a nice day together, but that didn't mean she wanted to tumble him into bed.

Or did it?

Would it make things better if she scratched that itch? Unlike with lovers she'd had in the past, she'd still have to see him again. This might be a trip out of their normal routine, but next week they'd both go back to their rival businesses, and that was always going to sit between them.

The water reached the perfect height. She stripped and carefully lowered herself into the tub, moaning as the almost too-hot water caressed her muscles. God, this felt good. She'd like the bath even better if strong hands were there to massage her shoulders.

She indulged in the fantasy for a moment, imagining leaning back into a strong chest while muscular arms encircled her from behind. Hands with new calluses brushed her skin, creating delicious friction that gave her goose bumps. She looked up into familiar warm brown eyes.

Damn it. She had it bad for David. Now what the hell was she going to do about it?

****

David juggled his hotel key card and the bag of takeout and successfully managed to make it inside his room. He put the bag on the tiny table before he went to the window and pulled open the curtains. Atlantic City never slept, but it wasn't quite as bright as Vegas. Maybe in another lifetime he would have been out there, seeing a show or throwing some money at a poker table.

All he wanted to do right now was crawl into bed.

His stomach chose that moment to growl, which reminded him that food came first, then sleep. The convention had worn him out, but he couldn't wait to go back and do it all again tomorrow. He'd made contact with new vendors and gotten lots of new ideas for his next grand opening.

And of course, there was Elena.

He wished he had been able to convince her to have dinner with him tonight. Instead he had a sad sack of takeout. David sat at his lonely little table and pulled out his food. This had been his life when he wasn't working his tail off. Nobody had waited for him at home since Laura left, and he had gotten used to having dinner alone.

That didn't mean he liked it. He missed having someone to talk to, to share the woes of his day with. At least grabbing takeout at The Greatest Escape meant he had company when he ate, but he wanted more than chatting with his own employees over pizza.

He'd enjoyed spending that time with Elena today. It reminded him of what it had been like to be one half of a pair, to have someone understand and, yes, laugh at his jokes. Of course, she was gorgeous, the kind of beauty that reminded him of autumn that lasted only so long and must be appreciated before it slipped away.

He found himself thinking of her hair, of how he'd like to catch his hand in her locks as he bent her head back to kiss her. He'd start with her soft pale lips but wouldn't be content there. No, he'd nibble along her jawline, down her neck, until he got to those collarbones that taunted him, that creamy skin that looked good enough to eat.

His phone vibrated against his thigh, and he stood up with a shout, knocking his takeout container over and spilling french fries everywhere. He might have gotten a little too caught up in his own fantasy.

"Tony, I've got to say you really have some timing," he answered.

"Okay, that's great and all, but where do you keep your Allen wrenches?"

"Why do you need... You know what? Never mind. There are probably some in the toolbox in my office. Check in the cabinet."

He waited while Tony rummaged around. "Everything going all right there?"

"What?" Tony sounded distracted, despite the fact that he was the one who'd called David. "Fine, fine. New drywall got installed. Painters come tomorrow. I'm trying to reconfigure your network cables. You should really be using a wire closet."

"Do whatever you need to do." Even as David said it, he knew he was going to regret it. To be fair, when it came to tech, Tony knew what he was doing. Interpersonal relationships? Not so much. "Except you need to lift the ban on Spano's delivering across the street."

The sounds of rummaging stopped. "Oh, you heard about that."

"Honestly, did you think I wouldn't find out? That's not the kind of thing I want to be known for. We don't do petty revenge." David rubbed his forehead, fighting a sudden headache. He needed Tony to stop acting like a twelve-year-old.

"They started it," he grumped.

"Well, I'm finishing it. Got it?"

"Fine."

David sighed and cleaned up the mess that remained of dinner. "There's lots of great stuff here. Do you want me to bring you back anything?"

Tony made him write it down, and David didn't think he'd remember otherwise. He scrawled his notes on hotel stationery and hoped he'd have time tomorrow to find vendors that sold this kind of electronic equipment. He told Tony to be good before ending the call to his manic laughter.

He tossed his phone on the table before digging around in his overnight bag for the charger. He was almost out of juice.

After plugging it in, he sat on the edge of the bed and considered calling his mother. He wanted to tell her about the convention, about the puzzles he'd seen that she would love. Part of him wanted to talk to her about Elena. But talking about her would make it more than what it was—an attraction to a woman he couldn't have, no matter how much they seemed to be getting along.

And after the whole Laura thing, he didn't want to break his mother's heart by getting her hopes up.

He wanted a serious relationship. Tony had told him to pick up some rebound girl and have a little fun, but David had never swayed that way. He wanted to get to know someone, to have shared jokes, to curl beneath a blanket on the couch and watch TV. It wasn't the most glamorous of fantasies, but the thought of that made his heart sing.

Doing this escape room thing with Elena tomorrow

was probably a bad idea. He couldn't help wanting more. Maybe she did, too. Maybe their rival businesses didn't matter so much, not in the long run.

He could only hope.

Chapter 17

David spotted Elena the moment she entered the convention center, carrying a heavy-looking backpack that had her slightly bent over from the weight of it. He waited under the banner where they'd arranged to meet the night before. He enjoyed the opportunity to watch her without her realizing it. She deftly avoided strangers in the crowd, dodging them with a smooth grace. When she finally saw him, her face erupted in a smile that made his heart twist.

He smiled back as she came up to him, and for a moment they were the only two people in the crowded convention hall lobby.

He handed her one of the to-go cups of coffee he held. "I guessed how you liked your coffee."

Her eyebrows went up. Ah, probably skeptical. One of his many talents was picking up on someone's coffee preferences. If he got this right, that would go a long way toward proving they had a connection.

She took a tentative sip, and her eyes widened, although whether at the taste or in surprise that he'd guessed correctly, he didn't know.

"How did you know I drank it black?"

He grinned and looked down, embarrassed at having to explain his logic. "You seem like the type of take-no-crap woman who likes her coffee black. Also, I didn't want to risk it if you were lactose intolerant or allergic to nuts."

She chuckled. "How do you like your coffee?"

He held up his cup as if she could see inside. "Light with a dose of chocolate syrup. It's never too early for chocolate."

"It's a little too early for me." She laughed. She squared her shoulders, tugging at the straps on her backpack. "Are you ready to try Lorraine's sample room?"

"Ready as I'll ever be."

David followed Elena through the twisting maze of vendor stalls until they reached the back of the conference center where the sample rooms were. He couldn't help smiling as he walked behind her. She'd actually come and wanted to spend time with him. Now, granted, they'd both gotten roped into this at the mixer, but she could have blown him off. Instead, they'd had coffee together.

It wasn't exactly a date, but he'd take it.

The chatter and business of the vendor area soon quieted as they reached the back with the sample rooms. They looked like giant black boxes. These were temporary structures, but they were so enclosed that once he and Elena got inside, it would mimic the experience of an actual escape room. They'd be cut off from the rest of the convention.

Elena approached the two individuals standing outside the sample room marked *Ancient Egyptian Experience*. He recognized the woman from the mixer yesterday, but the young man was new. They sat surrounded by computers, and he guessed that would serve as the control room for the experience. Nice, they could show off how the room worked while people were inside, thus also advertising the control system.

"Hi, Lorraine. We're here for our ten a.m." Elena grinned.

"Great!" the guy said. He had white-blond hair sticking up in all directions, reminding David of that Food Network guy.

"I'm Martin from Night Eye Designs. I'll be your game master for the experience. Inside you'll see all of our props and puzzles. It's part of our new series, what we like to call 'rooms that reset themselves.' When you get out, please take one of our cards and brochures. We'd be happy to work with you."

"This is a shorter version of our room up in Montclair," Lorraine said. "You'll only have a half hour inside today."

"That's going to be nerve wracking." David frowned. Sometimes an hour seemed too short of a time to really appreciate a room and its puzzles.

Lorraine smiled. "I'm sure you'll do fine. I know how good Elena is at escape rooms."

Elena shook her head, her cheeks pink. "I hope you're right. Nothing like a little pressure before we go in."

"Are you ready to begin?" Martin asked.

David looked over to Elena who nodded at him. He turned back to face Martin and said, "Sure."

"This way, please." Lorraine led them to the door cut into the black temporary walls. "You have been trapped in the Pharaoh's tomb and are rapidly running out of air. The only way to get out is to find the golden scarab that is the key to the door. You have a half hour to find the scarab and get out."

Her words stirred David's excitement about the

room. At first, he'd focused on being able to experience this with Elena. But a good story always got him going. Although perhaps it could use a little more detail—why the heck was he in the Pharaoh's tomb to start with? Escape rooms with tangible objects that needed to be found were always more interesting to him than just escaping. Opening that final door with the treasure clutched in his hand always felt so damn satisfying.

David bounced on his toes, itching to get in there. He met Elena's eyes and nodded at her. "Let's do this."

She all but vibrated herself, like an impatient runner at the start of a race waiting for the pistol to go off. "Yes."

"Good luck." Lorraine threw open the door.

Elena ducked in first, and David hurried to catch up. This wasn't a competition. Hell, they had to work together in order to succeed.

His eyes adjusted to the suddenly dim light after the fluorescent bulbs of the convention-room floor. He felt like he had been transported to an Egyptian tomb as if the door had been a portal to another world.

This—this was what escape rooms should be. It should feel like a totally unique experience, like leaving real life for a while.

The room was lit by two sconces on the wall, a flickering light that mimicked real torches. Somehow, the walls looked like sandstone carved with hieroglyphics. In the center sat an ominous-looking rectangular sarcophagus, with a mummy carved into the stone lid.

"If that leads to another room, I'm sending you down into it," Elena said, running her fingers along the edge of the sarcophagus.

"No problem." David grinned. No way had they tunneled through the floor of the convention center. Hopefully. "Where do we start?"

"You take left. I'll take right."

He moved to the left wall and found five dials covered with nine symbols. Clearly, they had to put the symbols in the right order to do something, but he had no clue as to what yet. "Look for a set of five symbols. Somewhere."

"You think it's going to be that easy?"

He looked over to see her playing with a set of levers jetting out of the wall. When she moved them, three panels on the wall moved, two up, one down. He watched as she worked, slim hands against the handles, her lips pursed in concentration.

"I think you need to line them up."

"But how?" She took a step back, visibly frustrated. "They don't seem linked to an individual panel."

He became aware of what sounded like heavy breathing and moaning. He looked around but couldn't see the speakers. Smoke started to drift in through the ceiling. "They are certainly going for ambiance here."

She snorted. "Clearly. Here, I'll throw the first two levers up. You do the second two down, and let's see what happens."

After trying out a few different patterns, they eventually got all three panels lined up. *Pulley system,* he realized. Once they got it, something clicked. A large panel on the front wall had slipped down a notch, revealing a word beneath it. *Breathe*, it said.

"Puzzle one down." She let her levers go, and the panels immediately reset. *Ah*, he understood now. Nothing in here needed to be put back by a person. It was all mechanical and could probably be reset by the flip of a switch.

What happened when a piece of equipment failed? That had happened to David too many times already, and he'd just opened.

"Here." Elena circled around the edge of the sarcophagus. "There's a metal panel over here. How about on that side?"

He crouched down to look. "Got it. Along with a picture of a circuit?"

"Touch it and take my hand." She reached across the top of the sarcophagus. "I've seen a puzzle like this before."

He placed his palm against the cool metal and then reached to entangle her fingers with his own. This wasn't exactly how he'd imagined holding hands, and he had to quash a grin. He didn't want her to think he wasn't taking this seriously.

Her fingers were warm and smooth except for a callus on one finger. Perhaps unlocking so many locks had left their mark. He was so focused on how her skin felt that he nearly missed the panel shifting out of place right next to him. "We have symbols."

"Do they match anything else in the room?"

He squinted and then realized where they fit into. "Yes, those dials on the wall next to you."

She let go of his hand, and he found himself missing the contact. He squeezed his fingers into a fist. Luckily, the panel didn't slide back into place. Otherwise, this room would be impossible to do without three people.

"Can you read me the symbols?" She stood in front of the dials.

"I can try? The first is an ankh." At least he knew

that much. "The second kind of looks like a square with an X through it."

"Real ancient Egyptian there."

"Hey, you don't want to actually summon a mummy by using real hieroglyphics. That would be very poor for business."

"Or fantastic for business. How could you beat having a real live mummy?" She slid the second dial into place. "Next?"

"Um. Round with a trapezoid beneath it."

She turned, her forehead furrowed. He lifted his hands and used his fingers to demonstrate.

"Ah, okay."

The next two symbols weren't nearly as complicated, and she had the dials in place in no time. Once again, something clicked and shifted. The front panel had slipped again, revealing the rest of the message.

" 'Breathe my life to me,' " he read out loud. "What's that supposed to mean?"

She came over and glared at the wall. "How long do you think we've been in here?"

He looked at his watch. "Did we actually enter at exactly ten or was it a few minutes later?"

"I don't like not knowing. How are they supposed to give hints anyway?"

In most escape rooms, a message would flash on the monitor that counted down the time. It was how David did it. He also had speakers in his rooms so he could give voice instructions as well, so perhaps they planned on doing that through the speakers in the corners.

The heavy breathing sounds increased, along with a low musical tone that sent shivers down his spine. Well, he couldn't fault them for ambiance. It was suitably creepy.

Elena suddenly whirled, her hair flying behind her as she raced to the sarcophagus. "Here goes nothing," she said as she leaned down and kissed the mummy.

No, not kissed. She breathed into its mouth, blowing a soft breath that echoed like she was talking into a microphone. Just then he heard a snap. The base of the sarcophagus slid open, revealing the golden, glittering scarab.

He scooped it up with a yelp. "We did it!"

The door to the tomb opened, revealing Lorraine with the light from the conference streaming in behind her. "Congratulations!"

He had to blink to adjust his eyes to the light. Real life suddenly intruded on the little adventure he had been enjoying with Elena. He held out the beetle. "Thanks. I assume you take this at the end?"

"Yes. It's very easy to put back together." Lorraine took the scarab, placed it carefully back in the notch in the sarcophagus, and slid the lid back on. As soon as she did that, all of the panels in the room reset, going back to their previous positions. "Of course, the full room has a lot more puzzles. This is just a sample of what Night Eye designs."

"It's remarkable," Elena said, coming out of the shadows. "For a minute there I forgot we were in AC."

"Come check out the full room sometime." Lorraine escorted them out, handing them both flyers for her business in Montclair. He noted her other themes—a heist room and a secret-agent room. Both were very classic escape tropes.

David stopped to chat with the kid from Night Eye

Designs.

He was happy to hand over his business card. "We do everything from simple puzzle design to putting entire rooms together. Plus, we're local."

By the time David pulled away from the conversation, Elena was glancing at her watch. "I have to go," she said. "I need to make my train."

His brain stuttered to a stop. "You took the train down here? From New Brunswick? Didn't that suck?"

She grimaced. "I had to change trains twice. And go through Camden."

"Why didn't you just drive?"

Her face lost all color. "I don't drive."

His first instinct was to ask why not. Everyone drove in Jersey. But something told him not to push, especially with how pale she'd gotten. They were having such a great time, and he didn't want to upset her. He also didn't want this moment to end. He would do anything to spend a little more time with her, away from their businesses and rivalry.

"I'll drive you home," he said instead.

"What?"

"Have lunch with me. Stay the rest of the afternoon. And I'll take you home afterward. It's not like it's out of my way."

He had to say something else to convince her. "We're having fun, right? Let's not end it yet. And trust me, my car is a lot more comfy than the train. What do you say?"

Chapter 18

Elena hesitated.

Getting into a car with someone else driving required a whole lot of courage on her part. She had to grit her teeth and grasp the handle whenever Phoebe drove. Somehow, she'd managed the Uber ride last month, but she hadn't gone out of her way to repeat the experience.

She really didn't want to get back on that train. The train system was so poorly designed that she had to go west before she traveled northeast. On the way down, she'd had to change trains twice, in increasingly sketchier areas. The thought of being able to kick her feet up and be home in less than three hours was extremely attractive.

But could she trust David to drive her? Elena swallowed and tried to turn it into a joke. "This isn't a secret plan to get rid of your competition, is it?"

His eyes widened. "Shit. You're right. You have no reason to trust me."

Warmth filled her, and for one single moment, she thought that somehow he'd seen through her and knew exactly why she couldn't get into a car with him. And then the more rational explanation seeped in. "Not that I actually think you're a serial killer."

"I'll tell you what." He reached into his pocket and pulled out his phone. He tapped away at the screen. "You can give my device tracking info to one of your friends. Preferably the one that hates me. Phoebe?"

She stifled a giggle. "I'll give it to Quinn. She's more likely to know what to do with it."

"Right. Does this mean you'll accept my offer?"

He looked so unsure of himself, holding out his phone like everything depended on it. He had those soft eyes again, and the way he ducked his head made her want to ruffle his hair.

If she hadn't gone on that Uber ride, she wouldn't even be considering it. But now she knew she was strong enough. She took his phone. "All right. Let me get this information to Quinn."

Because she certainly wasn't going to be stupid about it. She would make sure to check off all the boxes—wear her seat belt and make sure someone knew exactly where they were at all times.

Quinn texted back immediately.

—Are you sure about this?—

Well, no, she wasn't. That was the point. Elena texted back.

—This will get me home earlier.—

—You know we got this place covered, right?—

—It's not that. I don't want to sit on the train for three hours.—

Elena didn't want Quinn to think she didn't trust them to run the place. They were pretty much the only people she did trust.

—Besides, this gives me the opportunity to learn all his secrets.—

—LOL, right.— Quinn typed back. *—Send me the device info.—*

She dutifully passed it along and then handed David

back his phone. "Where to?"

"Another workshop, then lunch, maybe?"

She tugged out her paper program. "Which of these sound interesting?"

They passed on the session about designing with kids in mind. That wasn't either of their markets, and Elena had let one family bring in a toddler who ended up stealing a key and flushing it down the toilet. She told David about it, and he laughed so hard he had to lean over to catch his breath.

"You laugh now, but wait until you've got applesauce smeared on your walls." She grinned. She loved seeing him like this, so relaxed and unself-conscious.

"We're definitely not going to the workshop on designing for the kid market." He straightened and cleared his throat.

"Not today, Satan."

That set him off again. She left him to catch his breath and excused herself to use the ladies' room. Once inside, she leaned against the wall and winced. All weekend on her feet had not been a good idea. She dug into her purse for some ibuprofen. Elena had left her stronger pills at home. She limited herself to taking those before bed.

She swallowed the pills, using water from the sink. Her ankles should be getting better. That's what her doctors had told her. As her muscles strengthened, if she kept doing her exercises, then she'd be able to eventually do something more strenuous than walking. Dancing on pointe was out of the question, of course, and she couldn't think of that without an ache in her chest. But, God, she'd love to not have to worry about overdoing it and feeling stabbing pains up her calves.

She and David ended up going to a workshop on story design given by some famous escape room bloggers. She put the URL of their blog in her phone. She wanted to catch up on their content later. It looked super useful.

"Lunch?" David asked as they exited the room. "The casinos are a bit out of the way, but there are actually some nice places to eat near the outlets. Those aren't too far from here."

They ended up at a cute little brewpub, sharing a plate of fries with their burgers—giant slabs of meat that oozed juices. Elena reached for a napkin to catch the dribble on her chin. She felt David's eyes on her, and when she looked up, he swallowed hard.

"So." He cleared his throat. "How did you get into escape rooms?"

"Jesse took me to my first one." She couldn't help smiling at the memory. He'd convinced a whole group from their company to go out. Eight dancers, giggling and not having any clue as to what the heck they were doing.

Her chest ached with missing them. Not them in particular, but the comradery of being in a production, of having a little family surrounding her and the dance. Although now perhaps she was in a different kind of production.

"I think I fell in love right then."

"With Jesse?" David asked.

She looked up. "What? No. With escape rooms. Jesse and I aren't like that. He's my best friend. And he's married."

She didn't know why she added that last detail. It

wasn't David's business. But she really needed him to know she and Jesse were not involved.

"It had a Sherlock Holmes theme. We had to work through one of his mysteries to get out." She turned the subject back to the escape room to cover her disconcertment.

"And then you decided you had to open one yourself?" He swiped another fry through the pool of ketchup in his plate.

"No. That didn't happen until a few years later." She hesitated. They'd been having such a nice day. She didn't want to talk about the car accident and why she left dancing. She only said, "I'm a retired dancer. I went looking for a second career, and I decided to do something else I loved."

He nodded. "I first went to an escape room during a work team-bonding event. It was like, yes, give me more of this. Only with people I like instead of coworkers."

She chuckled at that. "You said you were in corporate?"

"I did pharmaceutical research. I got tired of my work earning million-dollar bonuses for CEOs." He scowled. "It was the perfect opportunity to go into business for myself."

She held up her soda. "Here's to starting out on our own."

He clinked their glasses together. "I'll drink to that."

****

They spent the next few hours walking through the vendor area. David bought a bunch of things, mainly locks. Now, in theory, Elena could take stuff home with her, but she didn't want to start buying things willy-nilly. She needed a plan before she attacked that third room.

Still, she accepted cards and pamphlets from those who gave them out. She could always order for delivery later. In fact, a lot of the samples weren't for sale. They were just demos for the custom builds the vendors could do. Although she still wanted to do all the design herself, she admitted that having someone else build it for her was very attractive.

"Ready to head home?" David checked his watch. "I think this place is only open for another hour or so."

Prickles shot down her spine. This was it. Getting in a car with him.

It's just like Uber. He'd managed to drive himself down here. Most likely he'd get them back up to New Brunswick with no problem. Right. She had to keep telling herself that. "Yeah, we don't want to close this place down."

"I parked in the lot across the street this morning. That way we don't have to take a shuttle back to the casinos."

He had a dependable-looking sedan. It wasn't top-of-the-line new, but it looked sturdy. He popped the trunk and motioned toward it. "Feel free to put your bag inside."

"It's fine. I'll keep it with me." That way she had something to hold on to, and it wouldn't be immediately obvious that she was panicking.

The moment of truth came when he unlocked the doors and slid into the driver's seat. Elena had only sat in the back seat before, even when Phoebe drove. Statistically, the safest place was the center of the back.

She swallowed hard before opening the door to the front and getting in. She tucked her backpack between her knees before grabbing the seat belt and buckling up.

When he pulled out of the spot, she closed her eyes and tried to concentrate on her breathing.

One. Two. Three.

She started to calm down a bit once they got out of the city and onto the AC Expressway. David stuck to the right lane and followed the flow of traffic. If he'd been one of those drivers who changed lanes every five minutes, she would have had to have *words* with him. But instead he drove slowly, relatively speaking—this was the expressway after all—and steadily as if somehow unconsciously aware of her fear.

"Music preference?" He fiddled with the radio dial. "I have a highway playlist I usually listen to, but if you want a particular station…"

She thought about it for a moment. "Why don't you play your playlist?" The best way to get to know someone was to find out what music they liked.

His lips pressed together tightly, and his cheeks turned a shade of pink. "All right." He hit a button, and the happy tones of the song "Africa" blasted out of the speakers.

Elena gave it a few minutes before she started singing along. He joined in, and by the end of the song, they were both laughing too hard to keep singing. The next tune that queued up was yet another '80s top hit, and now she had a pretty good idea about his taste in music.

After a while the monotony of the road got to her. She leaned her head against the window and closed her eyes. It had been a long weekend.

Elena hadn't even realized she'd fallen asleep until the car started to shudder. She came awake with a gasp as David guided the shaking and thundering car to the side of the road.

"Are you all right?" he asked.

She unbuckled her seat belt and stumbled out of the car, her hands shaking as she climbed up the grass median. Traffic sped past them on the highway, cars too fast to notice. She covered her ears, desperate to cut the sound off. Her stomach twisted, and she couldn't catch her breath.

What the hell had just happened?

David exited the car, his cell phone in hand. "Okay, thank you. Yes, mile marker sixty-two." He ended the call and walked over. "It looks like a tire blew. I called Triple A because I'm not comfortable changing it myself on the highway, but I forgot they can't come on the parkway, so they're sending the parkway authority..."

His words stopped making sense, and a pounding sensation took up between her ears. Her stomach did a final flip-flop, and as David came over asking, "Are you okay?" she couldn't hold it in any longer.

She threw up all over his shoes.

Chapter 19

David shut the trunk of his car, a bottle of water and spare towel in hand. He'd replaced his sneakers with the shower sandals he'd brought with him for the trip. He didn't think the sneakers were salvageable, so he tied them in a plastic bag and tucked them next to his luggage for disposal once he got home.

Elena sat in the grass, shivering.

The tire blowout had unsettled him. He had to clench his hands to keep them from shaking. But mostly he worried about Elena. His erratic driving in an attempt to get to safety must have upset her stomach. He should have checked his tires before making such a long trip.

"Here." He handed her the water and held out the towel.

She grimaced but took the bottle, rinsed out her mouth, and spat over to the side. "Thanks." She accepted the towel and wiped her face.

She looked so sad and a little vulnerable. He sat next to her and touched her shoulder. He wanted to put his arm around her but didn't know if that would be welcome or not. "I'm sorry. For the bad driving."

She let out a little laugh. Only it didn't quite sound like a laugh. It sounded like a sob. "I wish it had been your bad driving."

He didn't say anything. He could sense a story there, and if she wanted to tell him, she would.

The silence paid off. She took a long drink of water and stared at the highway, her eyes bright and glassy. "I was in a really bad car accident. Two years ago. It's the real reason I stopped dancing."

An ache settled in his chest and wouldn't let go, especially when she kept talking.

"I was on my way to Jesse's wedding"—she shook her head as if she couldn't believe it either—"when some asshole missed a stop sign and plowed right into me. How can two minutes change your life?"

"All too easily," he said. "You haven't driven since?"

"Hell, no. When Phoebe drives, I sit in the back seat."

"Why didn't you ride in the back seat now?"

She looked over at him, and her cheeks went pink. "Didn't want to explain, I guess."

He understood that. He'd given her absolutely no reason to trust him with something so private. He'd been the one to insist on her coming with him when she wanted to take the train home.

"That's really why I got into the escape room business." She leaned over and picked at the laces of her shoes. "I had to do something else. Something that had absolutely nothing to do with dancing."

That ache dug into his stomach and then leapt out into his throat. "I didn't quit my job to start a new business. I got fired."

Finally, she turned and looked at him, her eyes wide and yet still so vulnerable. He swallowed and curled his fingers into his palms, anything to keep from giving in to the desire to touch her.

"What happened?"

"Well, the excuse was they were downsizing. I knew that was bullshit." He looked away. "We had just gotten bought by this big company. They put all new bosses in charge. The guy in charge of my team was a real jerk." That was putting it mildly. Remembering the embarrassed and terrified look on Lizzie's face still caused David to burn with rage. "He started harassing some of the younger women in my lab. So instead of going to HR like a normal person, I told him off."

"And that made you the bad guy." She leaned into him so they were touching all along their sides.

"Of course. I have the 'anger management' problem. Being laid off was a gift instead of being fired outright." At least Lizzie had found employment elsewhere—with one of the company's direct competitors. "And in a way it was. I really did want to do something new. Something where I wasn't making rich boys richer."

"Instead you're making people happy." She smiled at him.

"I guess that's one way of looking at it."

He leaned toward her, his head dipping down low. They were close enough that if he moved ever so slightly, his lips would brush hers.

A loud horn blare had them both scrambling to their feet. The tow truck had arrived.

****

Elena got out of David's car. She waved before shutting the door and walked up the steps to The Escape Space. He idled at the curb until she'd gone inside. How gentlemanly of him.

He'd refused gas money. Tried to joke that he shouldn't charge for his bad driving. She didn't tell him that his so-called bad driving had saved both of their lives, getting them out of traffic when the tire blew. He had to know.

The shaking had finally stopped.

Elena had to use every ounce of courage she had left to get back into that car with David once the tow-truck guy had fixed the tire. But she'd done it. Even sat in the front seat when he motioned that she could take the back. She refused to go backward. Only forward from here on out.

"Hey, boss. How did it go?" Phoebe popped her head out of the control room, which meant she'd been game mastering.

Elena forced a smile. "It was fantastic. I got a lot of ideas." She shooed Phoebe back into the control room and followed.

Phoebe hopped into her seat and pulled on her headphones. "No, you idiots. There isn't a code written on the bottom of the chairs," Phoebe muttered, her fingers flying across the keyboard as she typed a better-worded clue to appear on the screen in The Ballet Room.

Quinn looked up and removed one of her headphones. "Glad to see you made it back in one piece."

I almost didn't.

"Yeah. You can delete David's data from your phone."

"Sure." Quinn picked up her phone and started tapping at it. "How did you manage to get hooked up with him anyway?"

"We didn't hook up." Elena flushed. She tried again. "We both showed up at the same workshop. He offered me a ride."

Quinn stared at her for a moment. Then she smiled. "All right."

What was that supposed to mean? She decided to ignore it. "How are things going here?"

"This group is nearly done—if they ever figure out the last puzzle. Then we have a few more coming in right after."

Elena nodded. She needed to work, to get her mind off the disastrous car ride. She pulled off her backpack and tucked it in the corner of the control room. "All right. Let's get to work."

Hours later, she helped them finish the final cleanup and waved them off to their respective homes. With a sigh once she saw the time, she grabbed her backpack and retreated to her apartment sanctuary.

Elena filled a basin with cold water and ice to soak her feet, set it in front of her favorite chair, and got comfortable. She pulled out her phone, but instead of checking her email or reviewing the bookings for tomorrow, she found herself texting Jesse.

—Men are weird.—

Even after burning her restless energy with work, she couldn't get David out of her head. Something had happened between them on that grassy median on the highway, something she couldn't quite put a name to.

She'd had fun with him this weekend. They'd worked so well together at the convention, doing that sample escape room. She'd enjoyed having a partner, and they'd fit together, like no one else she'd ever done an escape room with. No matter how well they got along, she couldn't forget that he still was her biggest competition, the one thing preventing her from completely succeeding.

But they'd talked, really talked, about the accident, about his past. She wanted to do it again, and she couldn't. She shouldn't.

Her phone buzzed on her lap, and she realized she'd dozed off. It was Jesse, actually calling her.

"Don't you have a performance?" she answered.

"Well, you can't lead with that, darling, and expect me not to call." He sounded happy, which was good. "And I had the matinee today, so now I'm home, enjoying some quality time with my husband."

"I didn't mean to interrupt."

"If you had, I wouldn't have called. What's going on, hon? Who's this man that has you texting me?"

She sighed and leaned back, sinking farther into her chair. "You're going to laugh."

"I won't."

"Remember that guy who came into my place and started arguing with me while you were here?"

"Is he being an asshole to you?"

"No." She paused, thinking about the way David had leaned toward her, right before the tow truck showed up. For the briefest of moments, she'd expected a kiss. "I think he might like me."

And then Jesse did laugh. "I could have told you that two seconds after I met him."

"It's not funny." Except maybe it was. "He's my competition."

"So was Jaques Lefebre, and I screwed him," he reminded her. That had been pre-Phil, of course. Jaques and Jesse had been up for the same part, and as Elena recalled, Jesse got the role.

"It's not just…screwing." If it was about scratching an itch, Elena knew how to play the script. She'd had her share of lovers, men she wouldn't see the next day or ever again, really. "We sort of spent the weekend together. At this escape room conference. And then he drove me home."

"Hmm. Slightly date-like." Jesse's voice had a hint of amusement in it. "Did he try to kiss you afterward?"

"I'm not sure."

"That sounds like a story. How do you not know if he tried?"

She pulled her feet out of the water and reached for the towel she kept nearby. She really didn't want to tell him about what had happened with the car. He might worry, and she didn't want him to dwell on the accident anymore. "We got interrupted."

"Well, did you want him to kiss you? If he wasn't your competition, would you take him home and sleep with him? Or would you try for a second date?"

This was what she didn't want. She couldn't answer any of those questions. She didn't know herself. "I don't know how to do the dating thing. I'm not even sure that's what he wants."

"I know you hate uncertainty, but you want to know what I learned from being with Phil?"

"What?" She waited for what she hoped would be the answer to all of her quibbling.

"Sometimes you gotta let go and see where this takes you."

Elena had never been good at letting go.

****

David pulled into his driveway but left the car outside. He jiggled his keys as he walked up the front path, the automatic lighting flickering on to welcome him. It would be the only greeting he got. He unlocked the front door to silence. At one time he'd considered getting a dog. He had liked the idea of coming home to be adored by a big slobbering beast eager to see him.

Laura outright refused. She didn't want to be responsible for caring for the dog while David was at work. And he always seemed to be at work.

He should have realized then. He merely shrugged and agreed that he didn't really have time for a dog. Maybe a cat? She glared at him in response.

She'd left him a week after the dog conversation.

Now David came home to a house as silent as a tomb. He flicked on all of the lights as he moved from room to room. How many times had he come home to find Laura asleep on the couch, waiting for him? She'd been right to complain about him spending all his time at work. He had thought she accepted it as part of the job, that it was something else she loved about him. He'd been wrong.

He frowned at the stack of moving boxes lining the wall of his office. Of course he couldn't stop thinking about Laura. He had this reminder of her every day. Plastic crates of her crap still sat in the bedroom. Those needed to get out of there and stacked with the rest.

Once his computer booted up, he sent Laura a quick email—the only way they communicated these days. He asked if she was planning on picking up her things anytime soon. His house wasn't a damn storage bin. It sounded a bit more irritated than he'd planned. But what was the point in being nice? She had left him, and he didn't need boxes of her shit cluttering up his life.

That sent, he opened up an internet browser to do what he'd sat down to do. He stared at the blinking cursor for a moment. Guilt itched at his spine for doing this, but he couldn't stop thinking about what Elena had told him on the side of the road. About being a dancer and being forced to retire. Something that big would be online, wouldn't it?

He typed *Elena Evans ballet* into the search bar.

He ignored the first result—a newspaper article that read *Ballerina suffers career-ending car accident*—and scrolled down until he found an old biography on a ballet website.

Originally from New Jersey, Elena Evans began her dance training at a young age and moved to New York City to attend the School of American Ballet. She joined the Five Boroughs Ballet Company at age twenty-four and was promoted to principal dancer a few years later. Her most notable performances have been with partner Jesse Bartholemew in the filmed production of Romeo and Juliet*. She retired at age thirty-four.*

"Retired, yeah, that's a great way to put it." David clicked the back button and stared at the first article again. He had to know. *Click.*

The very first picture on the site showed Elena in mid-flight. Her hair had been pulled back into a severe bun, and she wore a white leotard and tutu. Her body curved into a statuesque arc, her arms stretched out like wings, her legs as graceful as a swan.

Beneath it the site had a grayed-out snapshot of her destroyed car. He swallowed and closed the browser.

His phone rang suddenly, the buzz startling him as if he'd been caught out doing something he shouldn't. He grabbed it and smiled at the display. "Yes, Momma, I forgot to call you again. I'm home."

"I don't mean to be a worrywart. It's just a very long drive."

He could hear the sounds of her cooking in the background, boiling water, pot lids being lifted. They were familiar and made him think of safety, doing homework at the kitchen table in their tiny apartment as she danced around him, making dinner for them both.

"It was fine," he said automatically. Then sighed. "Actually, it wasn't. I had a flat tire on the parkway." He didn't mention the blow out and having to navigate the car to the side of the road on three wheels. No wonder Elena had thrown up on him. The thought of it now had David faintly queasy.

"Jesus, Mary, and Joseph, thank God you're okay. And you were all by yourself! Did Triple A come?"

He smiled. "I wasn't alone."

He quickly explained about spending the conference with Elena and driving her home. He couldn't stop talking somehow, about the workshops and the escape room they did.

"Mmm-hmmm," his mother said.

"What's that supposed to mean?"

"Oh, nothing. When am I going to meet this girl? Didn't she throw you out of her business the last time you went over there?"

"Things are a little different now."

"Right. Be a good boy, David."

"I always am, Mom."

He ended the call and looked back at the computer screen where his search history taunted him. The Elena he'd seen on that website wasn't the woman he knew. She laughed at his jokes. She was brilliant at solving puzzles. She'd built her own business from the ground up. He wanted to know that Elena, the woman she was now, not the cold dancer or a woman portrayed as broken and injured.

He'd been attracted to her from the moment he first

saw her, defiantly doing his escape room and not disclosing her real identity. He had a taste of something more, and he wanted to chase it, to have Elena in his life as more than the competition across the street.

He needed to talk to her. He looked at The Escape Space website to see when they were next open.

And David knew exactly what he'd bring as a peace offering.

Chapter 20

Elena sat on the couch in the lobby, her feet propped up on the other end with some spare pillows. Her ankles still ached from the weekend shenanigans, but it had been worth it. She just needed to treat herself gently for a little while.

She'd gotten into costume, but they weren't expecting any customers until that afternoon. College students didn't sign up for early morning slots, so she had cut their opening time to noon. Between that and having Monday off, she felt like she had an abundance of free time. She had even managed the grocery store yesterday. Cooking any of that food was another matter entirely.

"I love these." Phoebe flipped through one of the pamphlets Elena had brought back from the conference. "Look, actual chains. We can turn the attic into a dungeon."

Quinn managed to dodge Phoebe's swinging legs as she spun in her task chair and grabbed one of the leaflets. "Yeah, let's chain people up. That sounds like a great idea. For a lawsuit."

"I wouldn't actually chain anyone up. But it would be great for ambiance."

"There are already so many horror rooms." Elena flipped through another catalog she'd picked up. "Look, this one even has a live zombie."

"I assume the zombie is not included?" Quinn leaned over to look.

"You have to provide your own live actor, yes. But the design and puzzles are all premade." Elena snorted. "And then what happens when something breaks? You have to wait until a tech comes out to fix it?"

"That's what I'm here for," Quinn pointed out.

"I think even you would have trouble with whatever proprietary software they're using. That's what keeps them in business. If they provide a perfectly working room every time, then you wouldn't have to come back for more." She tossed the catalog, tired of looking at designs she couldn't afford even if she'd wanted to.

Both of her rooms had her personal touch in every single inch. She'd spent weeks crawling through antique and thrift stores, searching for perfect pieces to complete the look to match her imagination. Honestly, how unfair that someone who hadn't spent months researching puzzles and design could shell out a little cash and have a gorgeous escape room without any of the blood, sweat, and tears she'd put into hers.

But, damn, she'd seen some nice prefab rooms.

"The sample room we did was gorgeous," she admitted. "It felt like we'd stepped back into ancient Egypt." Elena closed her eyes and pictured the room. Any words she'd use wouldn't do the place justice. "The sarcophagus looked like something I've seen in the Met. The walls felt like stone, with flickering lights. And this was just a pop-up version, not the entire room."

She opened her eyes to find both Phoebe and Quinn still—a bad sign because Phoebe never kept still—and staring at her.

"What?"

"You said we—*we* did the room." Quinn crossed her arms over her chest.

Phoebe leaned forward. "Are we finally going to talk about it? How did you end up spending the weekend and hitching a ride with Mr. Handcuffs from across the street?"

"We didn't spend the weekend…" Elena sputtered, sitting up. "It wasn't like that. I mean. You shouldn't call him Mr. Handcuffs."

How odd to remember that the last memory they had of David had been him shouting as he left, angry at not being permitted into Elena's room. That seemed a lifetime ago, instead of only last month. The man she'd spent the past weekend with seemed an entirely different creature, someone who fascinated her, who made her laugh. Who put his arm around her when she spoke of the most horrible night of her life.

"Then what should we call him?"

"David," she said, the word coming out hoarse. She cleared her throat. "His name is David."

Phoebe and Quinn continued to stare at her. Quinn raised an eyebrow and looked expectant.

"We just happened to meet up. It was nice to not be alone."

"Uh-huh." She didn't miss the look Phoebe threw Quinn's way. Before Elena could demand to know what that was all about, the front door opened, the bell above it jangling as just the person they were discussing entered the lobby. Elena's cheeks heated at the sight of him as if he had read her thoughts from across the street.

"I hope I'm not interrupting," David said. He held two pizza boxes and a white to-go bag, all marked with the Spano's Pizza logo. "I come bearing gifts."

Elena's mouth watered from the rich scent of the food. Spano's made some of the best Italian food around, and she'd missed it during the ban.

"Like that makes anything better since Spano's won't deliver to us." Phoebe had jumped to her feet.

Elena pushed herself off the couch, intent on nipping this in the bud. She didn't want Phoebe going off the handle again.

David had it covered. "I spoke to Tony, Tony Spano," he clarified, "my friend and sometimes overzealous employee. Cutting you off from pizza was his idea, not mine. And you'll be happy to know that ban has been overturned."

He opened one of the boxes of pizza and presented it to Phoebe. "I heard that you are a fan of pineapple on pizza."

Phoebe's cheeks had gone pink. "Um. Yes."

"Phoebe, that's gross," Quinn said, but her eyes twinkled. "Why didn't you tell me? You kept letting me order what I liked."

"Because of exactly that reaction."

He handed Phoebe her pizza and turned to present the takeout bag to Quinn. "And you, I heard, are a big fan of chicken marsala. This is fresh from the kitchen. I watched them make it myself."

"How did you know that?" Quinn took the bag and looked inside.

"You ate in once, and the waiter remembered the blue hair." He motioned toward her head. Then he turned to Elena.

"I don't think you know what I like," she said slowly. One weekend didn't give him that much information, and she found herself wanting to tell him.

He smiled. "True. But everyone loves pizza." He held out the second box toward her. "I figured we could share it."

She waited a heartbeat, unable to sort out exactly why she hesitated. She'd just been thinking about him, about how she did want to get to know him better. Now she'd been given this gift, out of nowhere, and she didn't quite know what to do with it.

She had to answer one question. Did she want to share this pizza with him? She looked at the hope in his dark eyes, and something inside her melted. She took a deep breath and checked the giant clock on the wall. They had forty-five minutes before her first customers arrived.

"I have some diet soda in my office. I hope that's okay?"

David grinned. "Perfect."

****

Success. If David had learned anything from his Italian-American mother, it was that food went a long way toward smoothing any situation. On a perfect day, he'd have brought something home cooked himself. However, Spano's would have to do, especially when it doubled as a peace offering. Hopefully, this whole feud thing could stop. And he could get down to serious business.

Like asking Elena out.

He followed her into her office, doing his best not to ogle her ass in that wispy 1920s dress she wore. It shimmered a greenish gold and did amazing things for her hair. He still wanted to wrap his hands in those strands and use them to pull her head back gently as he...

"Sorry. I only have diet." She emerged from under

her desk with two cans. She had a tiny college-student-sized fridge tucked under there.

He cleared his throat and tried to erase all not-so-innocent thoughts out of his head—which wasn't easy. "No problem."

"Let me clear some stuff out of the way for the pizza."

He took a quick look around. His last visit he'd been too angry to really get a view of the place.

Elena didn't keep any pictures or knickknacks on her desk. A single poster on the wall served as the only decoration. She snatched up manila folders stuffed with papers, set aside pencils, and hid a notebook in a drawer she quickly shut. He tried to get a look. Were those puzzle plans scratched in pencil?

David set down the pizza in the cleared space on the desk. He gestured to the poster, which showed a ballerina in white silhouetted in bright light, standing with one leg extended behind her and her arms reaching for something. It reminded him of the photo he'd seen in the news article, but he didn't want Elena to know he'd been poking around in her past.

"Is that you?"

She pulled out a roll of paper towels and handed him a wad. "It's not a photograph. It's an artist's rendition, but yes, it's supposed to be me. It was my first show as principal dancer."

"That's like the lead?"

She reached into that same drawer and pulled out paper plates. Maybe, like him, she spent too much time eating takeout in her office.

She smiled and shook her head. "Yes, it's like the lead." She took a slice of pizza and arranged it carefully on her plate. Her nails were painted pale pink—he couldn't help noticing the graceful motion of her fingers. Every movement she made had a delicacy to it, and now he understood why.

He didn't know if she could discuss the good days. She had seemed so hurt when she told him about the accident, but she had a poster. He wanted to know more about who she'd been before.

"Did you enjoy doing that show?" He couldn't pronounce the name sketched along the bottom in what he assumed had to be French.

The question seemed to catch her off guard. She took a tiny bite and chewed for a moment before responding. "It was a lot of work. Five hours of rehearsal every day. Working on one jump over and over again. When we finally got it right, Jesse nearly dropped me because he was so excited."

"So lots of fun, then."

She laughed.

"Thanks for the pizza," she said while he had his mouth full. "I appreciate you lifting the ban."

He took a long chug of soda before replying. "Hey, I prefer things fair. And you know it wasn't my idea. Tony can be a bit protective."

"I can understand that."

They ate in silence for a moment. Melted cheese made it difficult to talk and chew at the same time. David wiped sauce off his chin and winced at how he must look, covered in pizza grease. Perhaps the pizza hadn't been the best idea, not if he wanted to impress her.

He dug into his pocket for the printout. He'd saved it for last, in case things didn't go well. But Elena seemed glad to have him there, so he might as well give it a shot.

"I wanted to ask if you'd seen this." He handed her the paper.

She took it gingerly. "You know most people send links these days. No need to kill trees."

"Well, maybe someone didn't give me her phone number." He smiled to soften the blow. "But anyway, it's a new place that opened up in North Jersey. It's part escape room, part obstacle course. It sounds interesting."

" 'Your goal isn't to escape,' " she read aloud from the flyer. " 'This time you need to lock the serial killer out. Can you do it in sixty minutes?' Huh, I haven't seen anything like that before."

"Are you interested in going?"

"Well, someday, maybe. I haven't had much time to actually do escape rooms since I opened…"

He stopped her by placing his hand over hers. "I mean, are you interested in going with me? You're closed Mondays now, right?"

"Should I be concerned that you've memorized my schedule?"

"Hey, isn't that what any competition should do? I bet you've memorized my schedule, too."

By the pink in her cheeks, he knew he was right. "Next Monday. I'll book the room."

She hesitated a moment and then nodded.

"Great. I'll text you the time. If I can have your phone number?"

She shook her head and let out a little laugh. "All right, fine."

David stood up and fist-pumped. The chair fell over and clattered to the floor with a loud boom. They were still laughing when Phoebe opened the door in concern.

Chapter 21

Elena sorted through her packed closet, tossing discarded options behind her on the bed. She'd even grabbed one of the unopened moving boxes, but none of the clothes she pulled out were even remotely appealing. How had she accumulated so much useless clothing? She had always traveled light, but in the past few years, she'd started to hold on to things a little longer than necessary.

She blamed David for her indecision. He hadn't made it clear if he'd meant his invitation as a date or...or what? Trying to be friendly? Getting more information on his competition? She didn't have many possibilities to choose from. Elena pulled out a pink sparkly blouse that she didn't remember purchasing and threw that right back into the box.

They'd almost kissed during that moment on the side of the highway. His plump lips had been so close to hers. Another few inches and they would have touched. She'd vomited only a few moments before, which would have made that one terrible kiss.

Maybe David wanted another chance—a moment when they weren't reeling from nearly dying on the parkway and awash in vomit. Maybe if they went someplace they both enjoyed, they could find out if that same chemistry existed between them.

The problem? Elena still hadn't decided if she wanted him to kiss her.

Her phone buzzed, and she took a few moments to find it beneath the pile of discarded clothing on her bed. Jesse's smiling face appeared on the screen, and she swiped quickly to answer before it went to voicemail.

"Jesse. Thank God. I need your help." She tried to catch her breath from her panic at nearly missing the call.

Silence on the other line. "The dial-911 kind of help or you need help picking out a sweater kind?"

She laughed. "The latter." Hearing his voice calmed her. It reminded her of the times they'd spent picking out each other's wardrobes, getting ready for nights on the town in the city.

"Okay, that I can deal with. I'm too far away for the first one. It's too hot for a sweater. Don't wear one."

"Ha. Funny. No, it's… I'm going to do an escape room with David." She took a deep breath and closed her eyes. She could picture Jesse's reaction exactly—the way one eyebrow would raise and he'd give her a knowing look. "I don't know if it's a date or not."

"Okay, so things have clearly progressed on this front since the last time we talked."

"Shut up."

"I thought you wanted my advice."

"On what to wear. Not my love life."

"On what to wear to your escape room date."

She dropped onto her bed, knocking over a pile of T-shirts. At this rate she wouldn't make it out of the house. "Yes."

"What would you wear to a normal non-date escape room?"

"Well, this one is supposed to be a bit more physical than usual. It's an obstacle-course escape room." *Hmm.* That changed how she thought about it. She sprang back up and went to her closet to grab workout-appropriate attire that didn't look shabby.

He was quiet on the other end of the line. "Exactly how physical are we talking?"

At first she thought he was making some kind of innuendo. "PDA is generally frowned upon in escape rooms."

"No. No, I mean, can you do that? Physically, I mean?"

She stiffened. She hadn't considered that she couldn't. Getting up on pointe for hours a day? No, definitely not. But she had never limited herself, not even if it meant suffering from the pain afterward. As a dancer, she and pain were old friends.

For the first time it occurred to her that Jesse thought her broken. No wonder he still felt guilt over the accident. "Let me decide what my body can and can't do."

"I still think you should be cautious. I could tell you were in pain when I saw you." His voice lowered, and all sense of teasing had disappeared.

"Like I was in pain when I danced on an ingrown toenail? Or when you danced with a busted-up knee?" She'd had to bully him into going to the doctor afterward. He'd never liked downtime. "We've spent years dancing through it."

"It's different," he snapped.

Elena forced herself to move, to continue combing through her closet and not give in to her anger. "Can we not do this? You are not responsible for my pain or how I manage it. The accident was not your fault, Jesse."

"Fine. Excuse me for caring." He hung up.

She stared at the phone. He hadn't even said why he

had been calling in the first place.

She decided on black yoga pants and a blue tunic. *See, Jesse, I didn't need your advice anyway.*

****

David double-parked in front of The Escape Space, ignored the drivers gesturing at him as cars swerved around him, and honked his horn. He didn't have to wait long before Elena came down the steps. He hit the button that rolled down the window on the passenger door. "Do you want to sit in the back?"

She hesitated, and for a moment he could see the vulnerability in her eyes. Then she squared her shoulders and tugged the passenger door open. "I'm fine." She slid in and buckled her seat belt. "You did get your tires looked at?"

"Of course. Clean bill of health." He patted his dashboard.

Someone laid on the horn as they passed his car. He gave them the finger, and Elena laughed.

"I almost feel like I'm in New York again."

He pulled into traffic, noticing her wince in his peripheral vision. He had to stop looking at her and pay attention to the road although that was hard to do on normal occasions, never mind when he was worrying about making her nervous with his driving.

"How much do I owe you? I brought a check."

"It's okay. I had a coupon." He held his breath. He wouldn't be a gentleman if he didn't pay for a date, and while this wasn't technically a date, he wanted to do something nice for her.

After a moment she said, "Fine. I'll get the next room, then."

That meant she wanted to do more escape rooms

173

with him. He couldn't help grinning as he merged onto Route 18.

"I don't know how anyone makes money offering discounts like that," she said. "I really regret offering so many in the beginning. The percentage of profit is so low."

Precisely why he hadn't offered any discounts for his rooms. "I suppose the exposure is worth it for some businesses. Gets their name out."

"I guess."

In another world they could discuss their businesses without tension. But her comment reminded David that he couldn't forget they were competitors, that his business was a threat to hers. He gripped the steering wheel and frowned at the car that merged in front of him.

"What's our strategy?" she asked.

He didn't answer for a moment—Route 18 required all of his concentration. Once he took the exit for 287, he could take part in conversation. "Um. Look for clues and open locks?"

She snorted. "Well, yes, but this is a different kind of escape room. It's going to be dark, and we'll be doing other kinds of puzzles. What are your strengths?"

"Are you always this analytical?"

"Ask Jesse about how many times I went over the choreography before we actually danced it, and then we'll talk about analytical."

"I'm good with numbers," he answered her original question, not quite sure if he'd insulted her or if he should be glad that she'd dropped a bit more about her past. "If there's a math-related puzzle, let me handle it. I'm terrible with finding hidden objects."

She laughed. "That's why you don't have a lot

hidden in your rooms?"

"I try to make everything as open as possible. It might not be clear what to do with the object, but nothing buried in the back of a closet or in a dark shadowed corner. Nothing requiring you to dismantle a prop to get to it." He frowned. He had failed one room that simply hid the keys too well.

"Sounds like you are speaking from experience."

"Let me tell you about doing the Speakeasy in Cape May…"

He had her laughing by the time they reached the escape room. His phone chimed that their destination was on the right. At first he didn't see anything. The highway had let them off onto a busy road, and they turned into what looked like an industrial park.

Elena pointed at the sign he'd missed—once again proving that finding things wasn't his strength. "There. Dark Horse Escape Room."

"It's in a warehouse." He had known that, but knowing and seeing were two different things.

The building towered over them, a solid square of concrete and steel looking cold against the bright-blue sky. It had no visible windows and only tall garage-style doors that reminded him of a loading dock.

"Are you sure this isn't the home of a real serial killer?" Elena said lightly, but she chewed her bottom lip. Surely, she couldn't actually be worried.

"That would be genius on the part of the serial killer. Get people to pay for the privilege of being killed."

"I'm sure that's a metaphor for something profound. Or at least it sounds like it."

She opened the door and got out of the car. David followed, letting her lead. As they approached the propped-open glass door, something dropped into the pit of his belly. This wasn't like doing the mini escape room at the conference. They were going to be locked in together for an hour.

He didn't tell her that he'd paid extra for a private experience. They were going to be the only two people in the room. Maybe, just maybe, if it all went well, he'd ask her out for a proper date.

That's if she could get past the whole competition thing. It shouldn't matter. Rival businesses popped up next to each other all the time. Hell, even Spano's Pizza had to deal with another pizzeria down the block. And if people had a good experience at David's rooms, why wouldn't they want to check out another escape place? Especially when one happened to be across the street?

He would tell her all of this. After they completed the room.

"Hey, I assume you're our two o'clock?" an incredibly tall young man said as they entered. He wore a black T-shirt with the place's logo on it. He bounced with energy, not standing still even as David and Elena entered the lobby.

The walls were covered with horror-movie posters. The floor and ceiling had been painted black. With the only daylight coming in from the door, this place would look incredibly dreary when it was shut. David hoped the room itself wasn't so dark.

They signed the waivers acknowledging the physical nature of this room. The clerk kept up the conversation, asking them about other rooms they'd done, telling them about his theatre experience, an incredible roll of chatter that reminded David of his own employee Vanessa.

"Okay, so this is everyone in your party?" the kid asked as he checked the tablet. "We can get started, then."

He led David and Elena through a door, down a hallway that seemed artificially created. David recognized temporary walls from his own rooms. The ceilings were naturally high—of course, this was a warehouse. They passed the entrances for the two other rooms the location boasted until they got to the final room. The walls had all been painted black, and this one door had words in green spray-painted next to it. *Can you escape the forest strangler?*

"Okay, so the story goes that these woods are inhabited by a killer called the strangler. But you didn't think the stories were real. Until tonight, when you decided to take a walk in his forest."

Despite himself, a shiver went down the back of David's spine. Yes, this was what he loved—starting the tension early, making it part of the experience. He only hoped the room lived up to the story.

The kid threw open the door. "You have one hour to find shelter from the strangler. Good luck."

David took a tentative step inside to near darkness. Ahead, as far as he could see, stood painted trees, like the kind that might be found on a theater stage. The room was dim and lacked any sort of monitor with the time or clues remaining.

Elena seemed to notice as well. "Wait. What's your hint system?"

"You'll see." With a maniacal laugh, he shut the door.

"That kid enjoys his job way too much."

****

No monitor meant no timer. They wouldn't have any idea of how long they were in the room. Elena hated that, but it truly added to the immersive nature of the experience. She'd have no visible reminder that this was only a game. The room even smelled like pine. It was most likely air freshener, but she gave them points for the ambiance.

"It looks like we can squeeze through here." David pointed to a section between the trees. The quality of design was good—they looked real enough in the dim light, though she knew if she looked closely, she'd notice the paint, or if she poked the bark, it would give like the foam it had to be made from.

"Wait. Let's look around first."

"You're right." David grinned. "What did I say about me not paying attention to details?"

"That's why you brought me." She scanned the area, double-checking the floor that seemed to be a black tarp nailed down. She wouldn't be finding any unexpected rugs hiding keys down here. Next, she looked up—because most people never lifted their gaze from their general eye-level and tended to miss a lot.

She spotted something glittering out of the corner of her eye. It had been tucked into one of the branches at about knee level. She crouched and pulled it out, revealing a key attached to a photo keychain. The picture showed a young couple in front of a laser background with the inscription *Chad & Janet, 1996* written in puffy paint.

"A key but no locks," he said.

"I think the picture is important." She finished her perusal of the rest of the entrance and decided it was clear. "We'll find out soon. Let's go."

He held one of the branches aside for her, and she squeezed through. They emerged into what looked like a camp scene with a tiny tent and a fake fire flickering in the middle. Nice effect that, it even included a crackling sound. She didn't wait for him before crawling in the tent and finding a lockbox, which she pulled out.

"The lock for our key?" He crouched down next to her.

His breath was warm against her ear, and she inexplicably shivered. They had to focus.

"Maybe." She tried it, and the key worked. Inside she found a diary—another monstrosity from the '90s with hearts and rainbows. "God, I hope this isn't one of those rooms where I have to sit and read every page for clues."

A couple of related pages would be fine, as long as they were appropriately marked. She had done one room with Phoebe and Quinn where Quinn had spent a good twenty minutes just reading the backstory out of a heavily illustrated journal. Only a quarter of it had turned out to be relevant.

David took the book and flipped through the pages. "It's Janet's diary. I don't see anything bolded or underlined, except for the last page, and notice the last few pages have been torn out."

Elena leaned over his shoulder to read the final page. They were so close she could feel the heat coming off his body. If she moved an inch, they'd be touching. She kept herself still, not wanting to go further than this— certainly not in an escape room.

Chad is taking me on a camping trip for our anniversary the page read, every other word underlined. *I'm so excited. He rented a cabin. It's going to be so romantic*.

David fingered the tattered edges of the missing pages. "I don't think it turned out that way."

She laughed. That's when the crackle of static broke the silence. Had she missed something in the tent? She and David split up to explore the clearing, and after a moment he lifted a walkie-talkie above his head and waved it at her.

"Got it."

The speaker crackled again, and a voice emerged. "Janet. I'm sorry…"

"Creepy. Are we supposed to respond, do you think?"

In answer, he clicked the button. "Janet's not here right now."

No response came from the walkie-talkie.

He clipped it on his belt. "It might be important later. Come on. Let's get to the next section."

They searched through thick fake trees for a while until she realized they needed to crawl beneath the tree line, under a trellis wound with fake ivy leaves. She led the way.

He swore behind her.

"You okay?"

"Hit my head," he muttered back.

She came up out of the tunnel just as a flash of lightning lit the room, with thunder crackling right after. The sudden sound had her shrieking in shock. She turned to David with her hand over her heart, which pounded too fast against her chest. "I didn't expect that."

"It was nicely done. Remind me to ask them about the special effects afterward." He stepped forward and pointed. "We have our first real puzzle."

The way forward was blocked with a series of gates; however, in the middle stood a wall with what looked like levers attached to pulleys. It reminded Elena a bit of the puzzle at the convention. "The right sequence will open the gate?"

"Maybe. Let's try it."

After a few moments of trying, they soon figured out that one sequence opened the left gate, and the other sequence opened the right one. But which was the correct gate to enter?

"You don't think we should split up?" She frowned.

"No, because that would close a gate behind someone, and that doesn't make sense."

The walkie-talkie hissed to life. "Janet," the voice said. "Remember when we went to the docks to watch the fireworks? I never would have left you behind."

They waited, but the walkie-talkie remained silent.

David frowned. "Do you think that means go left?"

Elena shrugged. "We can only try."

The left path involved climbing a convoluted set of wooden stairs. Who the hell put stairs in a forest? The steps had been designed too tall, so they had to climb to reach the next one. Perhaps this was meant to mimic a hill. At the top, they could see their destination in the distance, a cabin structure, with a painted sky behind it.

Lightning crashed again, and she nearly lost her footing.

He grabbed her arm and stopped her from falling. "I'm right here. Let me go down first."

"So you can catch me if I fall?"

"I'm softer for you to land on."

He smiled at her, and though he'd smiled at her dozens of times before, this particular one had something inside her melting. She didn't know what to do with that feeling, especially with the way his eyes softened as he looked at her. The walkie-talkie crackled to life again, breaking into her mood and reminding her that they were fighting the clock here.

"Janet…" That creepy voice again. "I told you I wouldn't leave you…" Suddenly, it turned angry. "Why did you leave me!" he roared so loudly David fumbled with the walkie-talkie and dropped it.

Elena slid down the last step and bent to pick it up. A fluttering bit of fabric caught her eye. She stood and pulled the pink sweater down from a conveniently placed tree branch. Red splotches stained the front of it. "I don't think things went very well for Chad and Janet."

"You could say that." He frowned. "How much time do you think we have left?"

The walkie-talkie came to life again. This time the voice of their game master said clearly, "You have twenty-five minutes and forty seconds remaining."

Crap, that was cutting it close. Far more time had elapsed than she thought, and they still had quite a distance to go to get to the cabin. Wind started to pick up from unseen fans, and it made her glad she'd put her hair up in a ponytail.

David's tousled curls flattened against his head, and he groaned. "So help me if it actually starts raining."

"Let's do this." Elena narrowed her eyes. Time to focus. No more thinking about David's sweet smile or his tight ass. She had one goal—to escape the room.

The last half of the room didn't have too many puzzles left. It was exactly as advertised—an obstacle course that required climbing and crawling. The final leg had them snaking through a tight path, and Elena screamed when something fell out of the trees above them—especially when that something turned out to be an arm.

The voice on the walkie-talkie got more insistent and creepy, demanding to know who they were, what they'd done with Janet. They found the rest of Janet's diary, and what it revealed was not pretty.

Elena found herself out of breath as she climbed the plank that led to the cabin, David at her heels. She went to open the door and saw the number lock. "Four-digit lock. Any ideas?"

"What?" He leaned forward to look. "Absolutely none. Is there anything written on the walls? Did he say anything that even remotely resembled numbers?" He touched the fake wooden planks, looking for something hidden.

"No." Her belly cramped with nerves. They were so close.

Wait, she had seen a four-digit number before, hadn't she? The keychain with the picture. She touched her pockets, but she'd left it behind when they'd opened the lockbox. "The picture. What year did it have on it?"

"Oh, shit. I can go back and get it…"

"No time. Are you kidding me?" She flipped through the numbers. It was 199-something. She could brute force the last digit.

A ticking sound came from the walkie-talkie, like they were running out of time. She didn't let it bother her. She had to keep cycling through the numbers until she came to 1996, and the lock popped open in her hand. With trembling fingers she unlatched the door, pulled it open, and stumbled inside, David at her back.

It slammed closed behind them, leaving them in

complete darkness. She could feel his hands around her waist. By instinct, she reached for him, looking for something familiar in the cabin. Then, almost by accident, she felt his lips on hers, a gentle, seeking kiss that did nothing but accelerate her heart rate.

Suddenly, lights came on and a trumpet blared, reminding her that, yes, they were still in the escape room with cameras everywhere. She took a jump back, knocking into the wall.

"Congratulations!" a voice said from the walkie-talkie before a door opened on the other side of the cabin. Their game master appeared with a matching walkie-talkie in his hand. "You've escaped the strangler and made it to safety!"

She licked her lips and smiled. David had a blush on his cheeks, and it had to be because she'd put it there.

"Did you guys have fun? What did you think of the room?" The game master kept chatting as he led them back to the lobby to have their photo taken.

"It was definitely interesting," David deadpanned, and Elena couldn't help giggling.

When they posed with their signs, he put his arm around her, and she nestled into that warmth. Now she knew exactly where they stood.

This was a date.

Chapter 22

David's lips tingled. He barely remembered getting his picture taken and talking with their game master. Any intention of interrogating the guy about their special effects had fallen completely out of his head.

Elena had kissed him. Or he'd kissed Elena. They'd reached for each other in the dark, and all he could think about was doing it again. He thought about it the entire walk to the car, how he'd cup her head, carding his fingers in the luscious strands of her hair as he tilted her face back to give him access to her pink lips.

He slid into the driver's seat, the key in his hand. He hesitated before putting it in the ignition. He turned to face Elena who'd just slammed her door closed. Not knowing what to say, he opened his mouth to suggest getting something to eat.

He never got to say the words. She leaned toward him and gave him a proper kiss, one hand caught in his hair, tugging him down and into her. He breathed in. She smelled like sawdust and pine—like the escape room. It made him smile against her lips, and she took that opportunity to nip at his chin.

"You're killing me," he told her. They were stuck in his car, in broad daylight, with a fifty-minute drive ahead of them. His jeans already strained across his hips.

"That's for not telling me this was a date." She winked and gave him a dangerous-looking grin. "How about we stop for burgers on the way to your place?"

He swallowed and took a deep breath. He'd need some of his composure back before he started driving. "You'd like to come home with me?"

Was that doubt in her eyes? He grabbed her hand and squeezed tightly. He wanted her to come home with him, definitely, but he wouldn't push.

"Better your place than mine. I assume you have something larger than a twin bed?"

He turned the key and revved the engine. "King-size big enough for you?"

"It'll have to do."

****

The burgers ended up on the kitchen counter.

David found himself hungry for something else when he turned around to meet Elena right behind him, her eyes smoldering. He'd kept his hands to himself during the long car ride. The one thing he did not want to do was crash the damn car.

He took a step toward her, grasped her around the waist, and pulled her close. She slid her hands beneath his shirt and down and around to his ass, which she squeezed.

"Do you know how long I've wanted to get my hands on your ass?" she said when they were only inches apart.

Instead of laughing, he kissed her. Her lips were just as lush and sweet as in the darkness of the escape room. He'd hoped it was more than just the excitement of the moment, that they'd come together like this and it would spark. And, oh, did they spark.

"Then let me do this." He moved down along her neck until he could mouth along those collarbones that had haunted him for weeks. Her skin was pale and soft, and he worried if he pushed too hard, he'd leave a mark.

She let out a little moan, and it unlocked something inside him, the beast he usually kept pushed down deep inside. With a growl, he lifted her and then set her down on the kitchen counter. He moved between her thighs, pushing up her shirt until his hands reached the silky fabric of her bra. She shivered as he stroked her.

"More."

David pulled off her shirt, and Elena helped by unclipping her bra and sending it off in the direction of the dishwasher. Oh, now he could look his fill, see the soft roundness of her breasts sitting perfectly on her chest. He met her eyes, right before he touched. "This okay?"

"Yeah." She nodded and bit her lip.

He wanted to do more than bite her in return. He curved his hand around one breast, brushing his thumb over her soft skin, light teasing motions. Then he leaned forward, trailing kisses along her clavicle until he reached the other nipple, which, really, required all of his attention.

She gasped and shuddered. Then her hands were tugging at his shirt, and he stepped away long enough to pull it off. He shook from the intensity of it. He had never felt anything like this before. Even with Laura it had been quick, in and out, and now suddenly, embarrassment about that filled him.

But with Elena—he wanted to lay her out on his bed, take his time, get to know every divot of her skin, look for the freckles that hid in the most delightful places, like the one beneath her left breast.

He stroked down her thighs, along the black fabric

of her leggings, and pulled up one leg. He hesitated at the laces of her shoes. "Anything I should know about these?"

She let out a hitching breath. "Be gentle. Don't mind the scars."

His heart ached that she should have been scarred by her ordeal. He took care with her shoes, making sure to kiss up the arch of each foot, spending time on the too-white bits of silver that crisscrossed her ankles.

The sneakers were easy to get off. The leggings were another story.

****

Elena didn't realize how sensitive her feet had become. When David carefully removed her socks and kissed each ankle, she shivered, tears pricking at her eyes. She hadn't been with anyone since the accident, but even so, she'd never expected anything like this, so gentle and caring. The heat between them had sputtered to a simmer, and she enjoyed the slow burn.

He straightened up and kissed her. She pulled him to her, missing the warmth of him close to her while he'd worked on her feet.

"How—" He groaned. "—do you get your pants off?"

She giggled. She couldn't help it. Would he always make her laugh? "Lift me up a bit."

He took hold of her beneath her armpits and obliged. She reached down and shimmied her leggings and underwear past her waist. "Your turn," she murmured as he set her down—buck naked on his kitchen counter.

"I need a taste first." He tugged the leggings the rest of the way off, setting them down carefully next to her shoes.

Surely, he couldn't mean…

Oh, but he did. He spread her thighs with his large, well-formed hands, and she could feel herself getting ready in anticipation. He began with teasing licks along the inside of her leg, too firm to tickle, but not quite where she needed him.

She leaned back and gripped the edge of the countertop. She was going to need a solid handhold for what came next.

He stopped teasing, suddenly diving between the center of her legs, his mouth hot and warm and wet and exactly where she needed it. She let out a gasp, unable to hold back anything.

He knew exactly what he was doing. She appreciated that in a man. He kept her on the edge, pulling back every time it seemed like she might be close. She dug one of her hands into his mane of curls, determined to make him stay in one spot, damn it.

He chuckled against her flesh, sending vibrations all throughout her body. She arched her back, unable to control herself any longer, not with how he sucked and licked and touched her. She cried out, crashing into her climax without any sense that she'd been close. It merely was.

She came back to herself, clutching at his back as he held her through the aftershocks.

"Okay?" he asked.

She nodded, unable to form words at the moment.

"I have condoms in the bedroom. That okay?"

"Mmm. If I can walk that far."

"You don't have to."

She grabbed on to him as he scooped her up off the counter. Her heart raced as she buried her face in his neck, taking deep breaths of his scent—sweat and musk and something sweet. His sheer strength impressed her, and a pleasant tingle began between her thighs in response. She wanted to feel him inside her, feel that strength everywhere.

He managed to get them both to the bedroom without bumping her head on anything—which was pretty impressive. He moved with a grace that she hadn't expected of him and gently set her down on his giant bed.

He nuzzled against her neck, his palm firmly on her hip as he kissed her again. He was wearing clothes still, and she had to do something about that. She sat up and attacked his fly, undoing the zipper easily.

"Let me touch you," she demanded, wanting to know the feel of him, his length, how hot and hard he was for her. She wanted to inspect him before he got inside her.

He got up long enough to shove his jeans off, slipping out of his shoes in time before they got stuck. She watched him, her eyes drawn to that line of hair down his belly, a trail to the thick cock that hung hard against one thigh, flushed dark red instead of pink.

He groaned when she touched him, a slow, exploratory touch. His skin was soft, and he'd been circumcised. Many of her lovers had been European, so this felt unfamiliar to her, no foreskin to play with. Still, the ridge was sensitive, with the way he sucked in a breath when her fingers stroked there.

"Stop before I come all over you." He gasped.

She did, but not before looking him straight in the eye and licking her lips. She knew the power of a good performance.

He cursed. He threw open the top drawer of the side

table and pulled out a condom. He could have won a world record with the way he tore the foil packet open and wrapped himself.

"Come on." She slid her fingers down her own body, watching as his eyes grew heavy-lidded with desire. She needed him inside her.

"You're a temptress," he murmured, and it sounded like worship as he pressed her back against a ridiculous number of pillows.

She hooked her leg around his waist and took him inside. God, he filled her, splitting her open in the most delightful of ways. She clutched at his back, gasping as he rolled his hips. Who knew he had this vigor inside of him?

"Want to feel you come around me," he said, his words sounding like they'd been wrenched from him.

"Trying." She gasped. Unlike him, she'd lost the ability to say anything coherent.

He shifted their position, tilting her hips at a different angle, one that really worked for her. He bent to kiss her, his lips against her breast.

To her surprise, her climax rose up to meet her. She'd never come again this quickly. She let out a cry and clenched him tightly inside of her.

"That's my girl," he said, and then he really started to move, his hips pounding into her with no discernible rhythm. He let out a grunt, his eyes shut tight, and stilled.

He kissed her, cradling her face between his hands before letting go reluctantly. "Let me take care of the condom before it sticks."

She chuckled but was far too sleepy to do more than that. Elena melted into the sheets and closed her eyes, letting the soft sounds of David puttering around the bedroom lull her into a light doze.

****

The beep of the microwave and the strong smell of reheated burgers roused her. Elena blinked and looked around. She didn't see any of her clothes, but a clean T-shirt had been draped over the end of the bed. Once she put it on, she laughed because it said *I escaped The Greatest Escape.*

"Seriously?" she said as she walked into the kitchen. "You had T-shirts printed up?"

Perhaps she should have T-shirts. She'd have to talk to Quinn about that. Surely, she'd considered that as part of their marketing strategy.

David turned away from the open microwave and handed Elena the plate of warmed-up burger and fries. "It was for a contest I ran on Facebook. Winning team got T-shirts. I had a few extras that I kept. It looks good on you."

Her cheeks heated, and she took the food over to the island. She hopped up on the stool, but before she started to eat, she asked, "Um, you did clean these counters?"

He let out a laugh and slapped his hand down on the container of sanitizing wipes next to him. "Yup."

She shook her head. From what she'd noticed of his home—which was about fifteen minutes outside of New Brunswick proper—he'd kept it meticulously clean, decorated in pale blues and grays. It was almost stark in its cleanliness, like some pieces of furniture were missing. Maybe he didn't have time to fill up this giant—to her—suburban house. Her apartment could fit in here three times over.

He sat next to her and chowed down on reheated burger as if it were still fresh. "So what did you think of the room?" he asked between bites.

She had grabbed a packet of ketchup for her fries and now played with it while deciding how to answer. "Well, there were parts of it I liked—mostly the end in the cabin."

He made a face at her. "No question there—that was definitely the best part. But honestly, what did you think?"

"It wasn't a true escape room, was it? I mean, I get the obstacle course thing, but it felt like all that did was slow you down. The puzzles weren't particularly difficult or creative."

"I thought the story had potential. I liked the walkie-talkie as a plot device." He put his burger down. His forehead furrowed as he thought, and it was so completely adorable she wanted to kiss his eyebrows.

So she did.

"What was that for?"

"Because I could." She finished her burger, quieting her starving belly. "Do you have plans for the rest of the evening?"

"I have a very nice collection of board games. Some involve puzzles. I've heard you are fond of those."

"Are these clothing-optional games?"

"They could be." He curled his arm around her waist, stroking her side. "I threw your clothes in the wash. So you'll have something to wear tomorrow morning. If, that is, you'd like to stay?"

Elena leaned into him. "Depends."

"On?"

"How much fun those naked board games are."

Chapter 23

Elena woke to pain—a sharp stabbing sensation shooting up her left calf. To keep silent, she bit her lip so hard she could taste blood. *Don't wake David. He can't know.* One deep breath in, then out. David snored softly beside her.

She carefully peeled back the covers, keeping her movements slow to not disturb him. When she tried to slide out of bed, her feet wouldn't hold her weight. She crumpled to the floor in a heap. *Damn it.* These were the consequences to skipping her exercises and end-of-the-day icing. She liked to think she was completely healed, but some days her feet reminded her that she wasn't.

She might never be completely well again. And when she forgot her carefully regimented plan for managing her pain, she crashed.

Crawling on her knees, she made it to the bathroom and sat on the toilet. David had a bottle of ibuprofen, and she shook four of the little orange pills into her palm. She gulped cold water from the sink to wash them down. While she waited for the meds to work, she massaged each leg, pressing her fingers into the tender skin until the spasms eased.

She couldn't forget her routine again. Next time she needed to be better prepared.

Next time. Did she want there to be a next time with David? Elena wasn't used to relationships that lasted longer than a week. And while the sex had been fantastic—God, what he could do with his tongue—she didn't have any hope for anything more than that. She'd have to open up, about her pain, about not being perfect. While she'd talked about the accident with him, she wasn't ready to admit that it still affected her everyday life.

But she didn't have to talk about anything if she just wanted to sleep with him again. Sex didn't have to include strings. Despite waking up in pain, she'd do it all over again, simply for the feel of David around her and inside her.

Once she could stand, Elena made her way back to the bed, guided by the light of David's alarm clock. Four a.m. She had plenty of time to sleep.

He rolled over at her reappearance and threw one arm around her. She snuggled into his warmth, breathing deeply. God, he smelled so good. She closed her eyes and let herself drift, her legs still aching but a bearable ache for the moment.

****

"The disappointing news is that I have nothing decent to offer for breakfast."

The scent of the coffee hit Elena's nose before she registered the words. She blinked and opened bleary eyes. David sat on the edge of the bed with a steaming mug.

Somehow, she'd managed to sleep through him getting up and showering since he looked way too fresh for someone who'd just rolled out of bed. And his dark wavy hair looked damp. She wanted to comb her fingers through it.

She took the mug and breathed in deeply, hoping the

caffeine would fire up her brain through osmosis. "What's the good news?"

"There's a really good bagel place not that far from here. I put your clothes in the bathroom. Why don't you grab a quick shower? By the time you're done, I'll be back with warm bagels."

She sipped the coffee—he'd put in a dash of milk and sugar, which, while not how she normally took her coffee, felt almost luxurious, a special treat after last night. "Sounds great."

He leaned forward and kissed her nose, making her laugh. "I'll be right back."

Once he left, she set the coffee on the end table and stretched. The ibuprofen had done its job, and she felt mostly human today. A hot shower would be even better.

David had left her clothes on the bathroom counter along with a large fluffy towel and a toothbrush still in its package. She stopped in the doorway when she saw that and swallowed hard. For some reason being taken care of like this felt almost too much. She didn't want this to mean more than it did.

David was overly prepared for everything. That had to be it. Former scientist, he probably had boxes of extra things in case someone had an emergency and stayed over. Nothing to do with Elena at all.

The water beat hot down her back, and she closed her eyes, reliving the feel of his hands on her body. They'd been so good in bed. What would they do the rest of the day? She did have to go in to work, but she didn't have to be there until eleven or so. They could spend the morning together.

She dressed quickly, hoping David hadn't done anything so foolish as to launder her bra, but since it still fit, she assumed he knew better than to throw it in the wash and dry. She picked up her coffee cup again when she heard the lock jiggle in the front door, like he was having a hard time getting it to open.

Maybe he needed help with all those bagels.

"That was fast." She opened the door to reveal not David, but a woman holding a key. Two men walked up the sidewalk behind her, dragging along a hand truck. A white moving truck parked in the driveway.

"Um." Elena blinked at the woman who stared back with wide eyes. What was going on here? "Can I help you?"

"Is David in?" The woman was taller than Elena, with pale hair. Gold dangling earrings clinked as she spoke and tilted her head.

"He went to grab breakfast."

The woman nodded. "Jason's Bagels will be packed this time of the morning. Well, I'll get my stuff and leave, then. We'll be out of your hair in no time."

"Excuse me? Who are you?"

She blinked. "I'm Laura. His ex. I assume he hasn't mentioned me."

"Not recently, no."

"I left a bunch of crap behind when I left. He's been nice enough to store it, but I guess it was time."

Elena stepped aside and let her in. An ex. One that used to live here. That would explain the minimalist furniture. "When did you leave?"

"Six months ago." She seemed to know exactly where she was going, striding across David's living room and toward a door Elena hadn't noticed before. Laura threw it open to reveal a room filled with packing boxes. That was a lot of stuff to have left behind. How long had Laura lived with David?

Elena was struck with the urge to be anywhere but here. She found her purse slung over one of the kitchen chairs where she'd left it. Her shoes had been placed neatly on the floor below. Ignoring the men who'd come in with the cart, she pulled on her shoes and tied the laces carefully—it took her a few tries with her shaking hands.

Laura stepped out of the room just as Elena reached the front door. "Oh, you don't have to leave. We won't be long."

"Yeah, I was planning on going anyway." She forced a smile before waving and making a hasty retreat.

She walked a few blocks before pulling out her phone and texting Phoebe.

—*Can you pick me up?*—

She sent her location via the maps app. Then she sat on the curb to wait. Good thing she hadn't expected anything serious. David had already been there and done that.

Chapter 24

The smell of warm bagels filled the car as David turned onto his street. However, the thrum of happiness he'd felt that morning plummeted when he saw the familiar sports car parked in front of his house. *Laura.* How? Why?

He pulled up behind the moving truck parked in his driveway and knew, with a sinking feeling, that she'd come to get her stuff at exactly the wrong moment. Anger simmered in his belly as he got out of his car, slamming the door behind him. With each step toward his house, it grew hotter until it was a boiling pot of rage inside him. By the time he got to the open door, he nearly collided with the man carrying one of Laura's boxes out.

"Tyler." He nodded at Laura's brother.

"Oh, uh, hi, David. Laura's back inside, coordinating." Tyler shuffled around.

David let him go. Tyler wasn't the one he was mad at. He stalked toward the spare room where Laura had loaded several boxes onto a hand truck. Another unknown man helped her. He took one look at David and made a quick escape with the hand truck.

"Laura," he gritted out. He'd expected it to be hard seeing her again. They'd lived together for two years. He'd thought at one time that they were endgame, that she would be the woman he'd spend the rest of his life with. He braced himself for the heartbreak, but it never came. He didn't feel wistful or sorry that he found her dragging her things out of here. The only emotion that thrummed in him at the sight of her familiar face was annoyance. He'd been so close to moving on. He and Elena had shared an amazing night together. And now Laura had come back into his life to screw everything up. "Why the hell didn't you call first?"

"Hello, David. Nice to see you, too." She crossed her arms over her chest and glared at him. Oh yeah, he knew that glare well, almost as well as he knew his own reflection.

"Really, we're back to playing nice?" This was the whole damn problem. Toward the end they had been polite roommates, reduced to making small talk over meals. *Nasty weather we're having today. Oh, it looks like the Yankees beat the Red Sox. Nice.* Their conversations had stopped being about anything deeper, about their hopes and dreams for the future. He should have figured it out a long time before he walked in to find Laura with her bags packed and sitting on his couch.

"You're the one who emailed me and told me to get my stuff."

Once again they were both on completely different pages. "I didn't expect you to show up at my house with no warning!" Exasperated, he slammed his hand against one of the walls.

"Honestly, I'd hoped you'd be working." She looked away, the fire dying a bit from her eyes.

She wasn't wrong. He normally spent so much time at work that she was right to expect him not to be home.

"Then we wouldn't even be having this conversation. I admit I didn't expect you to have a woman over on a Tuesday morning."

God, he'd been so angry he hadn't even stopped to look for Elena. What had she thought when his ex-girlfriend had shown up like this—with the key to his house? Ice prickled down the back of his neck. "Where's Elena?"

"She left. Said she was on her way out."

Of course she had. What else could Elena have done when confronted with all of his mistakes? His blood thrummed, and he wanted to turn on his heel and go after her. She couldn't have gone far on foot. He needed to explain and beg for her forgiveness. But first, he had to deal with Laura. "What the hell did you say to her?"

She stalked toward him and then poked at his chest. "I wouldn't have had to say anything if you'd told her you had an ex-girlfriend. Christ, David, all my shit was still here."

"It's still my house, Laura."

"Right, it's always been yours. Nothing was ever ours. You have no idea how to make a relationship work."

That stung far more than it should. Just because their relationship hadn't worked out didn't mean it had been his fault alone. "There were two people in our relationship."

She barked out a laugh. "Only two? I had to compete with your job and your mother. When you started talking about getting a dog, that was the last fucking straw. I was right here, and you never saw me, David."

"Maybe there was nothing to see," he snapped, wanting to end this conversation and find Elena.

Laura recoiled as if she'd been slapped. "Wow. Thanks for reminding me why I left."

He swallowed. Guilt stabbed him. He'd let his anger

get the upper hand, and he'd taken it out on her. She didn't deserve that. "I didn't mean... Finish getting your crap out of here."

"Working on that."

"And leave your key when you're done." He strode out of the room and fished in his pocket for his phone. He had a missed text message waiting for him from Elena.

—Got a ride from Phoebe. Don't worry about me.—

The squeezing sensation in his chest eased a bit. Still, he couldn't leave things like this. David went to his bedroom, closed the door, and hit *dial*.

****

Elena didn't have to wait long before Phoebe pulled up along the curb. She got in and buckled up before sending David a quick text message. She didn't want him to worry, and she had left rather abruptly.

To be fair, she hadn't expected to be suddenly confronted with his ex.

"Hey," Phoebe said, thankfully keeping her eyes on the road as she drove off. "What happened?"

Elena made a face as she leaned her head on her hands. She didn't want to talk about it. "Date didn't quite end like I planned."

Phoebe pulled the car over. She threw it into park and turned to face Elena. "Did that son of a bitch hurt you? Because we can drive straight to the police station after I take a baseball bat to his car."

Elena seemed destined to be surrounded by overprotective friends. She tried to smile but for some reason burst into tears instead. "Wait, Phoebe, no."

If she didn't say something, Phoebe would make good on the baseball bat threat.

"We had a lovely evening. It was really good." Elena wiped her eyes, not knowing where the sudden burst of emotion had come from.

It had been a fantastic night. David had been skilled and gentle, and he seemed to really care about what she thought. She had wanted more.

"Then what happened?" Phoebe placed her hand on Elena's shoulder and squeezed gently.

"He went out to get breakfast, and his ex-girlfriend showed up to pick up her things."

"That asshole! He was hiding an ex?"

"They've been broken up for six months. I guess he let her store her stuff there." But why? Wouldn't it be a priority to get rid of everything when ending a relationship? Elena's only similar experience had been a bad roommate situation in the city, and she'd dumped all of Elena's stuff on the curb after changing the locks.

"Still, he didn't have the decency to tell you about her?"

"It didn't come up in conversation, no." She cleared her throat and blinked away the last of the tears. Should she have expected it to?

Maybe if David was heading toward something more serious with her. Then, yes, definitely. But when she'd gone back to his home, she had no illusions that there would be anything more than sex. She'd wanted that, and it had been fantastic.

But now something in her felt hollow. It had been a crappy way to end the date. Was that the only thing bothering her? She knew there couldn't be anything more between them. They still owned rival businesses. Although at the moment that reason seemed less important.

Her phone chose that moment to ring. She swallowed when she saw David's number. "It's him."

"Tell him off," Phoebe urged. She threw the car back into drive and got on the road.

Elena clicked *answer*. "Hi."

"Elena." His voice sounded panicked and breathless. "Are you okay?"

She pictured him, standing there with his worrywart expression on his face, his hand caught up in his curls, making them look even more mussed than usual. Warmth spread throughout her chest. "Yes. Phoebe picked me up. We're on our way back to The Escape Space now."

"I'm sorry," he said. "I'd emailed Laura to come pick up her things, but I had no idea she was going to be coming over today."

"The bigger problem," Elena said slowly, trying to get her wording right, "is that you didn't tell me about Laura in the first place."

He didn't respond for a second. She thought he might have hung up or lost connection.

Finally, he said, "You're right."

"I usually am." She injected some teasing into her voice to gentle it a bit. All things considered, she didn't want to end things with David. Although she wasn't sure where she wanted them to go.

"Let me make it up to you. Coffee, tomorrow morning?"

However, she didn't want to appear too eager. He would have to work for it. "I'll have to check my schedule. I'll text you when I'm available, okay?"

She knew he wouldn't like that at all, but she needed to take some of the power back in this situation. Let him wait on her.

"All right. I really am sorry."

"I know. Talk to you soon." She ended the call and dropped the phone in her lap. She looked up in time to see Phoebe blow through an orange light and winced.

"Are you seriously seeing him again?" Phoebe asked.

Elena shrugged. "It's not like I'm going to make it easy on him. He'll have to prove he wants to meet me."

"And how will you manage that?"

"Oh, I may have an idea or two." She grinned because something sparked in her brain. She knew exactly how she'd make David work for it.

****

David kept his phone on at all times, constantly pulling it out and checking it between customers. One time he got a buzz, and he eagerly pulled it out only to see the notification that his phone bill had been paid.

"Chill out, man. You're like a teenager in detention." Tony looked up from his laptop. He was busy designing something for the fourth room. He had some science fiction idea, and David was letting him run with it. Whatever Tony came up with, it had to be more creative than one of the stock escape room setups that he could buy online.

He'd spent his free time scrolling through those, trying not to think about Tuesday. He hated how things had ended with Elena. One moment he was kissing her and promising breakfast, and the next, she was gone.

However, he was grateful she hadn't seen his meltdown with Laura.

"I'm going in the back to make a phone call. Watch the front?" No rooms were scheduled at the moment, but someone could walk in at any time.

Tony waved at him, still looking at his screen, which did not give David confidence that he'd be a great receptionist, but David would take what he could get.

He checked in on the control room where both Sean and Vanessa were guiding customers through their rooms. Those players looked like they would take up the entire time. No record breakers in this group. David continued to the back of his business, to the empty space that would become his fourth room once Tony finished his design.

Then he pulled out his phone and dialed his mother. He usually called her once a week on Sundays, except when he was panicking over getting the business set up and called her every night to vent. He hadn't told her about having a date with Elena yet, knowing how upset she'd been when Laura left. He hadn't wanted to give her any unrealistic expectations.

"Hi, Mom."

"David, I was just about to go to bingo."

"You mean you don't have time for your only son?"

She chuckled. "I always have time. But not too much. It takes me fifteen minutes to walk to the senior center."

He ground his teeth to keep from saying something he'd regret later. The last thing he wanted was to start a fight with his mom, too. But he hated that she was alone in the big city, no matter how much she loved it.

"I wanted to tell you that I met someone," he said instead.

"Oh, now this I have time for."

He laughed. "I don't know if it's anything serious yet." He heated at the thought of Elena in his bed, her red hair bright against the paleness of his sheets, her smile wide, and her eyes heavy-lidded with desire.

Some things he didn't tell his mother, no matter what Laura accused him of.

"But at least you aren't alone," Mom said. "When are you going to introduce me?"

"When it gets serious," he promised. "When are you going to introduce me to one of the many men you've been picking up at bingo?"

She laughed, and he already felt much lighter. If Elena didn't text him by Friday, he was going to march on over to The Escape Space, no matter what. He'd given her a few days to "check her schedule," and while even he could read between the lines and know she needed space, he wasn't about to let her get away.

His phone buzzed, and he froze. "Have fun at bingo, Mom. Talk to you Sunday."

"Be good."

As soon as she hung up, David looked at the text message he'd received. It was from Elena, but it didn't contain any words. Instead it was an image. He poked it until he could blow the picture up and saw what looked like a bunch of gibberish, squares and triangles and dots.

He laughed. She'd challenged him with a puzzle. He nearly charged out to the lobby to get Tony to help him decode this.

But no. He could do this himself. He went to his office and got out a pen and paper. He recognized the symbols as a pigpen cipher. The only question was whether or not Elena had used the standard configuration for the symbols, or if she'd switched things around a bit just to make them interesting.

He kept getting interrupted—first by customers and

then by Tony who wanted David to look at his plans. But finally, he decoded the text message.

—*Coffee Friday. Eight a.m. Coffee shop on Fifth.*—

David grinned and typed a simple un-encrypted response.

—*I'll be there.*—

Chapter 25

David walked into the downtown coffee shop at exactly eight a.m. He looked around and didn't see Elena. His heart jumped into his throat. Had he decoded the message wrong? Maybe he just needed to wait a little longer. He resisted the urge to pull out his phone and check the cipher again.

Instead, he got in line, ordered a coffee, and then found an empty table, no easy feat this morning. Even though the Rutgers campuses proper had coffee shops, some college students still found their way here. In addition he spotted professionals from the hospital up the road—easy to note in their scrubs or bright-white nursing shoes. This city had a lot going for it, and David felt confident in his choice to set up shop here.

Surely, New Brunswick could handle two escape rooms.

Sipping his coffee, he took stock of the people coming in and out. His brain took a turn, and he entertained the thought of creating a coffee-shop-based escape room. Brew the espresso properly to earn a key. He found himself grinning at the thought as Elena walked into the shop.

She wore a T-shirt and another pair of those damn leggings that had so flummoxed him when they were intimate. How the hell did women get in and out of those torture devices? But no matter what she wore, she always looked stunning to him. Even walking up to the bar to grab a coffee, she moved with such grace, striding with those long legs that had been wrapped around his waist.

His hand twitched, and he grasped his own thigh to keep it steady. He wanted—no, he ached to touch. Heat flooded his cheeks, and he had to look away, unable to stare at even the color of her hair without growing hard.

He had it bad. He only hoped he could fix things between them.

She came to his table, carrying a tall iced drink. If she insisted on sucking on that straw, he didn't think he'd be able to control himself.

"Hey."

"For a minute there I thought I'd gotten the message wrong."

She slid into the seat across from him. "I had every confidence that you could solve it."

"I guess puzzles are the one thing I don't suck at." He cleared his throat and took a sip of his coffee.

"I wouldn't say the only thing." A trace of a smile spread across those pink lips, and all he wanted was to lean across the table and kiss them.

His cheeks heated, and he tried distracting himself by drinking more coffee, but that would only make his heart race more. "Does that mean you've forgiven me for not telling you about Laura?"

She looked away, and her shoulders dropped. "I mean, you didn't have to tell me. It's not like we're dating."

He heard the question in her voice. "Then what are we doing?"

She swallowed. "I don't know. I've never been in this situation before."

"You've never dated anyone before?" He found that impossible to believe. How could someone as amazing as Elena not have found someone before? Had no one ever looked on that stage and really seen her?

"I've always been a bit of a workaholic." She shrugged. "A relationship never fit into my schedule."

He knew that too well. "That's what broke me and Laura. To be honest, I never put her before work, and that killed any chance we had."

Silence, as they sipped their coffees.

Fuck it. The past didn't dictate the present. David had spent so much time worried about becoming his father that he kept a distance between himself and Laura. Work had only been the excuse. The revelation hit him like an epiphany on the road to Damascus, and he sucked in a breath and consequently choked on his coffee.

Elena pounded on his back until he could breathe again.

"I never told you," he started, chewing the words around in his head before he said them, "why I like puzzles? I mean, you don't end up in the sciences if you don't like figuring things out. You need to be a bit curious about how the world works."

"It wasn't because you were dragged to an escape room against your will and caught the bug?" She leaned her chin on one hand, and her eyes softened.

He forced himself to look away so he could say what he had to say next. "When I was growing up, my mom and I always worked on puzzles together. She had these brainteaser books she got from the library and…" He wasn't sure he could finish. He found he wanted to tell Elena. He wanted her to understand.

"When my dad was having one of his bad days, we'd

go hide in the attic loft. She'd make me focus on the puzzle instead of the sounds of things breaking downstairs."

He could see the moment it crystallized for Elena. Her forehead wrinkled, and her eyes narrowed.

"When you say bad day, you mean…"

"When he was so drunk and pissed off that he didn't give a shit about what got in his way. I learned at a young age not to care too much about something. It was bound to get destroyed that way."

"David." She reached across the table and squeezed his forearm.

He covered her hand with his own. He'd never spoken about this before, not to Laura or any girlfriend before her. He'd kept it wrapped up in its own little box, like if he didn't speak, then it didn't happen, hadn't scarred him. "It's fine. It was a long time ago. My mom divorced him when I was thirteen. Raised me on her own. I still like to bring a brainteaser to her every now and then."

"I think she did a wonderful job."

****

Elena didn't know how to do this. When she walked into the coffee shop that morning, she had decided she didn't care that David hadn't told her about Laura. They hadn't made any promises to each other, and she'd happily keep this about sex. She hadn't been looking for a relationship. Hell, this was the worst time to be distracted by one. She needed to be focused on building her business, not screwing around with David.

That decision had been the result of texting Jesse most of the night although he disagreed with her conclusion that she and David were only "friends with benefits."

—*You obviously like the guy*— Jesse texted. —*Are you sure that's all you want?*—

Elena had deflected the question. She couldn't give him a true answer, mainly because she didn't know herself. She knew she wanted to see David again. She loved spending time with him when it was just the two of them, not having to worry about the real world and their business rivalry. He was a kind and generous lover, and her body tingled when she thought about the chance to be in his bed again. Mostly, she liked his smile, liked being the person that put it there, in bed and out.

That didn't mean she wanted to marry the guy. Absolutely not. She had been on her own for a long time. She didn't need a man to complete her.

And yet the abstract concept of a "boyfriend" or "husband" didn't seem to match up with the reality of David sitting in front of her. David, who'd just shared something heartbreaking with her. She ached for the child he'd been, hiding from an abusive father and using puzzles to pretend the rest of the world didn't exist. Had he ever spoken about this before? The way he talked about it seemed like it had been hard for him.

She swallowed, and warmth flooded her body.

"I'll be sure to tell her you said that." David did smile then, a soft sweet smile. "Although she'd probably yell at me for not introducing you to her."

She took a sip of her coffee, surprised to find herself at the bottom of the cup. They'd sat here and simply talked for longer than she'd thought possible. "I don't think we're at that stage yet." No, she couldn't meet his mother, not now when she didn't even know what she wanted. She'd been so certain that morning, but at the moment she couldn't say which end was up. He had her spinning in circles. She wanted more, somehow, but she couldn't have it. Not like this. They were still getting to know each other.

His shoulders dropped. "Maybe not. I'm not asking for anything you're not ready for."

She studied his face, trying to read whatever the heck was going on in those eyes. He seemed to have picked up on her own uncertainty. How did he always seem to know what she was thinking? And could she afford to let him go? When would she meet anyone like him again? "Then what are you asking for?"

He shrugged. "A chance? To see where this goes? We both love escape rooms—hell, we're great at solving them together. And we're compatible in other ways as well."

"You mean we're both raging workaholics?" she teased. He wasn't wrong. All of her commitment to keeping this a fling seemed to want to desert her. No, David himself was working this magic. He wanted her, and hell, Elena wanted him, too.

His cheeks went red, and she delighted in making him blush, like she had the upper hand now.

"No, I meant, you know. The bedroom."

She sat back and pretended to give it some thought. *Let him sweat for a moment.* "Do you have any other secrets I need to know about? An evil twin perhaps?"

He laughed. "Unless my mother forgot to tell me something, then no. Now that Laura has finally moved out…I think I'm ready for a fresh start."

That's what she had wanted from the beginning. This was her new life, and she got to decide who deserved to be in it. Staring at David, she made a decision. "All right. Now that we've established that…would you like to see my other escape room?"

He dropped his coffee cup as he was about to take a sip. Luckily, it was nearly empty, and he managed to catch it before it completely upended. "Seriously?"

"We're not opening until twelve today. Phoebe won't be in until eleven. We have the place to ourselves." She didn't realize the innuendo in that until the words left her lips in a purr. Elena shook her head. "I really want to know what you think of my puzzle design. Honestly."

"I'd be honored. Let's go."

Chapter 26

David stood behind Elena as she unlocked the front entrance to The Escape Space. They were close enough to almost touch, and he could feel the heat of her body close to his. He nearly put his hand on the small of her back but kept to himself. Being allowed into her space was an intimate, private thing, and he didn't want to push too far.

It hadn't been that long—had it been only two months ago?—that he'd nearly screwed up any chances of being let inside. He had been so angry, and he'd let Tony talk him into cheating his way in. Now Elena was letting him in on her own terms.

His glimpse at her first room had given him a taste of who she really was. He wanted to know more. Sometimes she was still a mystery, a beautiful complicated puzzle that he wanted to solve.

"Both rooms are up on the second floor." She turned on the lights as they entered, illuminating the quiet lobby. "I haven't decided what I'm doing with the third yet. I had so many ideas after the conference, but I haven't settled on one yet."

"You could try bouncing them off me," he offered. "And I'll make sure not to have anything similar in my fourth room."

She turned around, her hand on the bannister. "I thought you were going speakeasy?"

"Everyone has a speakeasy," he grumbled. "I want to do something interesting. Tony is working on a spaceship design…"

He still didn't know if it had been a good idea or a terrible one to give Tony carte blanche. Knowing Tony, it could go either way.

Elena's eyes lit up. "Oh, I haven't seen anything like that before. Let me know if you need a beta tester."

He grinned. "This time you won't have to pretend to get in."

"And hopefully, you won't be violating any fire codes either." She gave him a stern look followed by a laugh.

They climbed the stairs up to the second-floor landing. Seeing it in person made the place come alive. Sean's little spying jaunt could not replicate the sheen of the wood or the lemon scent of its polish.

"This is Uncle Enzo's Study." Elena put her hand on the door. "But you've seen that one already."

David's cheeks heated with embarrassment. The tone of her voice had him feeling like a kid called to the principal's office. "Um. Yeah. Sorry."

She reached out, took his hand, and squeezed it. "This one is a bit more personal."

He searched her eyes, looking for all the things she hadn't said. He nodded, slowly, and squeezed her hand in return. "I understand," he said, though he didn't, not really. But, damn it, he was going to try.

She opened the second door, stepped inside, and flipped on the light switch.

They were transported to another world. Inside stood a rack of clothing filled with sparkling dresses and costumes. Opposite that sat a row of tables in front of mirrors surrounded by round light bulbs. David took in the boxes with locks as almost an afterthought.

The walls had been painted black, which made the entrance to the second room difficult to see—of course, that was the point. Elena led David around the room as she pointed out the puzzle chain, including the diary of the ballerina that showed her becoming increasingly unhinged. "You don't get the full story until you get to the second room."

She pulled on two ropes hanging in the corner that he hadn't even noticed. A portion of the black wall slid open. When they stepped through, they were onstage.

Several red velvet seats had been set up in front of the platform, and beyond, a mural had been either painted or wallpapered onto the wall, showing a rapt audience waiting for the performance. Curtains hung on either side of them, moving slightly from their entrance.

"It's not quite the same." Elena stood in the middle of the stage and lifted her arms, creating an arch above her head.

David slid into position behind her and placed his hands on her hips. He had no idea how to do this. He'd never danced ballet before. But right now he needed to have his hands on her, to touch her and give whatever support he could.

She laughed and spun out of his grasp, twirling like a creature in a music box. He couldn't do more than stare in awe at her beauty in motion. She stepped toward him and held out a hand.

He grasped her palm and gasped as she bent forward, moving one leg behind her so far into the air she looked like a swan.

She winced and stepped out of position. "I'm out of

practice."

"Can you dance?" he asked softly. "Your feet." He wasn't sure exactly how badly she'd been hurt. But he knew ballerinas needed strong ankles and toes to dance.

"I've been working on strengthening them. There's always going to be pain, I know. But I hope I'll be able to dance for fun again." Her face had gone pale, and she turned away from him, giving a sad bow to the faux audience.

David couldn't leave it at that. He stepped toward her and put his hands around her waist once more. "Is this all right?" he asked as he lifted her so her feet didn't touch the floor.

She laughed as he spun them both around, making up his own version of dance. She held her arms out and closed her eyes as he moved. His heart pounded, and he knew he could never let her go. No one would ever hurt her again.

****

"Do you miss it?"

Elena wiped at her eyes as she regained her footing. She was still a bit dizzy after David set her down. "That's a complicated question."

He held her gaze, his brown eyes soft in the intense light she had set up on the stage. This room had a puzzle that involved the lights, and she was actually quite proud of it. She'd planned on showing it to him. She'd really wanted his opinion about the puzzles and the room design, but this had turned into something else, something she wasn't sure she was ready to dive into with him, not yet.

Elena carefully stepped off the stage and sat in one of the velvet seats that served as the front row. He sat on the edge of the stage directly across from her.

"Short answer is yes, I do. There is nothing like being up on stage and performing. And getting lost in the dance until there's nothing but you and your body pushed to the limit." She held out her arms, moving smoothly into fourth position, with one arched above her head and the other reaching out toward David. She pulled back quickly, her cheeks heating. "But I knew going into it that it's a career with a clock attached. You're lucky if you go out before your body gives out. I wish…"

"What?" He leaned forward.

"That it had been my choice. That I walked away because I wanted to, not because I had to." She'd sworn that she was done crying about this, so she breathed in deeply, keeping those tears from falling.

And then he hopped off the stage and kissed her.

Those lips were just as soft as she remembered. She opened to him, her hands gripping the arms of the chair as he cupped her face carefully between his hands, his thumbs tracing lines along her cheeks. She could taste the coffee on his tongue, and she breathed deeply of his scent, a bit sweet and warm.

She gave in and dug her hands in his curly hair, keeping him in place as they kissed. It started so soft and gentle, but then she bit at his lip, and he growled in response.

Oh, she liked that sound. It stirred something deep inside her, a need to hear it again. She pulled back long enough to nip at his chin, to taste his skin and tease at the hint of stubble there. She loved how he tasted.

"You're wearing leggings again," he grumbled, as he sat back on his heels and drew her with him onto his lap.

She laughed. "Is that a problem?"

"They are very difficult to get off."

She cupped his face in her hands and met his gaze straight on. "David, we are not having sex in my escape room. Do you know how many people have been through this room?"

He threw back his head and laughed. "What? You don't want to be on the top-ten list of what people really do in escape rooms?"

"Not when my employees might be here any moment." She gave him one last long lingering kiss, one that had him groaning and clutching her closer. Then, regretfully, she pulled away. "Come on. I have some hand sanitizer in the hall."

David adjusted himself before he stood, and Elena got a kick out of causing that reaction. She winked at him as she led the way out of the room, making sure to put a little wiggle in her walk. She laughed at the sound of him swearing in response. Thank God for him changing the mood. Her sorrow would always be there, a sliver inside her that would never fully go away, but now she had something else to think about whenever she stepped inside this room.

"You know, you still haven't shown me any of the actual puzzles."

Right. And she'd wanted his opinion, too. She took his hand again and showed him around the room, pointing out where she'd cleverly hidden boxes and how to work the light puzzle—if her players hit the right buttons, backlit numbers appeared in the lights above. The finale for this room opened a trap door in the stage, with the ballerina's confession of murder.

David fingered the missing diary page and shook his

head. "That's quite a story."

"It is fiction, by the way. Lest you think I actually did murder one of my rivals."

"Hey, I've seen *Black Swan*. I know how it is."

"Not quite that cutthroat, but close." She gestured to the door, and he followed.

He stepped out onto the landing and pointed to the third floor. "Is that where your next room is going to be?"

"I hope so." She took the steps up, David at her heels. She had so many ideas for this space, but she had yet to choose one. Plus, unless she wanted to spend thousands of dollars to purchase a premade design, she was pretty limited in what she could do. She'd already sunk a lot of money into the construction of The Ballet, and that room was less popular than Uncle Enzo's Study, which had been much cheaper to build.

She threw open the door and sneezed, revealing the dusty attic space.

"Bless you." David blinked as he looked around the room. It was a single open area that held nothing but some boxes of supplies in the corner. The attic took up the entire length and width of the house. "With some temp walls, you could have a three- or four-room game up here."

"Yes, but what? Creepy serial killer is way too obvious. I want to do something different and unique." She had considered dozens of ideas, but nothing had really jumped out at her. She wanted to commit to whatever she spent time and money on. Plus, it had to be marketable. If it didn't draw people in, then she'd wasted her funds on a poor room.

David tapped his chin as he wandered around the attic, poking at the support pillars. He turned back to her with his eyes lit up. In two steps he was across the room and had his arms around her. "Elena…will you let me plan your escape room with you?"

She laughed a little as she stuck her hands beneath his T-shirt. They were both starting to sweat up here, and Phoebe would be in soon. "Helping the competition?" Although the words were teasing, she meant the sentiment. Whatever was going on between them, they couldn't deny the fact that they were still rivals.

"We'll just make sure it's different from anything in my space. We aren't competition. We complement each other."

Against her better judgement, Elena nodded. Putting a room together sounded fun.

He grinned before kissing her again. "Great. I can't wait to get started."

Chapter 27

"Okay, I think I have the list done."

David looked up as Tony handed him a sheaf of papers, which consisted of a color-coded spreadsheet. He blinked and flipped through the information. Well, Tony had been thorough; David had to give him that. Though he wasn't entirely sure where they were going to get some of these items.

"Everything in red I can find," Tony said, seeming to sense his hesitation. "The decor is up to you. I have some suggestions…"

"Lots and lots of silver spray paint, it looks like," David said dryly.

He'd have to ask Elena about her prop source. The quality of her designs was impeccable, and she might have some ideas about where he could look for good stuff. This was so different from purchasing an entire room from a company. He looked forward to the creative aspect of it. What could he paint silver to look like a space captain's chair?

He loved that he could text her and ask such a simple question. They were still rivals, yes, but in this business, owners should build each other up. A good experience at one escape room business only encouraged someone to try another.

Who was he kidding? He wanted to talk to her simply because he liked talking to her. He found himself texting her random things, usually escape room related, sometimes not. She always responded with something funny or insightful. He couldn't wait to see her again and pondered where they could go next. He'd been looking up new and innovative escape rooms to try all day.

But first, he had to have a conversation with Tony.

David wasn't sure how Tony would take the news that he was seeing Elena. Although this thing between them was still so fragile he couldn't put a name to it, not yet. Still, he didn't want Tony to find out the wrong way. He was still sore about the fire inspector.

"This looks good."

"Really?" Tony stepped back and ducked his head.

Damn it, someone in Tony's life should have told him he was doing a good job. David knew Tony and his dad didn't quite get along, but he'd like to have a few words with Mr. Spano sometime. Tony was good at a lot of things, but those things didn't always intersect with the pizza business.

"Yeah. Let me write up a project timeline, and we'll get started." This way he'd be sure not to have any problems with the fire department.

"Great. I'll start ordering parts."

"Let me give you a budget first," David grumbled. He went digging in his desk for a pencil and some paper. Tony might like the spreadsheets, but David always preferred to sketch stuff out first.

He came up with the pencil and rolled it between his fingers. "Listen. I've got something to tell you."

Now was as good a time as any.

Tony dropped into one of the extra seats. "Who died?"

"What? Nobody. Why would you ask that?"

"You got all serious for a second. I mean, unless you're about to tell me you don't have a budget for the new room…"

"It's not about the new room." David set the pencil down and rubbed his jaw. He couldn't stop fidgeting, mainly because he couldn't figure out quite what he wanted to say.

"I'm seeing someone," he settled on, figuring it was the safest way to start.

Tony visibly relaxed. "You are? That's great, but when the hell did you find the time? You're always working. Hell, the last trip you took was to that escape room convention in AC."

"Funny you should mention that. It's because of the convention that we got together." Hard to think about it now—a month ago on the side of the highway, with a blown out tire and Elena opening up to him. "Elena and I, I mean."

Tony narrowed his eyes. "Elena, as in the woman across the street who called the fire inspector on you?"

"Well, to be fair, that was one of her employees."

"David, will you listen to yourself? What the hell are you doing, going to bed with the enemy?"

"She's not the enemy," he snapped. "She happened to open her business across the street from mine. It's one of those coincidences, and you know what? I'm glad she did, because if she hadn't, then I never would have met her."

Tony rolled his eyes. "What, you managed to meet your soul mate right after Laura left? You're on the rebound hard, my friend."

"There's no such thing," David grumbled. "Laura's been gone almost six months now. I think that's plenty

226

of time to have gotten over her."

"And then you immediately hop into another relationship? Does that sound like a good idea to you?"

"I didn't say it was a relationship. I said that we were seeing each other."

Tony got up and paced the length of the room. That set David at ease, because Tony had been far too still. If he was his usual fidgety self, then all was right with the world.

"This could be a good thing. Has she let you see her other room? What are her designs like? We can—"

"Tony!" David slammed his hand on the desk. "Enough. Stop worrying about competing with her. You've got an amazing room design here. Let the work speak for itself."

Tony shook his head. "Do you honestly think that you can date her and not worry about it? You're not that naive. It's always going to be between you. Either you'll tank her business or she'll tank yours. Can you forgive her for that? Do you think she'd forgive you?"

David's heart started to pound, so loud he could barely hear himself think. He hadn't thought of that. Somehow, he'd expected them to continue on as they had, two businesses separate from Elena and David themselves. But Tony was right, at some point they'd reach the tipping point, and he didn't know what would happen then.

He did know he'd rather try than not. He didn't want his life to be like it had been before Elena had walked into it: boring, lonely, obsessive.

"I think she's worth it. Whatever happens."

Tony whirled and pointed at him. "You'd better be careful, David. You're starting to sound like you're in love with her."

The words hit him like a shot to the chest. He turned them over carefully in his mind, wondering if Tony had figured out some essential truth that he hadn't realized.

The shrill sound of the business phone ringing on the desk cut into the conversation. David reached for it. "We'll talk about this later."

"Don't think we need to." Tony turned and walked out of the office.

David would have to deal with him later. He put on his best customer-service voice and picked up the phone. "Hello, The Greatest Escape Room, how can I help you?"

"David Brant, is that you?"

After a moment, he recognized the voice. "Charlie Burke, you son of a bitch, how are you?"

Charlie had been his supervisor before that other asshole had come in and ruined David's life. Charlie had left for another position before the company got sold, and, honestly, he'd made the best decision out of all of them. They'd worked well together but had lost touch recently. David had been a bit busy the past year.

Charlie laughed. "I can't complain. I hear you're doing pretty well for yourself."

"How'd you hear that?"

"Well, I started looking around for some team-building activities for my staff here, and when I looked up escape rooms, a review on your place came up. Congratulations, by the way."

Review? David turned to the computer and pulled up Google, tucking the phone between his chin and shoulder. This was the first he'd heard of any review. None of the big escape room reviewers had come through as far as he knew, or at least, no one had disclosed they were reviewers before playing.

"I said to myself, why am I going to go book with some other company when a guy I know is running an escape room? What do you charge for corporate bookings?"

David stopped fiddling with his browser and straightened up. Charlie had been the boss who'd taken them all out to do escape rooms as a team-building exercise. In a way, he owed his whole business to Charlie. "You want to book my place?"

"If it's an option. How many people can you handle?"

He ran the math in his head. "I can fit ten to twelve people in a room, and I have three rooms. If we run them all at once, that's thirty-six."

"That's doable. I can take two teams over. What's your group rate?"

David had never considered this before. Honestly, he should have. This was what that marketing session at the Escape-a-Con had discussed. He'd been paying more attention to Elena than the session, of course.

"Since you're a friend, I'll give you a good discount." David grinned.

He rattled off a number, and Charlie agreed.

"Stop in later and sign the contract."

That would give David some time to come up with said contract. He was sure he could find a model online. He might have asked Tony, but right now he should give Tony some space. By tomorrow Tony would be over it and would probably be thrilled at this latest development.

"Great. See you later."

"Looking forward to it," David said. He meant it, too. Charlie had a lot of connections. If he liked David's setup, well, that could open a whole lot of new doors for him.

He ended the call and went back to his computer. He'd need to draw up that contract. But when he clicked back to his browser, the results of the search he'd put in at the beginning of the call had populated. There at the top of the hits was the review Charlie had been talking about.

It was called "A Tale of Two Escape Rooms." He skimmed it, curious about what they had to say about his room designs. This article wasn't just about David's escape rooms, and it looked like the reviewer had a bone to pick.

Oh no. Poor Elena.

Chapter 28

Elena sat in her office, staring at the computer screen. Her eyes watered from looking at numbers all morning. Jesse's husband, Phil, had done her taxes and set up accounting software to help her better keep track of her business.

She didn't like the bottom line on May. They were in the middle of the month, at the beginning of finals week. Of course the students were too busy to come out. But still.

Now she would have three long months of summer before the students came back. She needed to find another strong client base. She couldn't afford not to. Maybe Quinn had some ideas about who they could market to beyond the campuses nearby. If they started now, she might get some more business soon.

She rubbed her eyes and stepped away from the computer. No time like the present to ask. She left her office and ducked into the control room only to find it empty. Shouldn't Quinn be watching a room right now?

Elena went out to the lobby and found Quinn standing behind Phoebe and staring at the computer over her shoulder.

"Hey. Who's watching the room?"

Quinn sprang away from the desk, a guilty look on her face. "I've got the video feed on my phone." She held it up for Elena's inspection. "I'll see if they wave for clues."

"No, seriously, this isn't like you. What's so important that you're not in the control room?" Elena came around the desk to see what was so interesting.

"Wait, boss." Phoebe covered the screen with both hands. "What is seen cannot be unseen. Are you sure you want to look?"

"Unless it involves nudity." She paused, considered what she knew of Phoebe, and asked, "It doesn't involve nudity, does it?"

"I wish."

Elena rolled her eyes and shooed Phoebe out of her seat. She settled in to see what was so interesting—and so concerning that they wanted to shield her from it. At first she didn't know what she was supposed to be looking at. They were reading a blog post, done up in white text on a black background.

"It's a review blog. For escape rooms," Quinn said.

"Although the asshole never said he was a reviewer when he came in."

"Stop. Wait, did they review one of our rooms?" Elena leaned forward and scrolled to the top of the page. She hadn't seen any reviews that weren't on popular location review websites—she had mostly four and five stars on those sites, thankfully. Elena didn't think she was big enough to attract the attention of one of the admittedly niche escape room review blogs.

"Something like that."

The headline said "A Tale of Two Escape Rooms." Elena felt cold, then fiery hot as rage curled up her spine as she continued to read.

The escape room industry is fairly new. Everyone thinks they can hop into the scene and make a fast buck.

There's little to no overhead, after all, and at thirty bucks a head for each person, it looks like easy money. We covered why that's not the case in a recent blog post.

We bring this up because escape room businesses are popping up everywhere, but very rarely do we see two businesses set up directly across the street from each other. Except in New Brunswick. Now, this makes sense. With the college nearby there should be no shortage of customers.

However, you have two places with very different levels of quality.

Let's take the better of the two first, The Greatest Escape, located in the Spano strip mall on Gregory Street. The location boasts a gorgeous lobby with a variety of brainteaser toys and plush couches while waiting. The bathrooms rate an eight out of ten (see our escape room bathroom rankings post).

But what stands out about The Greatest Escape is the quality of their rooms. There are three different experiences, all newly renovated thanks to some trouble with the fire department.

Elena scrolled past all the gushing about David's rooms, his use of technology, how great that they could go for a bite to eat directly next door, blah, blah, blah. She hadn't been so annoyed about The Greatest Escape since, well, since they first opened up. David had said New Brunswick was big enough for two escape rooms, but now she wasn't so sure. Her phone buzzed in her pocket, but this was too important at the moment.

The review went on.

Now, directly across the street—which is a pain in the ass to cross—you have The Escape Space. There is limited parking in what used to be the backyard of a renovated home. The houses on this side of the block are mixed use, so you have doctors' offices, shops, and a very tiny escape room business.

Escape Space has only two rooms, and, honestly, two rooms is too many for the size of the location. You can probably only fit four to six people in each experience although their website advertises eight to ten. Don't bring a big group!

Both of the experiences are first-generation rooms, consisting mostly of four-digit locks and keys. While there are a few nice technological touches, most of the time you'll be looking for numbers and trying to figure out which lock they belong to.

"That's not true," she muttered. "It's exactly clear which lock belongs with which puzzle." Did she have too many four-digit locks in her rooms? She'd have to go and count.

The biggest failure is The Ballet experience. This concept clearly needed a much-bigger space. The first room is tiny, and you spend most of your time looking through drawers and reading a diary. There is way too much reading involved.

And while we typically don't give spoilers here, the second room is way too ambitious for the space. It would be more suited to a larger venue.

So while you do have two places to choose from in downtown New Brunswick, we highly recommend The Greatest Escape. It's perfect for larger groups and corporate events, plus the rooms are creative and fun.

Elena sat back and pushed the mouse away. "This is an unreasonable comparison. We are both trying to do different things with our rooms."

"Yeah, he bought all of his rooms. You made yours

from scratch." Phoebe had tightened her hands into fists and looked like she wanted to punch someone.

Elena understood the sentiment. But, unfortunately, she had no one to punch. Except maybe the reviewer.

"I'm going to comment on the post." Quinn started typing on her phone.

"No!" Elena protested. "That will make things worse. I'll look like one of those crazy business owners who try to squash one-star reviews."

"You have to address it! Especially since they didn't identify themselves as reviewers when they showed up. That's totally not cool. At the very least we need some kind of rebuttal on our website." Phoebe paced the lobby. "Yeah, we're not very big, but here you can get the cozy, family-friendly escape experience you can't get across the street."

Elena rubbed her head. Her forehead had started to pound. Here, for the first time, she had evidence that David's business was directly harming hers. She should hate him. She should be angry with him. But right now she wanted to call him and complain about the unjustness of the review.

"She's right," Quinn said. "We have to spin this. You know if you google escape rooms in New Brunswick, his room comes up first? We need Google ads, Facebook ads, anything we can get. You need to be more visible."

"All right." Elena waved at them. She trusted Quinn's ability to advertise. "But don't respond to the blogger, all right? The last thing I need is a horde of trolls descending on us." She'd seen that thing before in dance message boards. They were not pretty. "And get back in the control room before someone breaks something upstairs."

Before Quinn could respond, the front door opened, the bell oddly loud in the sudden silence. David stood in the entrance way and seemed nonplussed to find all three of them there in the lobby.

"I tried texting you. I take it from the look on your face that you've seen the review?" He stuck his hands in his pockets and looked so adorable all Elena wanted to do was walk over there and kiss him.

So she did.

They pulled apart when Quinn cleared her throat. Elena turned to face her employees, her cheeks heating. She was prepared to say something—maybe how she was the boss and could do what she liked—but apparently, Quinn meant her sound for Phoebe, who sighed and took a twenty-dollar bill out of her bra. Quinn pocketed the money with a smile.

"I don't even want to know. Quinn, back to the control room. Phoebe, find some new marketing opportunities. And you"—she turned back to David—"come back to my office with me."

"Yes, ma'am." He smiled that same sleepy-eyed wide grin that had her melting.

Elena was in far too much trouble to stop now.

****

"You know I had nothing to do with it." David watched as Elena paced the small confines of her office. She seemed to have too much pent-up energy and to not know what to do with it. He didn't blame her. If the same thing happened to him, he'd be doing more than pacing. He would be tracking down the blog owner and telling him off.

He wouldn't mind it if she used that energy to kiss

him again. That had been a nice surprise. Clearly, her employees were more okay with it than Tony was.

Elena stopped pacing and turned to face him. Her eyes were wide, and she looked horrified. "God, David, aren't we past that now?"

"Just checking." He put his hands on her waist and held her still for a moment. He planted a kiss on her forehead. "Tell me what I can do to make it right. Do you want me to contact the reviewer? Tell him to take it down?" Find the guy and punch his lights out? He had to admit he found that idea somewhat satisfying.

"That wouldn't be fair."

"The review wasn't fair," he growled. "They didn't appreciate the beauty of your rooms, how your simple design tells a story. A story that's far more intricate and enthralling than any of my rooms. Sure, I have things that light up, but you have drama."

"You sure know how to butter me up," she teased, pressing a kiss against his lips.

He reveled in her warmth, his fingers finding the bare skin beneath her shirt.

"David, there are always assholes online. This is tame in comparison to the ballet forums, trust me."

"That doesn't mean it didn't hurt," he said softly.

She untangled their bodies and stepped back, and he regretted his words. Why did she always pull away whenever things got a little bit serious?

"True."

"How can I help? I can't change the review, but…" He held his hand out and let it fall.

"Well, you did say you'd help me with my third room." She cocked her head to one side and poked him gently in the chest.

"Of course." David relished the idea of working on a room with Elena. He wanted to see her creative mind in action. That reviewer didn't know what the hell he was talking about if he couldn't see the uniqueness of the storyline in each of Elena's rooms.

"That's what we'll do. I'll create something spectacular, and then we'll invite other reviewers to come take a look, and that will fix the Google algorithms that Quinn goes on and on about."

Her eyes lit up, and he could see the brilliance of her mind working.

"When can we get started?" He felt the same excitement at the chance of not only designing with her, but the prospect of creating an original room from scratch. They wouldn't be buying any prefab rooms, so the possibilities were endless.

"Are you free this weekend? We need to hit the flea market for props. Can you pick me up at six a.m. Saturday?"

"You can count on me." He cupped her cheek in one hand, brushing the pad of his thumb against her soft skin. "And then maybe dessert afterward."

She laughed and pushed him away. "Go back to your own place. I have work to do."

"Yes, ma'am." He remembered how she felt about PDA in her escape rooms. They probably should avoid fooling around in her office.

He waved at Phoebe as he left. She seemed intent on doing something on her computer, so busy typing that she didn't even look up to acknowledge him.

He darted across the street back to The Greatest Escape when his phone buzzed. He pulled it out as he made it to the sidewalk, curious if Elena had texted him any more info about Saturday. Instead, it was a private message.

Before going over to see Elena, he'd put out a post on the private escape room-owners Facebook group, asking if anyone else had been blindsided by LockUp Reviews. He hadn't heard of that group before, because of course everyone knew the more famous escape room review group—Escape Room Rock Stars—and wanted to be reviewed by them.

Someone from the group had messaged him. The name sounded familiar—Lorraine. Right, he'd met her at the convention.

—Just an FYI, it's an open secret that the Escape-o-Rama owner is behind that review site.—

David stared at the words, at first not comprehending. Why the heck would an escape room owner run a review blog? Unless he wanted to fix the market to his own benefit.

Sven Svenson was the owner, and he'd tried to get David and Elena to franchise with him once before. What was this weird plan? To get David's business to increase so much that he'd be desperate to work with Svenson to handle the strain?

No. Ice settled in David's belly as he remembered Svenson's words about not being able to set up in New Brunswick because of the two escape rooms there already. He was trying to drive Elena out of business. If he couldn't have David's, then he'd destroy hers and open up space in the market.

David had to do something about this. The question was what?

Chapter 29

Elena woke suddenly, her body drenched in sweat and her heart racing. She tried to shake the sounds out of her head—a car's wheels screeching, the crash of metal on metal. She hadn't dreamed about the accident for months now. She'd actually thought she might be free of the nightmares that had dogged her since. The event might have left a mark on her body, but she'd been determined to move on. To start a new life. And she had succeeded, damn it. Why did this keep happening?

Clearly, she wasn't over it. She pushed the covers off, unable to bear them on her sticky skin. A drink of water and a walk should clear her head. Perhaps she'd even be able to get back to sleep. She'd come a long way from being afraid to close her eyes, of seeing the streak of headlights behind her eyelids again and again.

A creaking noise echoed from the ceiling above her. Elena froze. She'd gotten used to the sounds of settling the old house made during the night. This…wasn't that. This was the sound of people walking above her, in her Escape Space. No one should be upstairs. They'd been closed for hours now.

Some part of her wanted to believe that maybe Phoebe or Quinn had forgotten something and come back to retrieve it. Phoebe had a habit of leaving her schoolwork at the reception desk. Still, even Phoebe had more sense than to come back here at—Elena squinted at her clock—three a.m. No, she'd text first at the very least.

The sound of footsteps was followed by the crash of something falling and then voices. Male voices.

Elena's heart squeezed itself into a vise. *God, please, no.* She snatched her phone from its usual place and shot off a text to David with shaking hands.

—I think someone broke into The Escape Space.—

She kept the phone in her hand as she crept to her door to check the lock. Then she pulled a chair over to stick it under the doorknob. How long would that hold? If someone really wanted to get in…

Her phone buzzed, and she dropped it. "Crap!" She knelt and felt around on her floor until her hands came in contact with the slim metal case. Of course she'd dropped it screen down and only had the dim light of her alarm clock to see by.

—Did you call the police?—

She stared at the words. Why hadn't she thought of that?

Maybe because, for the past few weeks, David had been the person she'd gone to for advice. He was the person she texted all the time while they were both working, the person she asked about her new room design or the tech needed to achieve what she'd dreamed up. She wanted his opinion, and that was for more than escape room basics. She talked to him early in the morning and before she went to bed.

Not talking to David would be the strange thing.

But, shit, she really should have called the cops first. She tapped out a quick response.

—Dialing 911 now.—

He replied immediately.

—I'll be right there. Hide. Stay safe.—

Everything was going to be okay. David would be there soon. Elena dialed 911, swallowing down the panic in her throat. When the operator answered, her voice was clear, despite her having to whisper. "I need to report a break-in. Yes, I'm still in the home."

Elena kept the phone pressed to her ear as she ducked into her closet. She closed the door and wedged herself behind piles of clothes and moving boxes. Hopefully, nobody could hear the pounding of her heart or the way her blood pounded against her forehead.

Please, David, get here soon.

****

David had forgotten to turn off the sound on his phone before he went to bed. That was the only reason he'd heard the text come in, and it startled him out of a deep sleep. Still groggy, he trekked across his bedroom to where the phone had been plugged into the wall. Normally, he'd have plugged it into his computer, but tonight he'd been so tired he jammed it into the charger before bed. He didn't have to back it up every night.

Look at me, being slightly less of a workaholic. That would make Momma proud.

He looked at his phone screen and shook off any sleepiness he had left. Elena. She was in trouble. He tapped out a response before putting on his shoes. Her reply came back as he realized he didn't have any pants on.

Damn it. Maybe he wasn't as awake as he'd thought. He told her to stay safe, his fingers trembling as he tapped out the message. He pulled on clothes and grabbed his car keys. He shook his head and slapped himself before getting on the road. His heart raced as he made his way through the almost-deserted streets. Nothing good happened at three a.m., his mother always used to say.

She was right.

By the time he made it to The Escape Space, police cars blocked the road and flooded the streets with blue and red lights. He pulled into the parking lot for the strip mall across the street and darted through the traffic, intent on finding Elena.

He saw her from a distance, wearing an oversized sweater with her arms wrapped around herself as she spoke to a tall policeman taking notes. The lights did horrible things to her hair, which stuck up in all directions. As if she sensed him, Elena looked over in his direction, and their eyes met.

David knew at that moment that he loved her. He loved her, and he'd find whoever had done this and make them pay for hurting her. The emotion rose up inside him like a wave—no, a tsunami—crashing against the shore, and he had no defenses against it.

He stepped onto the sidewalk and threw his arms around her, holding her close. "Are you all right?"

She nodded against his chest but didn't speak for a moment. Then she pulled away, and her eyes were determined. "They took all my AV and computer equipment. All the cameras, mics, everything."

He went cold. Without that equipment, she couldn't run her escape rooms. She'd be out of business until it all could be replaced. He knew she couldn't afford the downtime. "I might have some stuff I can lend you."

All the equipment Tony had put aside to use for the fourth room. David would give every bit of it to Elena. They'd find a way to make it work.

"Quinn is on her way over. She'll have a solution."

"Ma'am?" The police officer got her attention and pulled her over to the side. David watched them speak, the officer nodding every so often and Elena looking so still and strong as she talked.

David waited on the sidewalk and crossed his arms over his chest to warm himself as a sudden breeze kicked in. The temperature had dropped during the night, and he was hardly prepared to face it. He'd pulled on whatever clothes he'd found first—a T-shirt and shorts—and now he shivered in the night.

He saw Quinn as she approached, walking down the sidewalk, her blue hair obscenely bright underneath the streetlights. He waved her over, not wanting to interrupt Elena's intense conversation with the police officer.

Quinn—who'd dressed sensibly in a black hoodie—stuck her hands in her pockets and came over. "What happened?"

"Someone broke into The Escape Space and stole all her AV equipment." David scowled. His hands itched to go over there and hold on to Elena and never let her go.

Quinn stilled. "That's fucking horrible." Her forehead wrinkled. "It's weird this happened right after that review. Like, adding injury to insult."

He opened his mouth to tell her it was the other way around, and then closed it with a snap. She had a point. "That review company," he said tightly, "is owned by Sven Svenson."

Her eyes widened in shock.

Before she could respond, Elena made her way back to them. "Quinn, I see you got my text."

Quinn stepped forward and hugged her. "Fuck, boss. Thank God you're okay. And holy shit, good thing you didn't call Phoebe. Can you imagine?"

"I think if Phoebe were here, the burglars would have run from her," David said.

Those words brought a wry smile to Elena's face. She shook her head. "Those assholes took off before the police got here. Took all of the computer and AV equipment."

Quinn whipped out her phone. "Not a problem. I'll run to The Computer Shop with Phoebe once it opens, and we'll have everything up and running by noon."

"That's a little ambitious. It took us weeks to get it set up right the first time." Elena bit her lip. David put his arm around her and tugged her close. She put her head on his shoulder and let out a little sigh.

"Yeah, but that's because I was still figuring things out. Now I know exactly what we need. Plus"—Quinn waved her phone at them—"I have all the info stored in the cloud."

Elena abruptly pulled from David's arms, and he felt bereft.

"Quinn, can I talk to you privately for a moment?"

They moved over toward The Escape Space, and David had to strain to overhear with the sounds of the police finishing up their investigation.

"…won't be able to reimburse you until the insurance money comes in…" Elena's voice drifted by as if on a breeze.

He frowned. Things were much worse than he'd thought if that was the case. He didn't hear Quinn's response. One of the officers came up to him, and David introduced himself as Elena's boyfriend.

He probably should have confirmed that with her first, but oh well, too late.

They spent the next few hours boarding up the backdoor where the burglars had gained entry, and then making sure every other lock was secure. The police finished taking statements, and the forensics crew got into their van and left as the sun peeked over the clouds.

Elena yawned and pressed herself against David's side. He stuck his nose in her hair and breathed deeply. Yes, she still smelled like cinnamon. "Come on. You're catching some sleep at my place."

He could tell how tired she was because she didn't protest. He told Quinn where she'd be and waved.

"They'll catch the guys," he told her as he drove them back to his place.

She shrugged. "Even if they do, I still have to fix everything. The place is such a mess."

"Okay, one problem at a time. Sleep first. Then we'll make a to-do list."

She turned and gave him a tight smile. "Thank you."

He felt like he'd aged several years by the time he tucked Elena into his bed. She pulled up the covers so far he could only see the tufts of her red hair. He went to plug in his phone before joining her.

Quinn was right. The break-in seemed conveniently timed—right after that bad review. And the burglars took stuff that needed time to remove—the cameras and AV equipment. Why not grab the computers and run?

Unless this was more than a smash and grab. They'd taken things that would cause the most harm to her business and managed to get out before the police got there. It seemed too perfect, too well planned.

If Sven Svenson thought he could ruin Elena's business, he was wrong. David would stop him and anyone else who tried to hurt Elena.

Chapter 30

Elena woke to the smell of freshly brewed coffee. She moaned in response, burying herself beneath soft luxurious sheets as she stretched out her entire body...and didn't touch wall. Her eyes snapped open as the events of last night came crashing back. She was in David's bed again and not for any fun reasons.

No, because some assholes had decided her business was ripe for the picking. She gripped the covers between her fingers, taking deep breaths to try to regain some measure of calm. *In and out. Breathe. One. Two. Three.*

Her skin crawled with the violation of it all. Her business, her home, her sanctuary. They had no right.

"Hey." David appeared in the doorway, the sunlight framing him like a giant halo. "You're awake."

On one hand, she was glad he'd come to her rescue last night. She had no idea how she'd have boarded up the back door or where else she could have gone to stay the night. Quinn might have offered if he hadn't stepped in, but that wasn't the point.

She didn't like having to depend on him. When they started this whole thing, they'd been equals—their businesses had chances of succeeding or failing based on their own merits. But now she felt like she was indebted to him, and she hated that.

"Barely. What time is it?" She looked around for her phone, which she'd left on the end table. The battery held out at ten percent, and she had a text from Quinn.

—Canceled all bookings for day. Going to take a little longer to get this fixed.—

Great. She couldn't afford to lose today's business. This would probably end up in the media, too, and, *ugh*, she had no idea what that would do. Customers might be afraid to come in, knowing her place had been a target for thieves.

She debated texting Jesse, but she didn't want to worry him. She'd tell him. Maybe once she felt normal again.

"It's about noon. I scrambled up some eggs if you're hungry."

Elena rubbed her forehead, which had started to throb. She needed to get over to The Escape Space and help Quinn out. She had to put in an insurance claim and figure out her next steps. Her belly growled and reminded her she shouldn't do any of that on an empty stomach.

David looked at her with a hopeful smile on his face. It made her angry, all of a sudden. How dare he stand there and look so happy? She'd almost lost everything, and he still had his perfect business across the street.

She threw the covers off and dug around for her sweatpants. She vaguely remembered tossing them on the floor last night. She'd been so damn tired. Tired and frightened and she'd melted into David's arms and let him take care of everything. That's not who she wanted to be. She had never relied on anyone but herself.

"Actually, if you could drive me over to The Escape Space, that would be great. Quinn's already there, and I have a lot of work to do."

He came over and put his hand beneath her chin,

forcing her to look up at him and away from her phone. "Elena. You have time to eat. You don't run on air."

She pulled away, not wanting to be touched right now. "It's been a rough night."

"All the more reason to eat. I made yours with extra cheese."

"Well, then. If extra cheese is involved."

****

Elena held the borrowed travel mug as David drove them back to The Escape Space. Every so often she sipped at the warm coffee, desperate for the caffeine to finally kick in. Right now she still felt like a zombie, which was not conducive to going back to work and figuring out how she was going to save her business.

David had offered to help. But she couldn't accept it. She would not be dependent on him. She'd started this venture on her own, and she damn well would continue on her own. This was a minor setback. She had good employees, and together they'd dig her out of this hole.

Even if she had to call up Phil and see what he could do about them getting a loan. All she had to do was make it through the summer. With the influx of college students in the fall, she'd be fine. Absolutely fine. And she didn't have to depend on David one bit to do it.

He pulled in to the parking lot behind The Escape Space. Elena hesitated with her hand on the door release. For a moment fear coiled in her belly as the terror of last night came flooding back.

His hand on her knee returned her to reality. She looked over and forced herself to give David a smile.

"It's going to be okay," he told her.

"Yeah." She got out of the car. Time to do her job.

****

David didn't like the look in Elena's eyes. They didn't have the spark he was used to, that fire that said she could take on the world and the world itself wasn't ready. She was too pale and quiet.

Not that he blamed her. Living through an experience like that must have been a nightmare. He couldn't even think about it without his heart racing and his fist itching to punch someone.

It made him all the more determined to make Svenson pay.

David followed Elena inside. He needed to see with his own eyes that she was going to be okay and not alone inside The Escape Space. Maybe he'd ask her to stay over another night at his place.

He opened his mouth to broach the subject, but once they entered the lobby, they found Quinn wasn't alone. She leaned over the receptionist desk where Phoebe sat along with Sean. All three sprang apart when the door slammed shut behind David and Elena.

Clearly, they were up to something.

"Sean?" David asked. "What are you doing here?"

"Oh." He ducked his head. "Phoebe called me to come over and help them install a new back door."

"We needed him to hold it while I screwed in the hinges." Quinn made finger guns. "Because apparently I am the only one who knows how to use power tools around here."

"I can't believe you guys got that fixed already."

Quinn shrugged. "I called Phoebe in early. We started cleaning up and doing inventory. This way you know exactly what we need to replace."

"I totally have the best employees ever." Elena smiled as she said it, but her eyes had a sheen to them.

"I believe Sean still works for me," he said.

Phoebe pursed her lips. "For now."

Quinn gestured to the steps. "Elena, I want to show you what's going on upstairs. This is why it's going to be trickier than I thought to fix everything."

"Got it." Elena waved to David. "I'll text you later." And she followed Quinn up the steps.

David waited until he heard one of the escape room doors open and close before turning on Phoebe and Sean. "Well? What are you three up to?"

"What makes you think we're up to anything?" Sean asked, his voice squeaking on the last word.

Phoebe rolled her eyes. "You are a terrible spy. I don't know why they tried sending you over here in the first place."

Sean's cheeks went bright red. David was careful to hide his smile. Honestly, what had he and Tony been thinking? They hadn't been thinking, which was the problem. He'd been so angry at Elena that he'd have done anything to get into that room.

Now anger simmered under his skin but for a different reason. In defense of Elena.

"Quinn told us about Svenson being behind that review." Phoebe leaned against her desk. "We were trying to figure out what to do about it."

"Did she mention how odd it was that this break-in happened now? When Elena's already taking a hit?" David's jaw clicked from the force of him clenching it.

"Totally. But do you really think he's that much of an asshole?" Phoebe shook her head.

"I don't know, but I'm going to go find out." David clenched his hands into fists. "And tell him to stay the fuck away from Elena."

Sean took a step back.

"Normally, I'd say that would be useless, but you looked really scary for a second there." Phoebe patted him on the shoulder. "Go forth and defend fair Elena!"

"And make sure you guys take care of her. She's going to need you." Elena would rebuild this place, better than ever.

Phoebe gave him a salute. "Yes, sir."

****

David got into his car and put the location into his GPS app. He'd been to Svenson's office once before—when the man had tried courting David—but didn't know how to get there offhand. It hadn't been an experience he wanted to repeat.

That stupid son of a bitch. Svenson had made no secret of his attempt to get into the New Brunswick market. He'd gone as far as creating a fake review. Would theft be the next logical step?

David didn't know for sure, but he was going to find out.

At the very least, he'd make Svenson take down the horrible review. Elena didn't need that when she was trying to rebuild.

Who the hell did Svenson think he was? Running a secret review blog to discredit his competitors. Hiring thugs to rob Elena's place. Did he think he owned the damn escape room world?

By the time David pulled into the parking lot, he'd worked himself up into a fury. His knuckles had turned white from gripping the steering wheel so hard. If he could get away with punching someone right now, he'd do it. He stomped up to the office building's front door and for a moment was stymied by waiting for the elevator. That didn't help his mood any.

"I'm here to see Svenson," he demanded of the bored-looking secretary.

"Do you have an appointment?"

"He can make time to see me." He strode past her through the open door that led to the room filled with carnival crap that Svenson called his office. He hadn't changed things at all since the last time David had been here.

Svenson rose from his seat, a sly smile licking his face. "Ah, Mr. Brant. A pleasure to see you again."

"Wish I could say the same." Now that he was face-to-face with the man, some of the wind had come out of David's sails. What evidence did he have, really? He had a hunch and some flimsy evidence. But he'd come too far to let this go, not now.

"I assume you've reconsidered franchising with me?"

"Are you fucking kidding me?" Now the rage was set loose. "You have the nerve to ask that? After what you've done?"

"I believe I've done you a favor." Svenson sat back down and folded his hands into a knot. He grinned at David.

"The review. It was you," David sputtered.

"I own a review blog, yes. I hire honest reviewers. If you're doing well, David, be proud of it. Only one can come out on top, after all."

Not an admission of guilt. David pushed on. "Is that why you hired someone to break into The Escape Space and steal Elena's equipment?"

Svenson's face didn't break, and that was a sign in itself that something was off. "It's Elena now, is it? How close are you with Ms. Evans?"

"None of your business." And how had David ended up on the defensive? "What you did was wrong. Stay away from The Escape Space and Elena."

"Or else? Is that a threat?"

"What do you think?" David held his gaze. Heat flushed up the sides of his neck. At the slightest provocation he would beat the shit out of Svenson.

Svenson lost the smile, but he didn't look too upset. "You have my word that I will not interfere with The Escape Space."

"And you'll take that damn review down."

Svenson chuckled. "Fine. But, Mr. Brant, have you considered that the only threat to The Escape Space is your own business?"

David didn't answer as he walked out the door. He didn't buy Svenson's innocent act, nor did he trust the man to keep his word. He had to do something to protect Elena. If Svenson got away with this once, he might try something again.

He got into his car and hit a number from his contacts list. No one was going to ever attempt to rob The Escape Space again.

Chapter 31

"This is why we should have bought that coffin. Anybody breaks in and sees that? Totally craps their pants and runs the other way." Phoebe chatted on as she sorted through the racks of vintage clothing at the flea market.

Even though two days had passed since the break-in, Elena couldn't get it out of her head. She'd refused David's offer to sleep at his place. No one was going to make her afraid of her own home and the business she'd built. But she'd spent the past two nights lying awake, listening for every creak of the floorboards above or for the sounds of voices.

Quinn had nearly finished rewiring in the new cameras. Elena couldn't wait to get back up and running again. Every hour without working rooms, she lost money. She'd taken to pacing the lobby, which apparently annoyed Quinn enough that she told both Elena and Phoebe to get out of her hair.

Which was why Elena had Phoebe drive her out to the flea market to look for stuff for the third room. She'd planned on going with David later that week, but she found she didn't want him there, not right now. Part of her was still angry with him although it was irrational.

He'd said the town was big enough for two escape rooms. She'd ignored every sign that he was wrong. She couldn't ignore it anymore, no matter how she felt about him.

She'd left his texts on read for the past few days, not knowing what to say. She had to focus on her own business and get herself on track. That's what she should have been doing the past month, not screwing around with David.

"Why are you so obsessed with coffins?" Elena pulled her attention away from David and onto the reason they were here—finding props for her escape room. She looked at a shimmery shift dress and evaluated it for use as a possible backup for her flapper costume. Maybe.

Phoebe grabbed a long black dress. "I don't know. Have you considered a vampire room? It would go great in the attic. Dark and creepy, comes with its own spider webs."

"Who's going to carry the coffin up three flights of stairs?"

"Sean might." Phoebe's cheeks went pink, and she put the dress back on the rack.

"Mmmm-hmmm." Elena didn't comment. Whatever was going on with Phoebe and Sean was none of her business unless Phoebe wanted to share.

A horror-themed room for the attic space wasn't a bad idea at all. It would be especially popular for Halloween, and she had the entire summer to make it perfect. She could reboot her business by drumming up marketing for the event. College students loved Halloween. It might save her yet.

She picked up the black dress Phoebe had put down and considered it. Perhaps a witches' haven for the theme?

"Finals are next week," Phoebe said out of nowhere,

sorting through dresses and not looking at Elena. "And I'll be going home for the summer. I live too far away to drive here to work. I mean, I can come back in the fall if you'll have me."

For a moment relief spread through Elena—she wouldn't have to pay Phoebe's salary during what was shaping up to be a slow summer season. But it also meant one less set of helping hands at the escape room. She and Quinn would have to run the rooms, build the new set, and organize the new marketing plan themselves.

"If I'm even still open in the fall." Elena folded the dress over her arm and decided she'd take it.

"Stop it, you'll be open. Quinn is going to fix everything. And before I leave, I'll do an aggressive social media push. Your numbers will be better than ever."

"Finally putting that business major to use?" Elena grinned, but her smile faded. "It's just that everything seems set against me. That awful review and now this? I don't even want to think what else could go wrong."

"I already reached out to some other review blogs. They'll see how great your rooms are." Phoebe pulled out a bright-red dress, made a startled face at it, and draped it over her arm. "None of them are run by Svenson, like the other was."

Elena paused in the middle of pulling out her wallet to pay for the dress. "Excuse me?"

Phoebe went still. "Crap. You didn't know."

"No, I did not. Who told you that?"

Phoebe's cheeks went very red.

"Phoebe?"

"David. David told Quinn, who told me and Sean. But none of us wanted to upset you."

He didn't want to upset her? Too bad, because now she wasn't just upset. She was royally pissed off. Who the hell did he think he was? Talking to her own employees about her? Not telling Elena that Svenson was behind the review?

She strode over to the cashier with her black dress, her happy shopping mood totally soured.

Phoebe ran to catch up with her. "Elena, I'm sorry."

"It's fine, Phoebe. It's not you I'm mad at." No, that would be David and Svenson, both for different reasons. She expected Svenson to be an asshole. She'd trusted David.

And maybe she was looking for reasons to be pissed at him. He might have mentioned it in one of those unanswered text messages, though a quick scan of them showed nothing about the review. Elena was going to have to have words with him, and she didn't think it would end up well at all.

"Come on. After we get these, I want to look for more stuff. I think I've finally decided on a theme for the third room."

Witches. Right now Elena wanted to cloak herself with the image of powerful women.

****

They filled the trunk of Phoebe's car with anything even remotely related to witchcraft—wooden spice racks, interesting glass bottles, tarot cards, and even a crystal ball. Elena had already started to think of a puzzle surrounding it on the drive back to The Escape Space. The break-in might have gotten her down, but she wasn't out, not by a long shot.

And she didn't need David or anyone else's interference.

She'd tell him that she didn't need his help with her new room. She had to set boundaries. This thing between them had been fun, but, well, now she had to be realistic. They had no future together, not when he was still her competition. Not when he kept things from her.

The drive back seemed quick, and maybe she was starting to get used to Phoebe's driving. Elena didn't even have to hold on to the door handle. She frowned as they pulled into the driveway. Two security company vans were parked outside—one in the front, the other in her lot. A man in a matching uniform exited The Escape Space, holding a clipboard in one hand.

This aggressive marketing was ridiculous. She knew the break-in had made the papers, but she hadn't expected alarm companies to show up without warning. They usually called first.

Elena got out of the car as Phoebe slid it into park. She walked up to the guy. "Excuse me. I'm the owner here. Shouldn't you be talking to me?"

The guy seemed taken aback. "Uh. Maybe? I'm just here putting in the new security system."

She blinked. "What? What security system?"

"Maybe you want to check with the guy who hired us?" He shrugged and started walking back to his van.

She gaped at him for a moment. Who had bought her a security system?

Oh. She swallowed hard and stormed into The Escape Space to find Quinn chatting with another guy in a red shirt. "What's going on?"

Quinn blinked at her. "I thought you hired them. They showed up about an hour ago with work orders to install a security system."

None of David's text messages had mentioned this.

When she failed to call him, had he decided to do whatever he wanted? The annoyance from before twisted into pure rage, a fire in her belly that had her face heating and the blood pulsing in her temples. *How. Dare. He.*

"Hey, Clive. How's the install going?" David's voice filtered through the open front door.

Elena whirled and charged outside, aware of Quinn on her heels. "You and I need to have a conversation."

David looked over and smiled. "Hey. You haven't responded to any of my text messages."

"Well, none of them mentioned hiring a security company to do work on my business without talking to me first."

"You read them. Didn't feel like responding to any of them?"

She pointed her finger at him. "Stop changing the subject. The security system."

He stepped forward and put his hands on her shoulders. He lowered his voice. "I couldn't stand the thought of you being in there unprotected. This was the best way I could keep you safe."

She pulled out of his embrace, not liking how it felt to be touched, not when she was so damn pissed off at him. "Have you thought about how I'm going to pay for this?"

"Elena, you don't have to worry. I've got it all covered. It's my gift to you."

She hated that even now, looking at his soft brown eyes and sweet smile, she wanted to say yes, let him do this. But the circumstances hadn't changed. And she wasn't about to let him interfere with her business. Not anymore.

"I didn't ask you to do that. I don't want you to."

He seemed confused. He still held his hands out, like he didn't know what to do with them now that she had stepped away. "Elena, I care about you. Let me help you."

"You should have asked me first!" she spat. She took a deep breath and tried to calm down. "I didn't get to choose my retirement from dancing. Most dancers know it's coming, but we know when it's time to quit. I had that taken from me. So I chose this. My business. My way of doing things. Mine."

"I understand that."

"Do you? You also didn't tell me about Svenson being behind the bad review."

His face went white. "I was trying to protect you."

"I don't need that kind of protection! The kind where you keep shit from me. If it weren't for you, Svenson wouldn't have targeted me in the first place!"

He went bright red, and his eyes narrowed. "Fine. Have it your way. I'll leave you alone if that's what you want."

He turned and stepped into the street on the other side of the security van. Elena had seen David do it a thousand times, dart across to his own business in the strip mall on the other side. This time he didn't look first.

She saw the car come speeding down the road.

As if in slow motion, she watched it hit him and send him flying through the air.

Elena screamed.

Chapter 32

Elena sat wedged in between a vending machine and the wall. It seemed to be the only place in the emergency room where she could get any cell service. She'd called The Greatest Escape first to let them know what happened. Sean answered and then gave the phone to David's friend Tony.

"Oh my God, are you serious?"

"Why would I make something like this up?"

"Sit tight. I'll call David's mom."

That had been an hour ago. She shivered, the metal cold against her back. Then she called Jesse and burst into tears. "It was the most horrible thing I've ever seen."

She hated the smell of hospitals, the sound of them, the way footsteps echoing down the hallway could make the skin on the back of her neck crawl.

"Elena, are you alone?" Jesse's voice brought her back. This was why she'd called him. She had so much to tell him, and she'd been avoiding telling him about the break-in because she hadn't wanted to be lectured at. But he kept her calm and from freaking out the moment she'd blurted, "David's been hit by a car."

The ambulance had driven off with David, leaving her behind. It had taken him away, and she'd had no idea if he'd live or not. *God.* She didn't even have his mother's phone number. She had to rely on Tony, and who knew if he'd tell her anything?

"I sent Phoebe back to The Escape Space. There's no point in me even being here. They're not going to let me see him." She swallowed. "It was my fault, Jesse."

"No, it wasn't."

"We were fighting. God, it's so stupid now. He was just trying to do something nice."

"Elena, if he hadn't gotten hit by a car, would you still be mad at him?" He sounded so reasonable.

She sniffed back something between a laugh and a sob. "Well. Maybe."

"Sometimes shitty things happen. That doesn't make it your fault."

They were both silent for a second. Then she said, "Are you going to finally believe that?"

He laughed. "I guess I'm going to have to. Now get out there and charm a nurse into telling you forbidden information."

"I'll do my best. And Jesse? Thanks." She ended the call and stared at her phone. She squared her shoulders. She'd find out how David was doing even if she had to break in somewhere.

It had to be easy. They did it on TV all the time. And she was something of an expert on locks at the moment.

She started back to the main desk in the emergency room just as an older woman with bottle-red hair stepped up to the nurse. "Excuse me. I'm trying to find out where they took my son. David Brant?"

Elena stopped and took a breath. That was David's mom? This wasn't how she'd pictured meeting her. Hell, she hadn't ever thought she would meet her. Elena had kept things between her and David as light and fluffy as possible, a simple affair, nothing more. Sex, with no strings.

But now that she could very well lose David forever, she realized she needed him in her life. She loved him.

She swallowed her pride and went up to the woman as the nurse typed on her computer. "Are you Ms. Carlucci?" David had told her his mother went back to her maiden name after the divorce. "I'm Elena."

To her surprise the woman smiled. "Ah. Elena. It's a pleasure to finally have a face to go with the name. David talks about you. Quite a bit."

"Ma'am," the nurse interrupted. "If you'll have a seat, someone will be right with you."

Elena stepped to the side, but Ms. Carlucci beckoned her over to one of the rows of chairs in the waiting room. To the right a tired-looking woman was sitting with three kids, one flushed red and huddled in her lap. Near the door sat a man with an icepack on his head. Otherwise, they had the place to themselves while a TV blared in the corner, telling everyone how to makeover their kitchens.

"Now, my dear, tell me what happened."

Elena swallowed and could feel the tears welling up again. "It was my fault," she blurted, conversation with Jesse notwithstanding.

Her eyebrows rose. "Unless you're the one who hit him with a car, I highly doubt that."

"I haven't driven a car in two years." Elena sniffed. "No, we were fighting when he tried to cross the street."

"Then I believe it's my son's fault for not looking both ways first." She dug around in the giant purse she'd plopped on her lap and pulled out a pack of tissues. She offered it to Elena. "Which will be the first thing I tell him when I see him."

Elena took a tissue and blew her nose, hating how

disgusting she felt.

"What were you fighting about?"

Elena crumpled the tissue in one hand and stared at it. For a moment she couldn't speak, and then it all spilled out—the robbery, the bad review, David buying her the security system without telling her. "It was my business. Not his. And I was so angry…" She trailed off, horrified at what had come out.

Ms. Carlucci patted her leg. "Yes, David can get quite protective. He comes by it honestly, I suppose. He was always protective of me in the bad days. Did he tell you about his father?"

Elena nodded.

"Yes. Mike was an asshole. I never should have married him. But things were different then, and I wouldn't have David now, would I?" She reached back into her purse and pulled out a ball of yarn and a crochet hook. She started a loop on the hook and kept talking. "It was hard to leave. Especially because at first I tried to do it all on my own."

Elena sank down into her seat. Ms. Carlucci's voice had a low soothing quality to it. "That must have been difficult."

"Eventually, I had to ask for help. I put myself through night school. No fancy online classes then." She clucked her tongue. "Our neighbor used to bring over dinner for David. And the church turned out to be a good place for him to spend time and not get into trouble. I bet he never told you he was an altar boy."

Elena laughed although it came out like a snort. They waited in silence as Ms. Carlucci continued to crochet and the TV continued to blather on. After twenty minutes, Elena felt like she could probably grout a kitchen backsplash herself.

Finally, a man in light-green scrubs approached them. "Ms. Carlucci? Your son is asking for you."

She stuffed her crocheting back into her purse and got to her feet to follow the man. Then she turned around and cocked her head. "What are you waiting for, young lady? Come with me."

"Yes, ma'am."

****

David stared up at the white ceiling of his hospital room, annoyed at the lack of cracks or anything remotely interesting about it. His head pounded, and if he even thought about moving, his stomach revolted in response. Doctors called that a concussion. His noggin didn't show any signs of internal bleeding, but they'd admitted him for observation.

What they were observing, he didn't know.

What he did know was this brain-rest thing was bullshit. No TV, no reading. Just quiet and darkness where he had to lie here alone with his own thoughts.

Right now those thoughts sucked. He didn't remember the accident at all—apparently common after getting slammed in the head. But he did remember very clearly the argument with Elena, how damn angry she'd been. He remembered how the pain in her eyes made him feel—ashamed and frustrated, so upset that he couldn't bear to look at her any longer. Hence the whole crossing the street without checking first.

I don't need that kind of protection. Her words spiraled around in his brain, over and over.

He'd screwed up. Because David knew her. He knew Elena from head to toe, understood that she was the kind of person who liked to stand on her own two

266

feet—and, God, did she, building up her business from nothing in the shadows of that horrible accident. And yet he'd done what he wanted to anyway in the name of protecting her.

Damn it, but he'd do it again. Every night he'd pictured the burglars discovering Elena hiding in her basement, and the images were nightmarish.

It didn't matter. He'd lost her. Something good had been starting between them, and he had destroyed it. That hurt more than the ache in his brain.

"Knock, knock."

David looked over at the door, a flood of relief rushed through him when he saw his mother standing there. For a moment it was like he was a child again—Mom would make everything all right. "Mom."

Her eyes softened, and her grip on the doorway tightened for a moment before she smiled. "I brought a friend." She stepped into the room and motioned with both hands as Elena walked in.

"Elena." His voice cracked as he said her name. He had never expected to see her again.

"I'm going to get a soda from the vending machine down the hallway. Play nice." His mother squeezed his hand and nodded at them both before leaving the room.

He started talking first. He had to get this out while he still had the chance. "I screwed up. I'm sorry." He tried to sit up and then, when he couldn't, fell back down on the pillow. His head throbbed. His broken arm and leg ached. "If I could get on my knees and beg forgiveness, I would."

"David, stop." Elena put her hand on his bed. "Don't try to move. Do I need to call the nurse?"

He must look worse than he felt. "I'm fine.

Concussed and with a few broken bones."

Her lips pressed together tightly. "I'm so sorry."

"For what? Defending yourself and your business? I should have talked to you first."

"Yes, you should have." She swallowed and looked away to stare at the beige wall across from his bed. "But when I saw you get hit by that car, I knew then that I didn't want a life without you in it."

Oh, Elena. That must have been so horrible for her. "That's like...when I thought about you alone while those crooks robbed your place, I went crazy. Couldn't stand the thought of anything happening to you."

She looked back at him, eyes wet with unshed tears. "We're both idiots."

He laughed and then winced. Laughing apparently was a bad idea with a concussion. He should try to remember that. "Maybe we should talk?"

He held out his hand, and she took it, squeezing gently.

"I think that's a good idea," she said. "I'm not...a relationship person. At least...I never was. But you make me feel things I didn't know how to deal with."

"We can make this work," he promised. "You and me. I can't let you go."

"David..."

"Oh, for God's sake, kiss her already!" The voice came from his mother, who'd returned from her soda errand.

Elena laughed and came over to the side of the bed. "I'll be quick because you need your rest." She leaned down and kissed him.

It might have been the concussion, but David was sure he saw stars.

Chapter 33

Elena paced outside of The Greatest Escape, trying to get up enough courage for the conversation ahead of her. None of her tricks were working—no matter how many times she counted to ten or did her deep breathing, the pit remained in her belly, a solid mass of nausea and anxiety.

Was she really going to do this?

She didn't need to. She could let David's friend Tony take care of this end of it. But if she committed herself fully to moving on and into a new future, then she needed to tackle this one last fear.

Squaring her shoulders, Elena pushed open the glass door and entered the lobby. How odd to look at it now, not as a place that threatened her business, but as the next step forward in her new life.

Tony emerged from the back, his phone glued to his cheek. "Oh, it's you. Let me call you back," he said, presumably to the person on the other end. He ended the call and tucked the phone in his pocket.

"Yeah. Um. I realize we've never actually properly met. I'm Elena Evans. David's girlfriend." She held out her hand.

He let her wait for a heartbeat before reaching out to shake it. "Tony Spano. David's *best* friend."

"Are we really going to play this game?" She thought they'd left all that behind months ago.

"You started it," he grumbled, lifting his hands as he paced around the lobby, touching the computer, the counter, until finally grabbing a solved Rubik's Cube, which he then proceeded to mix up. "I'm just looking out for David's best interests."

"And you don't think I qualify?" She would have been insulted, but she appreciated that David had someone who cared so much about him.

Tony made a face. He juggled the cube from hand to hand. "I didn't say that. David's been through a lot in the past year. And now there's that whole hit-by-a-car thing."

She flinched. She swallowed down any words of guilt—which still punched her in the gut when she thought of David being hurt. Instead she said, "One of the new rules in our relationship is that he must always use the crosswalk."

He laughed. He dropped the cube and bent to pick it up. "I guess you're all right."

"Thank you for the glowing endorsement."

"Don't break his heart." He didn't look up from the cube.

She smiled. David was lucky to have such a good friend. "I'll do my best."

She'd make sure they were both protected in this new business venture. She hadn't told anyone yet other than a quick phone conversation with Phil, who'd help with the financials. Plus, she didn't want David to make any big decisions right now.

She knew from experience—concussions were nothing to mess around with.

But once he got better and they both had time to really talk and figure things out…well, that was another story. She couldn't help but be excited about the opportunity to truly work with him as an equal partner in this business. She remembered the husband-and-wife team she'd met at the conference in Atlantic City. They'd made it work by being true to each of their own strengths. Elena could do worse than emulate their example.

Now she had to talk to Tony about the real reason she'd come. Bile rose in the back of her throat, and she fought against it. "I'm here for David's keys?"

He narrowed his eyes. "His keys? You mean his car keys?"

"He said he'd call you." Maybe David hadn't told Tony she'd be coming.

But no. "Yeah, and he also told me you haven't driven a car in two years." He crossed his arms over his chest and glared at her.

After all his fidgeting, to have his attention so focused unsettled her. "Right." She didn't elaborate.

"I'm not going to hand you the keys and take David's car. We're going to do some basic driving around the parking lot first."

She opened her mouth to object and then shut it. That actually sounded like a good idea. "Okay."

He seemed shocked that she'd agreed. Then a wicked grin showed up, and he rubbed his hands together. "Time for driver's ed, Spano style. Let's go."

What the hell had she gotten herself into?

Tony grabbed a set of keys from behind the front desk before leading the way to the parking lot. Elena hesitated on the sidewalk as he made his way to David's car. Could she actually do this?

She swallowed back the objections that wanted to rise up. Maybe he could take the car back to David's house. And then what? She'd rely on cabs and friends to ferry David around to his doctor's appointments and other errands? No, she had to do this.

Walking around to the driver's seat of David's car felt odd. She should be on the other side. Tony used the fob to unlock the car, and at the beep, she opened the door and settled in behind the wheel, only to laugh when she realized how much she'd have to adjust the seat. David was quite a bit taller than she was.

She expected to feel horrible, to have the night of the accident flashing before her eyes. But being in David's car during bright daylight was nothing like that. All she could think about were the moments she and David had had in this car—the way he'd look over at her and smile as they were on their way to an escape room. All happy memories.

Maybe she could do this.

"Okay, this is a key. It goes in the ignition." Tony leaned over and started the car. "Remember to always check your gauges before you do anything. Do you have enough gas? Is the oil light on? How about the temp?"

"I don't need that much of a refresher," she muttered. But she looked over the dashboard anyway. The gauge read at about a half of a tank of gas.

Elena put her hands on the steering wheel, grounding herself in the feel of the faux leather beneath her palms. The fabric was worn where David kept his palms, and she fingered the fraying left behind.

"All right, so put your foot on the brake. We're going to put the car in reverse, and you're going to, carefully and slowly, back out of the spot."

She put her hand on the gearshift and threw it into reverse. With a jerky movement she started to back out.

The sound of a horn had her slamming on the brakes, and they both were jolted back against the seats with the motion.

"Easy," Tony said. His voice had lost the mocking edge. "Take it easy. You'll be fine."

It wasn't quite like riding a bike, but her body remembered this. Like dancing, she'd need practice to get good at it again, but if she didn't take those first baby steps, she'd never reach that point. She looked behind her and then, once sure the parking lot was clear, tried again.

This time she managed to make it out of the spot, driving with slow, jerking motions. She winced. She hadn't driven so poorly since the first time she'd learned to drive. Her dad had had the patience of a saint, not saying a word as she made those first halting mistakes.

Tony was nothing like her dad. He didn't stop talking the entire time. "All right, easy does it. Keep your hands at nine and three. It's not ten and two anymore, did you know?"

Elena put the car into drive and made several slow, careful circuits around the parking lot. After a few tries she eventually figured out exactly how much pressure to put on the gas pedal to stop the jerking starts, and to ease on the brake to stop smoothly. After a few minutes, she felt almost comfortable.

"Okay, we need to take her out on the street now."

She turned to glare at him. "What? This isn't good enough?"

"I'd rather you find out when I was sitting next to you instead of by yourself."

Once again, Tony had a point. With a sigh, Elena made for the exit of the parking lot. Her belly fluttered as she merged into traffic. Perhaps someday she might be at ease while driving, but today wasn't the day.

She inhaled, realizing that the car smelled like David. That made her smile and gave her the courage to continue. She was doing this for him after all. Together, she and David could do anything.

After about ten minutes, she returned to the parking lot, confident now that she'd been able to navigate the busy streets, even with Tony chattering next to her. Right before she turned into the driveway, someone swerved in front of her and cut her off.

"Fucking really?" She gave the guy the finger.

Tony burst into laughter beside her. "That's it. You're ready. You have passed the Tony Spano driver's test."

She couldn't help but giggle. "Oh, I should have led with that." She smoothly pulled into the lot and then into the space in front of The Greatest Escape.

She couldn't say any of that had been enjoyable. A layer of sweat slid down her back, and her knees trembled. But she'd done it. Now she could pick up David tomorrow, and they could start their new life together.

"Thank you, Tony. I appreciate it."

He patted her on the shoulder. "Stick with me. I gotcha covered."

She laughed at that, but then he said, "Seriously. You and David need anything at all, you call me, okay?"

Elena nodded. It was a good reminder that neither she nor David were alone in this. They had friends, good friends, to count on.

****

Two days in the hospital had been long enough.

David wanted to bust the hell out of this place. He couldn't stand the medicinal smell nor the way the greenish-gray walls seemed to be closing in on him. None of that helped the throbbing of his head. Truthfully, he wanted to crawl into his own bed, pull up the covers, and sleep for about a year.

Of course, that might be a bit difficult with a cast on one arm and another on his leg. He'd gotten off lucky. The car hadn't been moving that fast. It could have been so much worse. He was grateful for that and grateful for this second chance. He would not screw it up.

"Ready?" Elena stood in the doorway, holding the door for the nurse who pushed David's wheelchair.

Seeing her was almost enough to quell the pain that simmered everywhere. They should bottle the essence of Elena and sell it. Although he was pretty sure he was biased and he was the only one she'd have this effect on. He'd almost lost her. But now they had a second chance, one he was determined to take full advantage of.

She smiled, and his heart sped up. Good thing he wasn't connected to any monitors. They'd never let him leave.

"Ready to get out of here."

Elena walked beside him as the nurse pushed him down the hallway. He'd be on crutches eventually, though David had let Elena handle the logistics of getting them. The cast on his arm was going to make that difficult, but he had plenty of PT appointments ahead of him to figure it out.

Step one, hobble on home so he could get that sleep in his own bed he'd been dreaming of.

When they got to the lobby, he realized that his dreams of being left alone to sleep would have to wait a while. A group of people stood in front of the exit, carrying get-well balloons and a fruit basket. As they got closer, David recognized them all: Phoebe and Quinn, Tony, Sean, and even Vanessa.

Phoebe stepped forward, clutching the fruit basket to herself like a giant basketball. "So. We've got something to tell you."

That was an awfully ominous introduction to a fruit basket. What the heck was in there? David could only make out shiny apples. They certainly looked delicious. He blinked. Perhaps the concussion had addled his brain more than he'd thought.

"What did you do?" Elena demanded. She stepped forward and crossed her arms over her chest. Clearly, she understood what was going on better than David.

What had their collective staff done together? This was like when he'd found Sean and Phoebe conspiring. "She's right. This is highly suspicious," David said.

No one responded at first. They all looked at each other and then away. David would have bet a twenty that Tony would be the first one to crack. But to his surprise Quinn stepped forward.

"Okay, so a bunch of us went over to one of the Escape-o-Rama rooms." She held up a hand when Elena started to interrupt. "We weren't going to say anything to them. We wanted to find fire-code violations we could report them for."

"Because that worked so well in the past," Tony said with a very slight tinge of annoyance to his voice.

"And we found them. They had crazy things like vinyl floor installed over carpet." Phoebe rolled her eyes.

Had she memorized the handbook or something? Phoebe was apparently a stickler for safety. Still, he didn't know why that merited this intervention at the hospital.

"Anyway, to keep from making this short story any longer"—Quinn took over again—"when the fire inspectors showed up, they also found a whole bunch of stolen equipment in the basement."

"Wait a minute. What does that mean?" Elena looked over at him, her forehead furrowed in confusion.

Quinn grinned, looking downright evil for a moment. "Since I dutifully used the label maker and marked all of the AV equipment, it's pretty good evidence that someone at Escape-o-Rama was behind the theft at your place."

"But we are going to let the cops sort that out. I've had enough of this amateur detective shit," Tony cut in.

"So happy ending, right? Anyway, here you go." Phoebe plopped the basket on David's lap, and he grabbed it to keep it from rolling anywhere. He had no idea what the nurse thought about all of this. She'd remained suspiciously quiet despite probably needing to deposit him in the car post haste.

David, his grip precarious on the basket, looked over at Elena, whose eyes were filling with tears. Oh, he did not want her to cry again. "Thank you. All of you. Working together, like a team. Doesn't that sound like a good idea?"

He and Elena hadn't hashed it out yet. It was still in the planning stages, waiting for his concussion to clear up. But he had already decided he'd rather work with her than against her.

She put her hand on his shoulder and squeezed. "I think that sounds like a fine idea."

"Okay, now you're going to have to explain that,"

Phoebe said.

"Soon, when we have all the details hammered out." Elena made eye contact with the nurse and nodded at her. "This one needs to rest first."

The nurse took the cue and pushed David through the crowd and the exit. He took a deep breath, enjoying the open air after being stuck inside the hospital. He would need some time to heal, but he was fine with that. He had Elena by his side, and with her, he could do anything.

Although he was a bit apprehensive when the nurse wheeled him to the passenger side of his own car. David didn't say anything while the nurse and Elena helped him get situated in his seat. He was too busy wincing since moving set everything throbbing again.

"Thank you so much," Elena told the nurse before slipping into the driver's seat.

"You told me you haven't driven in two years," David said, curling his good hand around the door handle.

She swallowed as she started up the engine. He found himself lost in admiring her face, especially that look of determination he'd come to know so well.

"I did practice a bit before Tony let me leave the lot with your car. Turns out it is like riding a bike."

David pulled on his seat belt and grabbed his spare sunglasses from the glove compartment. *There*. Now his head pounded slightly less. He closed his eyes and trusted Elena to take him home.

Epilogue

The timer ticked down relentlessly, reminding Elena that she had only minutes left. Sweat gathered on her forehead, at the base of her neck, and on her collarbones. She resisted the urge to swipe at it, not wanting to get her fingers wet and sticky. Her breathing sped up to match her heart rate as she charged forward, determined to win.

"Would you like to test something for me?" David had asked her.

She'd been sitting in their now-shared office in The Greatest Escape, sketching out plans for a new escape room. She wanted to do a pop-up holiday-themed room that they could bring to the college student centers and was deeply engrossed in the planning. "What is it?"

"I built a little escape room in the back storage room. Trying my hand at design." He ducked his head and looked down as he spoke, his cheeks turning pink.

How cute. She'd have to be gentle with any criticism since he seemed so embarrassed about it.

"Sure, I'll give it a try." She let her pencil drop and followed him to the back.

"I'll watch from the control room so it's more like a true experience." He held the door open for her. "Not actually locking you in, of course."

She laughed as she stepped inside. The room had been stocked with extra furniture—a set of bookshelves, a desk, some chairs. She grinned and got to work.

They'd merged their businesses months ago, with David's half specializing in corporate team building and her portion being dedicated to personal, private experiences. It allowed her to increase her production values. Quinn and Tony got along very well when it came to tech. During the long dry spell of the summer, she'd been able to revive her escape rooms with fresh decor and new puzzles.

Business had picked up briskly in September, and October was looking to be a showstopper. She'd been right about college students loving Halloween. The haunted escape room in the basement had a waiting list. Phoebe kept saying it was because she finally got her coffin.

The basement apartment had become available after Elena had moved in with David. At first it made sense—to help him after the accident. That first week had been so difficult and frightening. Concussions were nothing to play with.

But he'd gotten better, slowly, with her by his side where she belonged. Going back to living alone didn't make sense. And it had given her an opportunity. She could expand into the basement and create new rooms straight out of her imagination.

"Are you stuck?" David's voice came over the room's speakers.

"Not a chance," she called back.

She'd only stopped because she started to get suspicious. The first puzzle in the room had to do with fire codes. She had to look up the right one to get the number for the lockbox on the bookshelf.

Inside the lockbox she found a postcard from Atlantic City. It led her to find a collection of AC memorabilia around the room—a set of dice, a baseball cap, a deck of cards, and finally a cigarette lighter. Putting those objects on the shelf in the right order triggered a magnetic lock to open a drawer in the file cabinet. Inside she found a tiny figurine of a ballerina.

David's question had caught her at that point while she stared at the little porcelain piece in her pointe shoes and tutu.

"David, what have you done?" she murmured. He'd set this up for her and for her alone. All of these puzzles had to do with the events that had caused her to meet him and get them together. She half expected to find toy cars somewhere.

As long as she didn't have to use them to run down a little figure of David, she'd be fine.

Elena found the music box that had been sitting on the desk from the beginning. She put the little ballerina in her place, and a soft tune played throughout the room. The drawer to the desk shot open, and inside sat a single red-velvet box.

The door behind her opened before she could touch it. She knew without turning around that it was David.

He came to her side and took her hand before getting down on one knee. "I hope you'll answer my question before you open that box."

"David."

"Will you marry me?"

She couldn't speak at first.

"We work well together. You get my crazy ideas. You make me want to be better. Hell, my mom loves you."

She put her fingers on his lips to get him to stop. "Here's my answer." She opened up the box, revealing a pink opal ring—her favorite stone. She bit her lip, trying to hold back tears—he hated when she cried—and put the ring on her left hand.

Cheers echoed through the speakers in the room.

"David?"

"Okay, so, yes, all of our employees are watching from the control room. And my mom and your friend Jesse and his husband are waiting out in the lobby. Mom made cake." He stood and caught her in his arms.

"What would you have done if I hadn't said yes?" She grinned.

"Quietly escorted everyone out and thrown the cake out the window. Although that would have been a waste of a good cake."

"I love you," she said, laughing as she kissed him. Elena would never get tired of kissing him.

A word about the author...

CC Bridges spent her childhood visiting other worlds in books, comics, and the starship Enterprise. It's no surprise that she ended up a librarian, being surrounded by the books she loves so much. She writes about amazing worlds with honorable heroes.

Her hobbies include paying money to get locked in a room for an hour so she can solve puzzles to escape, along with the aforementioned reading. She lives with her husband, son, and dog on the Jersey Shore. She is currently pursuing an MFA from Southern New Hampshire University.

~*~

Find CC Bridges online at:
http://ccbridges.net